BOMBORA

TEGAN BENNETT

ALLEN & UNWIN

© Tegan Bennett 1996

Publication of this title was assisted by The Australia Council, the Federal Government's arts funding and advisory body.

First published in 1996 by
Allen & Unwin Pty Ltd
9 Atchison Street, St Leonards, NSW 2065 Australia
Phone: (61 2) 9901 4088
Fax: (61 2) 9906 2218
E-mail: 100252.103@compuserve.com

National Library of Australia
Cataloguing-in-Publication entry:

Bennett, Tegan, 1969– .
  Bombora.
  ISBN 1 86448 010 6.
  I. Title.

A823.3

Set in 10/13 pt Stempel Garamond by DOCUPRO, Sydney
Printed by Australian Print Group, Maryborough, Victoria

10 9 8 7 6 5 4 3 2 1

BOMBORA

Sandra Dows

Tegan Bennett was born in Sydney in May 1969 and has lived there all her life. She has written several books for children and teenagers. *Bombora* is her first novel.

Acknowledgements

With thanks to Ali, Blake, Danny, Michael and Steven K. Thanks also to Annette Barlow and Patrick McIntyre for criticism and laughs.

The author would like to thank Faber & Faber Limited for permission to reproduce lines from *Collected Poems* by Philip Larkin (ed) Anthony Thwaite, Faber and Faber Limited; and Music Sales Pty Ltd for permission granted to reproduce lines from 'All That She Wants' by Ace of Base. © Megasong Publishing via Polygram Music Publishing.

Contents

for Julia

BOMBORA

The bombora happens at sea. The tides run against each other across a submerged reef—two moving walls of water come together, advancing instead of retreating, and there is an almighty slap! as they hit each other. The water is hurled hundreds of feet in the air, as though some vast explosion had taken place just below the surface.

Someone must have seen the bombora, though whether anyone has been caught in the running of the tides is another matter.

Annabel ran quickly past the spiky bird of paradise, ducking its reaching points, and catching her foot on the coiled hose, fell forward into the grass. Buffalo grass. Cut about a week ago. Its edges paled, its stalks split, fat swords of green. Her eye caught a movement—a stalk flicked—up—back into place. And another. Flick. Flick. And around, and over, a black ant climbing through. Flick. Another stalk hid its progress.

She was lying on her stomach, lying still so that the bird of paradise would not get her. Soon she would edge forward on her elbows, pulling herself through the scratching grass, and if she moved slowly enough the bird of paradise would not see. It was sticky and it was threatening and it was in a corner of the garden that nobody ever went, except to mow the grass; her grandfather bending under the umbrella tree as he pushed the dirty-sweet smelling mower back and forth and the noise of it drowning out his hearing so you could stand at the safe edge of the lawn and yell and yell and he would never hear you.

Upstairs, on the second floor of her grandparents' house and on the verandah that looked over their garden, the people were talking and drinking. Her father drank a bitter, bitter red drink with soda and ice. Soda was no good—fizzy, but not sweet. Why bother? Leo drank his bitter drink and the people helped themselves to handfuls of chips and peanuts. Annabel had eaten too many salt-and-vinegar chips and had come down to the garden to feel sick, to sit in the sun and feel sick and wait for it to pass away so she could go back and eat some more.

When she stood next to her father, he put his hand on her head so that she could feel the weight of each heavy finger, and the warm separate weight of his palm. She could have stood like that a long time but the people came over and wanted to talk and he needed his hand to hold his cold, red glass, to plunge into his pocket, to pass over his eyes.

The absence was very strong. The absence was like a presence. It waited in a corner of the room or by the drinks cabinet, or at the window, not picking up the binoculars to look at the sea. It didn't catch her eye and smile, or promise that they would be going home soon, or reach out to push the dirty hair back from her forehead. She could run right through it. It was down here, in the garden, under the bird of paradise.

She dragged herself forward and then, when she was far enough away, climbed as fast as she could to her feet, stumbling and nearly falling again. The salt-and-vinegar chips moved in her stomach. She reached the edge of the lawn and sat down on the stone steps, breathing hard.

When the rushing in her ears stopped, she could hear the people upstairs. She couldn't hear her father's voice. Two of the people came out onto the verandah. She could feel them looking

4

down at her—the top of her head burned. They couldn't say anything. They wouldn't tell her to come back upstairs. They were watching her, and she bent down, between her knees, to look at the grass and put a hand out to pick at a blade or poke or do something. She was busy. They couldn't call her back upstairs. The top of her head grew hotter and at last she sat up and swung around, but they had gone back inside. They had looked at her and not known what to say and they had left her there in the garden in the sun on her own, with the currawongs swooping down from the Norfolk Island pine in front of her eyes and her bottom growing sore on the cold stone step and the sound of the children next-door playing under their sprinkler.

She shifted and swallowed and stared at the bird of paradise, and stood up on her stiff legs, watching it as she backed away, up the steps, holding onto the old painted railing. She backed right into the house and the bird of paradise never moved. The breeze made the leaves on the trees shift and change in the sunlight, but the bird of paradise stayed still as though the space around it was empty, empty of wind and empty of sky. It reared into the garden but it did not move.

It was not a long death. It was short—caught between the breathless, white face of her mother, suddenly unable to stand up at the side of the road, and the blue curtain of the bed in the emergency ward. That blue, almost green like the tails of mermaids. Annabel sat and stared, her eyes swimming in the blue and the green until everything and everyone about her was underwater; they shimmered and flashed and murmured past her and the aching disappeared. Everything was just turning to silver when Leo picked her up and carried her out.

The little mermaid wished and wished for feet and when she finally got them every step was like knives, walking on their angry blades. But when she swam again the pain was washed away.

After the wake the cousins had collected her and taken her

down to Maroubra Beach. It didn't seem to have ends—it stretched away in a yellow haze of sand and spray. Everyone was still in their funeral clothes. They undressed awkwardly, climbing down to underpants, to bras—for Annabel, her nasty new singlet and pants. Mickey had brought a packet of biscuits from the kitchen. They sat on the sand and ate Scotch Fingers until Annabel decided she wanted to go in. The cousins clustered around her like bodyguards, forming a phalanx as they trooped into the waves. Even when their feet left the ground they floated around her. She had a wall of cousins.

Waiting for the trance to descend, Leo sat beside the window and watched the street.

His guitar lay flat on the big heavy desk and the chair was wonderful. It had wheels and you could spin it right round. The house was quiet though, so full of deep pools of shadow. The smallest movement or sound would find its way to you. Once he had stopped in the kitchen, wondering why it was dark, and heard a squeak-squeak, squeak-squeak, squeak-squeak. And occasionally a thump. He followed it through to the study and, edging the door open, saw Annabel, eyes closed, pushing herself round and round, her legs splayed to keep her balance. Every so often she would hit the side of the desk. Thump.

Outside it was hot and clear and each cicada's voice came to you separately, a chirping on every register until the sky held no space for anything else. Leo sat by the window and watched the air throb with noise. You would not think such a street, such a quiet, neat street could be possessed, but this country does not forget itself, despite the deadening layers of tar, the hiding buildings, the heavy howl of traffic. It can make itself heard, and you will always remember that it is there. You can spend all day in the liquid cold air of an office and then step out into a heat so strong it will carry you home without your feet even touching the ground. You can hear the cicadas in the city, and see the twin gleam of a possum's eyes in the parks at night. And you can lie in the surf, you can be rolled and licked and loved by the water, the same water that has been cooling the sides of this hot island forever.

Leo swung, creaking, back to the desk, feeling a slow ache beginning in his thighs. He reached out to pick up the guitar—holding it by the neck, he pulled it onto his lap, easily propping one elbow on its waist. He sat like that, perfectly still, until he heard Madeline's voice, calling to him from their room.

He laid the guitar down and walked hurriedly along the hall. He stole into their room, his bare feet silent on the shiny wooden floor, and for a second he saw her, but she twisted, she twisted, and in one swing of the curtain was gone, and the breeze slipped coldly into the place that she had left.

This part was not too bad. This part he could put down to poetry—on this hot day he could believe he was dreaming. He found some Valium and dropped it down his throat, washed along on a tide of wine. It made him sleep and sleep, though at first it curled around him, turning his misery inside out, making his sadness a kind of rippling, half-cheerful exhaustion.

But there were other times when the dream disappeared and only the solid objects were left. They were grey and chill like iron left in the dark and he ran his head against them, and the pain was so sharp that he would lose his breath.

When he turned to ask her something in the pub.

When their daughter stitched with her smaller hands the tapestry of gestures Madeline had woven every day, woven so bright and thick around him he never realised there were other colours behind it.

When he found a pair of her underpants, slightly stained with old, old blood and held them, limp, in his hands, wondering what he should do.

Annabel's mother and father lived in a house in Newtown before she was born. They shared their house with two other people. In the sunny afternoons when no-one was home, they would make love and lie in each other's arms and hear the sounds of the street and the house.

Madeline had gone back to university when Annabel was four or five and slowly begun to finish her arts degree. The rest of the long, long week she spent at home in the house in Newtown, painting, lying on their bed with Leo as Annabel climbed and clambered around the room, or dreaming over the stove, dyeing clothes or making soup, letting the heat from the electric rings cloud around her face.

The household changed—the walls were painted, the landlord put the rent up, the gay couple upstairs moved into a flat in Darlinghurst—and Leo and Madeline's room with its covered verandah for Annabel's bed grew inwards like the nest of a bowerbird. The walls were thickly draped with bright-printed fabric, sarongs that Leo bought for Madeline to wear when one of his bands played up north, in the towns whose names she would roll around her mouth—Ballina, Bangalow; books gathered in piles in every corner; the dressing-table, decorated long ago with candles and jars and sticks of incense, took on layers of smoky, sweet wax, that Annabel would pick off with her soft baby's fingernails.

By the time Annabel was eight—and Madeline twenty-seven—they had more than half the house to themselves. They had been there so long that their possessions had begun to creep throughout the rooms, moving it seemed, at night so that nobody knew quite how they had gotten there. Occasionally one of Madeline's paintings sold and she took on a part-time job working at the new health food shop. Leo's third—fourth—fifth? band played almost nightly and Leo had a wage. They could afford to rent three rooms—one for themselves, one for Annabel and one as a studio, the big desk littered with canvases, paints and half-jars of turps. In the far corner stood Leo's guitars. The fourth room, the wide one at the pointed top end of the house, had a series of tenants; some who seemed to lurk in the shadows behind the long, billowing curtains, scurrying out when their backs were turned; others who elbowed cheerfully into their lives, adopting Annabel, organising house-meetings and economies with the shopping, building shelves and giving dinner parties; and some, all women, who came for Leo.

These women usually had long hair and an evangelical glint in their eyes. They had seen Leo play, and watched him at the pub, sliding easily through drink after drink until he could hardly balance on his stool. They saw Madeline smiling unconcernedly as he leaned against her, occasionally turning and lowering her head to listen to him speak, calm and interested. Leo's friends planted themselves around the bar—when he was on stage they would crowd closer together to talk, nursing glasses of beer or scotch and coke. Sometimes they disappeared to the back room to play pool or pinball, to dance in front of the jukebox, to hand their conversation around like a baton. Leo's set would finish and the woman—whoever she was—would use the moment.

When there were holidays at school and Leo seemed set to sleep all day, Annabel would go to the university with Madeline. She played in the long, blue corridors of the English building, running wildly up and down so that the students, murmuring together in their tute rooms, would lift their heads and frown at the thump-thump-thump of her feet. Sometimes she would get bored with pretending that she was in a ship—on a train—catching the tram in Melbourne (the windows flickering past as she raced from one end to the other)—and she would go downstairs to the quad.

In the quad there were cement mushrooms with limited possibilities—having climbed onto one, there was then very little you could do but sit there. Much more fun was the tall thicket of bamboo that grew against the building. Annabel had read in her picture encyclopaedia that bamboo could grow a metre, two metres overnight. She would stand and watch it carefully, waiting to see it change, or force her way into it. The light swayed and danced as the bamboo moved in the wind, scattering bright coins onto her face and hands. She was in the jungle—in the depths a tiger lurked, a monkey shrieked, a lost band of travellers marched. The bamboo squeaked and creaked to itself. In the jungle the passing of time was different. Her mother's face appeared after weeks had gone by, weeks in which she learnt jungle lore, like how to tread quietly so that your prey knew nothing of your approach, how to scale trees hundreds of feet high, how to tie a tourniquet after being bitten by one of the poisonous snakes who lay in wait, curled around the trunks of the vine-covered coconut palms.

Then she would be tired of her own company, the movement and colour dying, flattening out, and she would tiptoe to the door of Madeline's tutorial and hold her breath until she had gathered the courage to knock.

'What is it, sweetheart?' Madeline would ask, and the faces of the students and the professor would swing her way, pale moons of disapproval. She could never think of anything to say.

'I need to go to the toilet,' she'd quaver, hating herself, hoping that Madeline would leave the class and come with her.

'Well, you know where the bathroom is.'

You couldn't ask to be taken, not if she didn't offer. It was awful enough, having to say toilet in front of all these strangers. Aunty Helen would have corrected her. 'It's lavatory, Annabel.'

If stretched out, a visit to the bathroom could last ten minutes or more. Annabel sat on the seat and effortfully read the graffiti which she had read before and still failed to understand. 'Subvert the dominant paradigm.' 'No fees.' 'A woman without a man is like a fish without a bicycle.' This last would be different, she supposed, from just a normal fish—one that had never had a bicycle. There must be some kind of fish that *went* with bicycles. It was a meaningless, grown-up puzzle, like the books her mother read at the table during dinner, or the conversations she and Leo had about money.

The best days were when Leo turned up, drifting through the

open quad with a blurred, cheerful expression on his face. He might have fallen asleep on the bus trip up Anzac Parade. You had to snag him quickly or he would walk right past you.

Annabel ran up behind him and hooked her small hands into his jeans pockets.

'He-ey, baby!'

'Hey Dad!'

'Mum out yet?'

Annabel looked at her metallic digital watch. 'It's 5.31,' she said uncertainly.

'Yeah? She finishes at six I think. What'll we do till then?'

Leo would play any game Annabel wanted him to, letting himself be dragged through the bamboo or along the cold concrete alleys between the buildings. She could push and pull him around, saying, 'Stand there!' as she organised enemy troops behind him or took a run-up to swing on his hands as though she was on a carousel. If she was too rough with him his big warm hands would come out to catch her, holding her firmly until she calmed down. She hung panting in his arms while her heart slowed down, until she could feel his heart too, bumping against her shoulder.

When Madeline came blinking out into the quad, her arms full of books, they would be in the corner by the bamboo or perched together on a mushroom, deep in conversation. Her student friends separated and disappeared like clouds and her eyes became used to the light as she made her way towards them. A question mark and a comma, Leo curved over the small plump body of their daughter.

Evenings: if Leo was not playing they would walk out to where Madeline had parked the car and drive home, through streets softening in the twilight. Leo drove, Madeline sat next to him on the Kingswood's bench seat and Annabel crammed herself up against the window. It would not wind all the way down; its cold ridge pressed into her arm. She would lean out, mouth open, and the rushing air freeze-dried the insides of her cheeks. When they stopped at traffic lights tears would fill and warm her eyes, her stiff face relaxing.

Leo or their housemate Fabien would have cooked dinner. You could smell it as you climbed out of the car into the cool night air.

Once, when Annabel was three or four, the whole family had had the flu. At the time they were sharing the house with a handful of hippies, who had names like Cockatoo and Joanie. The hippies gave them massages and set fire to little piles of leaves for them. They whisked away the aspirin but let Leo gulp at a bottle of Scotch. One of them—an albino girl with pigtails like tiny horns all around the edges of her scalp—took charge of Annabel, who had such a sore throat that she could not swallow or speak. Madeline could feel Annabel watching her, waiting for the pain to be over, but she was too sick herself to be able to help. She and Leo lay tangled like snakes in bed, their skins hot and dry, the sheets caught around their ankles.

Madeline was the quickest to recover, but with her recovery came a tearing cough. If she was quiet she could hear her breath jarring in her ribs. It was interesting rather than painful—surprising to have to stop on the stairs until the air came back into her lungs.

It did not become frightening until the night her breathing cut out altogether, snatching her out of sleep and up to her knees in a world that had suddenly become two-dimensional. She gripped the iron bedrail, making a terrifying, consuming effort to pull air from the room around her, and Leo woke, some tug of the current or scrape of the reef knocking him into consciousness.

'What's wrong? What's wrong?' he'd said, his brain thick with sleep.

She could not speak or even look at him, trying to stay upright. She could feel herself growing dizzy. *But I am not ready!* Leo could do nothing but watch, his hands uselessly held out to her, his face stricken. Somehow, before blackness filled her eyes, her throat seemed to tear open, the air rushing into it in a freezing torrent, and she relaxed. She let Leo move forward and touch her, doubtfully, hands shaking.

This was where Annabel found them. She had struggled out of the arms of the white-skinned hippie girl and come bolting down the wooden corridor into their room. They looked as though they were praying, both kneeling at the end of their iron bed. The metal gleamed dully in the darkness.

Annabel sat up with her mother all of that night, in front of the blue flicker of the television, and every time Madeline dozed off she woke her. Every time Madeline dozed off she would begin to choke again.

This trouble did not abate as time passed. Once, she stopped breathing at a Thai restaurant after swallowing a chilli. Too much pepper on her food, humid nights, a cold—the family became accustomed to it and watched carefully for causes and symptoms. Leo read menus for her and surprised them all one night by saying to a waiter who had brought them a scaldingly hot curry, 'My wife can't eat this'.

They were careful but Madeline's breathing remained erratic. She went to a series of doctors. The first gave her an asthma inhaler that nearly killed her. The second, third and fourth said they could do nothing for her. The fifth, a woman with a brusque manner that brought tears to Madeline's eyes, told her to stop trying to breathe in when she had an attack—the problem was that she was letting no breath out. She tried it and it worked. All of a sudden she could control the attacks—she no longer had to wake Leo and make him rub her back or prop her up until she started breathing again. But they did not lessen in frequency; in fact, they happened more and more often. And so Madeline became one of the sleepless.

Sleeplessness is romanticised and overrated. Some people think best in the middle of the night. They spend the early hours painting or composing, or finishing the tasks too difficult to complete in daylight. Madeline, however, would not trust the things that went through her mind in the grey, angry hours between four o'clock and dawn. Weariness would grip her temples, pressing its fingers into her eyes, blurring her vision and making her head ache.

Sometimes, as the light began to wash into the blackness, water into Indian ink, Madeline gave up trying to sleep or think and got up to go for a walk. Leo never stirred. The cat would be a dusty shadow around her ankles as she made her way up the hall, hands against the wall as she went past Annabel's room.

King Street in least light was nearly empty of traffic, except for the big buses that swung down on the bus stops and the silent, upright figures beside them. Madeline was too tired to walk far or fast. She sat on the step of the delicatessen, hands wrapped around her knees, eyes cold and sore, and watched the street wake up. She tried to decide what she should do. The shops looked like children's building blocks, tumbled against each other, and their fluorescent night-lights singed the greyness.

Annabel was four. It was winter. They sat by the fire in the living room, in a tight circle that excluded their housemates, who lay on their beds upstairs drinking red wine, reading, watching television. Annabel held two plastic horses, one in each hand; she had been making them climb up the side of the couch.

'I'm stackin' zeds,' she said abruptly.

Leo and Madeline looked up from their Scrabble game.

'What'd you say, sweetheart?' said Madeline.

Annabel dropped one horse and drew a zigzag in the air. 'Zeds. Like sleeping. I'm tired,' she explained.

Leo let out a shout of laughter, scattering the Scrabble tiles with his foot. 'You better go to bed then,' he said, and lay back against the couch, laughing till tears rose in his eyes.

At the time of the holiday in Port Macquarie, Madeline spent the nights reading, or fishing on the dark shore of the river with whoever could stay awake.

It was a long drive up the black tar road to the Port Macquarie house, but it was a long, straight drive and you could see all around. On your left was the bay and the people windsurfing and the fishing boats moving patiently in and around the pleasure crafts. On your right were the houses. They stood on wooden stilts, fragile legs planted on holiday lawns. There were no flowers that needed to be watched and cared for, just hardy, always-green things: fat succulents, stripy shady gum trees and the grass fingering its way up the letterbox. Mowed every two weeks. The houses stood empty from family to family, from holiday to holiday.

Leo drove Annabel and her cousins along the road in the brown Kingswood. It was a station wagon, with a wide back window you could roll down. Annabel always chose to sit in the back. It was the best—it was bumpy, and sometimes she hit her head on the roof—fantastic. She would never be able to remember who shared the back with her—that's the way it is with memory; a single, clear picture becomes a small circus of colour and noise and people. Lots of kids in the back, shrieking and laughing as her father drove faster.

He always speeded up at the same point, because there was a dip in the road that they all knew. The rest of the road looked the same to Annabel—she couldn't tell how close they were until it curved so, so slightly, and the new church appeared, sitting on its own, its lap covered in a neat apron of green grass. That was when everybody started to scream and grab each other and her cousins shouted, 'Go, Uncle Leo! Go faster!' and she shouted, 'Go Dad!' and he would. He'd put his foot down and they'd race towards the dip in the road that was always full of water, whether it had rained or not, and straight through with a huge whoosh

15

of water on either side of them and all of them laughing so hard they thought they'd never stop.

Annabel's Aunt Helen did not like it when Leo drove so fast. Her feet, in hard, brown court shoes or her special holiday sneakers, would press against the thin carpet of the Kingswood's floor, desperately, tensely braking as Leo took the corners. The back wheels made fat seams on the road as they listed to one side—the Kingswood's behind like a cow's, swaying as the wheels struggled to find purchase. It was no use asking him to slow down. Years of loud music had stunned his hearing so that he could not unravel a tangle of sounds—a frightened voice and the roar of the car's engine were too similar in pitch to be taken apart and understood. He was better with sounds of different colours—the skeins of Madeline's low voice, the high jangle of a guitar, the hungry miaow of a cat.

Helen worried about letting her children ride with Leo, but she could not fight their noisy adoration of him. Even Tony, their father, was easily caught up in his younger brother's recklessness. Leo could give people the feeling that comes halfway through the second beer—that surprised, happy realisation of invulnerability. Drunk on his company, Tony forgot his fears for his children and never thought about the morning after. Helen, however, tasted the sourness of sobriety and disappointment even as she was holding the glass to her lips.

Leo's brother, Tony, was, in every sense of the word, a more solid version of Leo. Louder, bigger, and more than ten years older, his marriage to Helen had painstakingly produced four children—Marie, Daniel and the twins, Mickey and Claire. Each year the two families spent the Christmas holidays together—the larger engulfing and cradling the smaller. Helen cooked and Tony paid and the cousins took charge of Annabel.

A photograph in the Shearers' album showed Mickey and Claire on a wooden chair, each holding one end of a baby Annabel. They grinned into the camera but Annabel's face was red and puckered with rage. It was only in later years that everyone accepted that Annabel belonged to Mickey. The twins had been six when she was born and their presence during her growing-up, the transitions from crawling to walking, mumbling to speaking, imbued them with a kind of weary knowingness where she was concerned. Claire was more likely to silence her with a reference to some embarrassment of babyhood; Mickey smiled on her, fatherly, and proudly recalled the first word she had spoken and when she had learnt to read.

Leo had written a poem and Madeline had found it. She was nineteen—he was twenty-six. She was visiting the Erskineville house, waiting for Judy, her friend, to have a shower. She had her bag slung sideways across her body. She stood in the kitchen, in limbo in a stranger's house, running her fingers along the table edge, looking at the photos Blu-tacked on the fridge, reading the noticeboard. 'Get your arse out of here before the talent gets nervous.' 'Leo's turn to do the washing-up.'

There was a book on the counter that looked as though it had been dropped in water more than once, its leaves ridged and bumpy. It was black on the outside. She picked it up, glancing nervously around the kitchen. The only sound was the distant hush of the shower.

The writing in the book was pointed and scratchy and loose, in biro and pencil. Some of it looked to be years old and was difficult to read. She turned the pages, scanning songs and diary entries, too frightened to read anything from start to finish. And then she read, *Your breath, I imagine, is like avocados, new and green-sweet/ When I wake beside you in the morning it will mingle carefully with mine/ If we stay in bed for long enough the sun will leak onto the sheets/ And soon will flood us both . . .* she quickly put the book down as the bathroom door cracked open, her heart rising in her chest.

'Come and see my room, Maddie!' called Judy.

She straightened the book carefully, and pulled her bag firmly across her stomach. 'Coming.'

Judy was pink and small like a prawn, unfolding herself from her towel. Madeline sat on the side of the bed as she disappeared into her Gothic clothes again—draped black, a skirt that caught around her heavy boots, layers of ripped singlets and shirts. They watched themselves in the mirror—Madeline turning sideways to see her hair—Judy leaning into her reflection as she gave herself panda eyes.

'How many people live here?' said Madeline.

'Four of us . . . me, Nita, Andy and Leo.' Judy's voice was harsher now she was dressed again.

'What do they do?' Madeline half-listened as Judy recited until she came to, 'And Leo . . . well, he doesn't do much. Just plays in lots of bands. He writes songs. He's fuckin' hopeless.'

'What, at writing songs?'

'Nah, just at life. He's a pisspot. He's not that bad to live with, though. You can't help liking him.'

Madeline stored each sentence away. Later on she could remember very little about Judy, and nothing she had said—only her ripped, black clothes. At first her description of him had framed Leo—then, he had been framed by his songs and his guitar—and then they too had disappeared into the flesh of him. He was no longer definable for her. He was without edges.

Helen had tried to form a bond with Leo's new girlfriend because of Tony and the kids. They loved him and Tony felt responsible for him. The age difference, he explained, but Leo and Tony's parents were still alive, still providing for their boys. Leo already had a father.

Madeline's mother and father had moved to London in the same year that she started university, taking with them her younger sister and her kelpie dog. She had missed the dog most in the beginning, although it had not been pleasant company. She remembered once catching the yellow glare from its mean money eyes and feeling protected. It was nasty; it would snap and snarl at anyone who came near them. She did not like it, but it was hers and knew it. When her family left she owned nothing.

When Helen met Madeline, her lack of ownership had become a permanent state. She had not seemed to be able to claim anything or anyone since the emigration of the brown dog. Any time she spent with other people—at university, at parties, in the restaurants and cafes where she worked—made her feel like an amateur. She watched nervously as her friends conducted their lives and did her best to imitate them, correcting herself, repeating the steps to herself like someone learning a dance. When she was alone in the house she shared with other students, she found herself caught, confused; not knowing what move to make next. At these times she painted or read or lay on her bed, her legs aching with inaction, waiting for something to happen.

She would lie in her room in the middle of the day and stare out the window, seeing the trees hover in the silver sky and think, *Is this life? When will I know?* She wondered if there was a moment between sleeping and dreaming, between painting and reading, reading, reading, that she would suddenly wake, find herself alive. Her legs wobbly like a calf's.

She read Virginia Woolf's diaries. 'So the days pass, and I ask myself sometimes whether one is not hypnotised, as a child by a silver globe, by life; and whether this is living. Its very quick, bright, exciting. But superficial perhaps. I should like to take the globe in my hands and feel it quietly, round, smooth, heavy—and so hold it, day after day.'

It was a going-away party, an excuse for a drink, an excuse for people to throw arms around each other and weep into their beer, to take each other aside and whisper secrets, to watch each other and hope.

Madeline didn't know the name of the girl who was leaving. She was small and round, dwarfed by her enormous mass of dirty-blonde dreadlocks, upholstered like a cushion in a fringed purple dress. She drank quickly and happily, fat schooner glass constantly at her purple lips. She moved around the table to talk to all her friends.

Madeline sat at one end, next to Judy, her other side bare and exposed to the rest of the beer garden, her leg propped against the bricks to stop her from slipping right off. Her hands did not belong anywhere. She laid them flat on the table, curled them around her glass and, finally, sat on them. It was too early to leave.

When she was sure that he was occupied, she allowed herself to look at Leo. He was balanced on the back of the long bench-seat opposite, his legs askew, listening to the talk of two friends who sat below him. Occasionally he would laugh, a wild giggle that showed a red mouth, a white cemetery of teeth, a liquid brightness to his eyes. Madeline watched him and pressed down more firmly on her hands.

The night meandered on—Madeline talked to Judy and her friends, everybody was drunk and the long table began to lurch like a ship at sea, its passengers swaying dizzily against each other. Madeline, grinning to herself, still trying to stay wedged on the end of the seat, let her gaze rock tipsily around the beer garden, swinging over the heads of people, generously taking in the other tables, the shiny green palms in pots, the orange lights, until her eyes came to rest on Leo.

Just at that moment, someone up the other end moved and the whole row was shoved to one side. Madeline lost her balance and slid off the seat, her backside hitting the bricks with a thud that made her eyes blur and her shoulders crack. There was an instant commotion around her.

'Whoah, you poor old drunk!' laughed Judy, reaching down to catch her by the arm. Nita, Judy's flatmate, got to her feet and climbed over people's legs to help. Madeline blushed desperately and could not look up. She took the hands that were offered her and stood up stiffly, the base of her spine aching. She sat on the seat again as soon as Judy made room, waiting for the exclamations and laughter, the shouted apologies from the other end, to die down.

'Want another drink?' said Judy kindly, but Madeline shook her head. She was beginning to realise how horribly drunk she was. What had seemed like good cheer was now just a pitching nausea, the orange lights swirling towards her if she raised her head. If she kept very still she would not be sick. She stared hard at the table.

A long time later she was well enough to get to her feet and whisper goodbye to Judy, who threw her arms around her and turned back to her friends. She made her way carefully across the beer garden, concentrating on not staggering. She kept her arms crossed, holding herself in as she climbed the stairs. Once she swayed sideways and her shoulder thumped against the wall, but nobody else was in the dim-lit corridor and she pulled herself in and kept walking, straight through the front bar, head up, not looking to either side, eyes fixed on the middle distance as she pushed past the people around the pool table.

The street was cool and welcome, but she didn't break her stride or her line of sight, heading for home. She could not help herself listing to one side of the pavement, however fast she walked. There were still people around, and cars cruising along King Street. Madeline turned into Church Street and had gone one short block before she realised what she was doing. It was not safe to walk past the cemetery, down these ink-black streets on your own. She should have kept on up King Street instead of trying to cut across. Her step faltered—she stopped and looked back, but there was a couple behind her, following her confidently. She shook her head and kept walking.

The park was a vast, shadowy pool of silver. A small group of dark figures was crunched together on one of the benches. Madeline increased her pace and one of them called out, 'Hey!'. She walked faster, heart racing ahead, hoping the couple was still around.

'Hey, Madeline!'

21

She jerked to a halt—her heart clenched in her chest and then released, dropping off a series of loose beats. One hand against it, she peered into the park, trying to make out the faces of the group. There were three of them.

'Madeline! Come over!' the voice called again. It was male but unrecognisable.

'Who is it?'

'Andy. Judy's flatmate. We were at the pub.'

'What are you doing?' she asked as she made her way towards them, watching her feet so that she did not stagger.

'Having a party.'

Madeline reached them and saw Leo sitting in the middle of the group. Next to him was a Gothic girl who looked like a large spider; legs, arms and trailing black cloth clinging to the bench. She blinked slowly at Madeline but did not move or speak.

'Want a drink?' said Leo. He peeled a can from a six-pack of beer and passed it to her. She could not refuse the first thing he offered her. She split the can open and put it to her lips. A river of cold beer ran down her throat. It had been more than an hour since she had drunk anything. It tasted new and bitter—it sent a rush of clear air to her head.

The second time they met, Leo asked Madeline to a family barbecue. She said yes and wondered how long it would be before he found out she was faking it. Surely he would be able to tell when he saw her beside his relatives. Her limbs seemed to grind as she moved. He would be able to hear them.

Helen was the first person to name her. 'Madeline,' she said, coming down the concrete stairs with two trays of raw meat, 'do you like sausages or steak? Or both?'

Even this was too difficult. She looked frantically around at Leo who was leaning over the railings with his father, talking and drinking beer. Helen brushed past her.

'Are you a vegetarian?' she asked, setting the trays down by the barbecue. 'Don't worry, there's plenty of salad.'

Madeline could not answer. She would eat whatever was

offered to her. If nothing was offered to her, she would find that she was not hungry.

Leo's parents' house was a block-like red-brick house in Coogee. The backyard was on three levels—the first, a painted concrete platform with railings, a Hills Hoist and enough room to fit a table and chairs; the second, a flat rectangle of buffalo grass edged in by bricks; the third, a small jungle of frangipani, palm trees, the thick trunk of a Norfolk Island pine, and a bird of paradise flashing its angry orange spikes.

As they ate lunch, the Shearer family looked to Madeline as though they had been placed by someone with painting in mind—they made a composition that was balanced perfectly by Leo, who perched on a step and dipped his sunny eyes at her, and Tony, who stood sweating over the barbecue. In the middle of it all the twins, Claire and Mickey, swung round on the Hills Hoist, squealing and kicking and giggling.

Helen piled Madeline's plate with meat and watched curiously as the girl hovered by the wooden table where the salads and the sauces stood. She had the body of someone meant to be plumper, more rounded—though not thin, her arms and legs looked wasted and unused. She would put one hand out towards the tomato sauce and then withdraw it. Her movements were slow—she was not, at first, noticeably nervous or ill-at-ease but Helen wasn't sure that she knew just what she was doing. She wasn't like Leo's musician girlfriends, and she couldn't have been a groupie. They were invariably blonde and made a point of claiming him in front of the family, flinging skinny arms around his neck, whispering and laughing in his ear, flirting with his father and with Tony. This girl looked unplaceable. Her hair was thick, light brown, cut in a straight fringe above her black eyebrows. She wore leggings and a purple T-shirt that was obviously her best, and her arms clicked with silver bracelets. She had not used her voice enough for Helen to be able to tell where she was from—north shore or western suburbs, beach or inner city.

The other Shearers did not notice Madeline's awkwardness.

Lily and William were content with their sons, with Tony and his wife and their children, and Leo was everybody's loved one. He was their baby, their golden-haired, golden-voiced child. They watched him with awe and amusement, laughed at his jokes and hummed his songs. He had an excess of joy. When he visited, William would open the fridge and chuck him a beer which he caught as easily as he appeared to do anything else—one hand out, thwack, and the green can fitted neatly into his fist.

Eventually Madeline took her place by Leo. He moved over on the warm step and smiled at her. He smelt of coconuts—a streak of white sunburn cream still showed itself on his cheek—and of beer. Heavy, sweaty and sweet. He did not put his arm around her but hooked one ankle under hers. She didn't catch his eye. She had only known him a week.

Is there love and great love? Do we all have another half, walking the world in search of us? Is there a difference between waiting out your life with someone nice or friendly or interesting, and living alongside your other half? Madeline thought about these things as she looked down the slender length of Leo's arm. A finger drawn along it—just so—would smooth the goldy-brown hair almost flat, sleek like a seal's.

Her previous encounters with men or boys had been undertaken by her as one would an exam. As soon as they were over she forgot everything that she had learned except the one fact—she did not want to cover the subject again.

Later on she was to say to Leo, half-surprised, 'I was not me until I met you'. He would take her by the back of the neck and press his face against hers, and all their movements would have the frightening grace you feel when you are half-drunk. Everything would be easy.

∞

Port Macquarie. The children were having a conversation on the verandah. The adults sat inside, at the kitchen bench, drinking gin and tonics and listening to them.

Claire asked Annabel how many famous people she had living in her suburb.

'How famous?' Annabel sounded uncertain.

'Well, famous enough to be on TV. Famous so we've heard of them.'

There was a silence, enough time for the adults—for Leo and Madeline—to imagine Annabel counting on her fingers. And then a heavy sigh.

'How many?' said Claire.

'None,' said Annabel sadly.

'We have lots,' said Marie.

Inside, the adults smiled at each other and quietly filled their glasses. The gin was fragrant on the evening air, the ice sang a slight note. Madeline picked up a discarded half lemon and began to suck it.

Later on, when the children were in bed, the adults had run out of tonic so they were drinking the gin on its own.

'How many famous people in your suburb?' said Madeline to Tony, teasing, her hips swaying as she leant against the low coffee table.

'Hundreds,' laughed Tony, 'starting with me.'

'And Leo,' said Helen, watching them.

Leo chuckled. 'But I'm not from Balmain,' He stood up, catching on to Madeline for support, and climbed over the coffee table to where his guitar was resting against the television. 'I'm just a ring-in.'

'A loser,' offered Madeline.

'A nobody,' added Leo, and picked up the guitar.

'Play us a song, nobody,' said Tony, and tipped the last of the gin down his throat. He settled happily into the couch, hands behind his head, and watched as his younger brother began to play.

Leo had a quality that was difficult to describe—Madeline had once looked up the word 'sylph' in the dictionary to see if that was right—a kind of drooping grace. You could never be sure that he wasn't about to fall down, but as long as he stayed upright he could move like seaweed in running water, rippling and drifting on the current. The guitar was awkward and box-like on his thin knees, but he leaned comfortably over it, his mouth dropping open and hair in his eyes. His voice was deep. It seemed to growl out from somewhere behind him.

Late afternoon, and Helen came into the kitchen just as Leo reached for the gin. Their eyes met. She watched as his body flicked through two movements—the first, defiance, as he stiffened and frowned, his hand clutching the bottle's neck; the second, a kind of guilty goofiness, his mouth loosening into a smile as he pulled the bottle lovingly towards him, holding it against his chest as though it was a baby.

'Drink, Helly?'

'Oh, Leo . . . I don't know. What's the time?'

'About . . . 'bout . . .' Leo looked at his wrist, 'I dunno. Madeline's wearing the watch.' He went to the window and peered out at the sky. 'It must be past four.'

'Okay.' Helen slid onto a stool in front of the counter. She had been sleeping and was hot and hungover and achey, her hair sticky and warm against the back of her neck. 'Where're the kids?' she said.

Leo splashed gin into the red plastic cups. 'The beach. The river. Not sure. I saw Maddie with her fishing gear.'

'What have you been doing all afternoon?'

'We-ell. I went down to the pub with Tony, and then we took Bella to the beach. Then she and Tony went to get ice-cream, and now I'm here . . . with you,' he offered, and held out her drink.

Helen took a swig. 'Is Madeline with Tony?'

Leo sighed and said nothing. The beers he'd had at the pub swilled gently around in his mind. Helen had the angry, petulant look of someone who wants to cry but needs to be pushed, prodded—given a reason. It was more than he could manage.

They went back to the pub. Annabel and the cousins were out

in the beer garden, eating chips and drinking lemonade. Annabel's straw hat, covered in artificial flowers, flipped like a butterfly in the sun as she talked and laughed.

Leo said, 'Whose round is it?'

'Nobody's yet, mate,' said Tony. 'I thought you were going to take it easy.'

Leo's eyes widened in indignation. 'I've been good all fuckin' holiday!'

'Yeah.' Tony snorted and, in one movement, reached out and grabbed his brother, pulling him across his lap and smacking his arse. Then, just as easily, he put Leo back in his seat, his strong arms releasing him and stretching out again on the table. Leo had not had enough time to struggle.

Helen stood up, her eyes stinging with humiliation for him. 'I'm getting another beer. What do you want, Leo?'

'Same again, Helly,' he answered, draining his glass. His hair was not even rumpled.

∞

Leo and Madeline stand together in the deserted main street of a north-coast town. It is dawn, and already hot enough for the sweat to be running down their skins, making a pretty furrow in the space between Madeline's breasts. She is tanned a deep brown and her dirty-white maternity dress looks startlingly bright in the new light.

There is a strong wind, coming from the sea somewhere. Leo is trying to put on his shoes. They have just clambered, drunk with weariness, out of the Kingswood, and are looking for somewhere to eat breakfast. Leo leans with one hand on Madeline's shoulder but before he can pick up his shoes—tattered, years-old gym boots, the soles worn right through—the wind moves briskly along the street and the shoes move with it. Together, as though joined at the ankle, they are walking down the street.

'They're leaving without you,' Madeline observes, and the two

27

of them turn to watch. They sit down in the gutter of the wide main street, and the shoes go walking on, one in front of the other. The sun rolls redly over the fringe of roofs in the distance, and the street echoes with their laughter.

∞

Annabel's big, charming cousins called her Annabella and she loved them desperately. In the mornings she woke early and happy, so happy, she sat on the verandah and watched the river waltzing up to the stone shore and back again, she watched the river and ate Weetbix, dreamily pressing her spoon into the sweet sogginess of it, waiting for the house to wake up.

Each day she had about a dollar to spend and she walked up the long black road to the shop, swinging from one side to the other in the quivering heat, her sandals dirty with sweat. She bought a packet of strawberry bubblegum and a chocolate paddle-pop.

The day the whiting came she walked away from the shop, bubblegum in her back pocket, paddle-pop dripping down her arm, and wandered to where the grass met the sand. The water stretched away in a bright, sheer pool, ankle-deep forever, and she started to follow it out.

There were people with buckets way over on the edge of the horizon, dark, spiky shapes bent over in the shimmery silver. They appeared and disappeared as the light shifted. As she came closer she saw that two of the shapes were the twins, Mickey and Claire. She felt a stinging around her sandals, a prickling against her feet, and she looked down and the water was *alive*. It was alive with flickering jumping twisting dancing fish, each no bigger than her little finger; as she got deeper they fought around her knees. She finished her paddle-pop and bent down and scooped—a handful of mirrors, two handfuls of prickling mirrors, she threw them in the air and it was like the water shuddering out of a fountain, catching the sunlight until it joins itself again in the pool.

Claire and Mickey had one bucket each and they were dragging their buckets through the water—through the whiting—and with each drag they filled it, and filled it again. It seemed that they could never have enough, they needed more buckets, they needed buckets and buckets to contain this silvery avalanche. Annabel thought perhaps she should fill her pockets with fish. They looked at each other. Mickey upturned his bucket and they grinned and grinned, their faces aching with the pleasure of it.

They took the buckets of whiting home to use for bait, for midnight fishing and early-morning fishing. The worms they dug from the yellow sand were for bait too, long and spiny, but the crabs were not. The crabs were not for bait and not for eating. Just for looking at. But Annabel had never seen a live one.

They were blue, golf-ball shaped, with delicate eyes, and strong legs for scooping away the sand. They could dig as fast as anything, but their backs were soft, and every time Mickey dug down to catch one for Annabella, he came up with a corpse, its back crushed as soon as his hands found it. The two of them moved from place to place on the beach, Annabel growing more and more teary as each pale blue squash was held out to her. Finally she begged Mickey to stop, and he carried her home on his shoulders.

Leo was the only one at the house. He was sitting on the verandah with his guitar, bare chested, bare backed, in a pair of faded black jeans cut off at the knees. His face was shaded by a huge straw hat that belonged to Helen. A blue and red scarf was twisted around it.

'Hi Dad!' sang out Annabel, waving her arms. Mickey staggered slightly as she leaned forward, and clutched at her ankles. She was heavier than last year.

Leo waved back, putting his guitar to one side.

'Where's Mum?'

'Gone to the movies, baby. With Uncle Tony and the others.'

Mickey bent his knees carefully, tilting his head forward so that Annabel could slip off his shoulders. 'What did they go see?'

he said, panting slightly. Leo didn't hear; he was coming down the stairs. They were spiral, cement, welded to the verandah—the only way you could get to the top storey of the house.

As he reached halfway—as Annabel bounded towards him over the grass—the hat slid down, obscuring his vision. His foot missed the step and, unable to regain his balance, clutching at the air, he pitched forwards, his stomach hitting the curved railing with a thump! He did a neat somersault over it and onto the lawn below, landing on his back.

'Dad!'

The hat flopped softly onto the grass.

'Dad!'

Leo tried to open his eyes—it felt as though he had been cutting onions, clenched against the stinging pain. He could see Annabel, and Mickey looming darkly behind her. She came closer, and her skin looked like pearl—like mother of pearl, swirling. She had a bright white aura. So did the trees. So did Mickey. He shut his eyes again and tried to disappear.

Madeline was climbing the stairs, pulling herself up with her right hand. The others were still getting out of the car, finding bags and keys.

'Leo?' she called, reaching the verandah. She slid the glass door open. Annabel came bursting out from the bedroom, followed by Mickey, their eyes bright in the afternoon gloom.

'Dad fell down the stairs!' she said and then quickly, 'But he's okay. He didn't get concussion. He didn't hit his head.'

'What?' She stared at them. 'What happened?'

'He tripped or something. He's in bed.' said Mickey.

'He's okay, but. He's okay!' Annabel called after her mother as Madeline pushed past them to the bedroom. She turned to the others as they appeared on the verandah. 'Dad fell down the stairs!'

Leo was lying on his back, the sheet curled around his hips. The little well of hair that started just below his stomach was visible. He grinned when he saw Madeline.

'Did it again, Maddie,' he said. There was a wide, blue bruise like a bar across his navel—his hand moved to it, following her eyes.

'Jesus, Leo. Did the doctor come?'

'Yep. Bella called him.' Leo closed his eyes as Madeline kicked the door shut and came forward, taking the hand that stroked his bruise. 'There's nothing broken. I've gotta take it easy for a couple of days, but.'

'Does it hurt?'

'A bit.'

Madeline sat on the bed, and then lay down, her body warm against Leo's.

'I'm . . . ah! . . . I'm accident-prone,' said Leo, turning painfully on his side. Madeline felt his breath begin to slide under her T-shirt. 'This stuff always happens to me. Remember in Erskineville, when the wheelbarrow fell on me?'

Surprised, Madeline let out a snort of laughter. 'When you were sleeping in it?'

'Yeah. And I fell out and it turned right over?'

'Jesus that made me laugh.'

Leo opened his eyes, looking at her and smiling. 'Me too.'

And it was true. Leo had crouched under the weight of the wheelbarrow which had somehow swung right over so that he looked like a huge, awkward turtle, and laughed until he shook, laughed until the wheelbarrow shook, until Madeline was leaning against the back steps and crying with it, her knees bent, holding her stomach. The other people in the house had come out to see what was happening and stood perplexed, hands on hips, watching the strange little arrangement. The sun had shone and the leaves on the trees had danced in the light.

Leo gasped as the pain in his back suddenly bit into him, but moved forward anyway, bringing his hand around and under Madeline's waist. She reached out and pulled him on top of her. He pressed the breath out of her, flattening her hips against the

31

bed, but she shifted until she was comfortable, and then it was as if he weighed nothing, nothing at all.

A story from the Shearers (Where Leo Got To Be So Clumsy). Leo's father, William, is taking Lily Irene, his new bride, for a picnic down at the Royal National Park. It is a bright, hot day. Lily Irene is tall, long-legged and elegant. Her body dips and sways, or seems to, as she stands on the wharf in the summer breeze. William is slightly shorter, thickset and slickly handsome, in a hat from Anthony Hordern's and a suit with a barely perceptible pinstripe. They have a picnic basket that William has bought ready-packed with food and a couple of bottles of beer. Their boat whispers through the water to the wharf and William, loving the moment, hands Lily Irene across. She settles herself easily and watches as William turns to pick up the picnic basket and, swinging back, full of the joys of life, steps straight into the water.

'Leo should give up drinking, now.' Helen chewed at the sides of her fingers. She had a disease, an infection, that made the skin on her hands peel back and flake off. Looking at them in the mornings, she sometimes wondered if she was growing a new skin, like a snake.

Tony looked up from his magazine. 'Helen . . .' he said quietly.

'I know I've said it before! I know you've said it! But no-one does anything about it. Madeline just sits there and laughs at him, and you act like nothing's happening.'

'What do you want me to do?'

'I don't know! Something! What's going to happen to Annabel if he keeps on like this?'

Tony said nothing.

'And what about our kids? What must be going through their minds?'

'The kids love Leo.'

Helen was silenced, worrying at the loose skin on her thumb. Claire and Mickey, Marie and Daniel would never be talked out of loving their foolish, giggling uncle. They boasted about him to their friends, and the twins still begged him to take them for rides in the old Kingswood. Helen would sit low in the front seat, cringing with embarrassment when they drove up to the Port Macquarie shopping centre, exhaust rattling, windows forever halfway open.

Annabel, too, seemed to be happy, despite Helen's grim predictions for her. Born a scant ten months after her parents met, she'd waxed healthy and cheerful, not appearing to mind the living in shared houses, the regular disappearances of her father, the second-hand clothes and homemade toys. At eight she was much like Claire had been. It didn't seem right.

Tony tossed his magazine on the floor and turned over on the bed with a sigh. 'They do okay, you know,' he said into a pillow.

'And what happens when they get older and Leo isn't popular anymore? He can't be in a band when he's fifty.'

Helen angled her eyes down at Tony. He pulled another pillow over his head. 'Then I'll look after them,' he said at last, his voice barely audible.

Their kids and Annabel, and Daniel's girlfriend Linda, were sitting in the living room. The TV was on in the background, with the sound turned down—a re-run of *The Great Escape*. Mickey had Leo's guitar balanced on his knees, and he was improvising. He couldn't play, nor could he sing, but he spoke as he banged at the strings, sliding his left hand up and down the neck of the guitar as he had seen his uncle doing. He was making up a story, shouting over the voices of his brother and sisters:

'And then he went to *jail*,' (strum)

'And then it started to *hail*,' (strum)

'But he couldn't find a *pail!*' shouted Claire (strum strum strum).

'It sent him off the *rails!*' Annabel squealed.

Daniel and Mickey roared at their cousin. Her face was red with laughter and her thick blonde hair, its fringe cut crookedly across surprisingly fine, dark eyebrows, was a wild tangle of salt. Her mouth was wide and baby-toothed. Linda sat quietly, her back against the couch, watching them.

Annabel made a lunge for the guitar. 'Let me play! I'm the only one who knows how!'

'No way!' Mickey leapt to his feet and backed across the room, slashing madly so the room quivered with sound. Marie and Claire jumped up, Claire making a dive for him over the coffee table. The plastic cups and magazines shot on to the carpet. There was a distant howl from Helen and Tony's bedroom, 'Will you kids keep it down?', but it was lost as Claire clambered up and, followed by Marie, began pursuing her brother around the room. Mickey, long-legged and clumsy at thirteen, tripped and bounced off the walls, screaming with laughter. Annabel stared, half-terrified for her father's guitar, but unable to stop her own shrieks.

'Go, go!' Daniel yelled, adding to the noise.

'Jesus *Christ!*' Tony appeared at the door just as Mickey reached it. The two of them collided, Tony's strong arm closing around his son as he stumbled and would have fallen. The guitar clattered to the ground, ringing a hollow, unmusical chord. 'Just keep it bloody well down, won't you? And for Christ's sake, be careful with that guitar. Leo'll be furious!'

The children were panting, halted in their tracks. 'Leo doesn't mind,' said Marie. 'He said we could use it.'

Tony let go of Mickey, who slid down the wall, his body still convulsed with hysterical giggles. 'Leo is *asleep*. He hurt his *back*, remember? And you're keeping him awake!'

'No,' piped Annabel. They turned to look at her. 'Him and Mum went for a walk. I think they've gone fishing. Mum couldn't sleep again.'

'Well . . .' Tony shook himself, ' . . . you're keeping *me* awake.

Okay? Just give us a bit of peace and quiet or you can all stay home tomorrow instead of going to the beach. You too, Bella. I'll have a word to your mum, and you'll be in scrubbing the bloody floors. Yes? Right?'

'Yes, Dad,' said the older kids meekly.

'Yes, Uncle Tony,' said Annabel.

'Good.' He slammed out, leaving the little tableau still for the moment, and silent—Mickey sprawled against the back wall, Marie and Claire planted in the middle of the room, Daniel, Annabel and Linda ranged against the couch. Suddenly Linda got up. She was a shy, beige sort of a girl who only enjoyed being with the Shearers in retrospect—saying to her friends at school, *Leo Shearer's such a nice guy in real life.* 'I think I'll go to bed. I'm a bit tired.'

'Yeah? You sure?' Daniel jerked back his head to look at her.

She blushed. 'Yeah. I'll . . . uh . . . I'll see you later.' She waved at them, a ridiculous gesture in the living room, and turned away. They listened to her climbing carefully down the outside stairs to the room she shared with Marie.

Annabel got to her knees. 'Hey Mickey? Can I've the guitar? I'll do Dad for you.'

He passed it over. It was far too big for her, but she slid back onto the couch, crossing her legs and letting half its body rest on the cushions. Claire and Marie came and sat down.

'Which song?' she said, expertly beginning to tune the guitar.

'Do "Tired of Being Alone",' said Mickey, still leaning against the wall.

'No, "Rainmaker",' said Marie.

'No, do Leo doing Dylan,' said Daniel. The others giggled. When Leo began to play Bob Dylan songs, his audience were always halfway between laughter and awe. He could take-off the man perfectly, and without the least selfconsciousness, sinking his own deep, liquorice-black voice in Dylan's.

'Okay,' Annabel grinned and looked round at her cousins, strumming the first chord. Marie and Claire, their dark heads together; Daniel, stroking the first signs of a beard he was determined to grow; and Mickey in the corner, scratching unconcernedly at his pimples. They were so grown-up.

Helen, who had left Tony in the bedroom and was sitting on the edge of the bath shaving her legs with his razor, heard the singing and thought for a minute the voice was Leo's. As it went on and became recognisably Annabel's, her eyes filled with stupid tears. They dripped onto her leg and made a track in the soap.

Leo and Madeline were not in the house, of course—they were somewhere out by the black tide, arm in arm perhaps, or flinging out their lines to catch the big, lively fish who patrolled the beaches at night.

Midnight fishing. Who knows what you will catch under the dark lick and suck of the water?

Annabel was woken in the middle of the night. Madeline was leaning over her, cupping her shoulder with one hand and shaking it, saying, 'Annabel. Annabel.'

Her eyes twitched open to the sweet yellow light coming from the kitchen. 'What?'

Madeline said, 'Dad caught a shark. Come and see.' She was already leaving the room.

In the kitchen everyone was gathered, blinking, under the naked yellow globe. Tony lifted her up. In the sink there was something flat and white, about as big as a cat (its long tail bent backwards against the stainless steel). There was a desperate flap of water and it splashed her bare arms.

'It's a stingray!' she said, struggling to get down. Tony let her go and she landed, panting, on the wet lino floor. 'It's only a stingray!'

'It's a shark,' said Aunty Helen.

'It is not! We can't eat it, anyway!'

The thing flapped again and a jaunty spray of water flung up into the air, caught in a dazzle by the electric light. Annabel turned on Leo, who was standing against the fridge. 'Are you going to put it back?'

'If you want,' he said, smiling agreeably.

She looked around the circle of grown-ups. 'It's not a real shark,' she said again.

'Well, it is,' said Aunty Helen, 'but not the sort of shark you're used to.'

'I thought he'd caught a White Pointer,' said Annabel.

Everyone laughed. 'Sweetheart, I think Leo'd be a goner if he came face to face with the real thing,' said Uncle Tony.

'Would not!' said Leo. He pushed up his sleeve and flexed one slim, milky muscle. 'Just me and the deep blue sea. The White Pointer's next on my list.'

The stingray made a leap into the air, showering them with water before it landed with a slap on the lino. In the laughter and commotion—someone running for a bucket, someone trying to pick up the slippery, desperate creature with their bare hands—no-one noticed the appalled look on Annabel's face. She backed out of the kitchen and slunk back to bed, with the seawater wet on her cheeks.

Madeline and Leo came back from the beach one day, big with news. Helen was supervising the starting of a jigsaw on the coffee table. A cottage garden in England, an edge of thatched roof, an impossibly blue sky. Tony sat on the verandah with a beer.

'What's up?' he said, as the two of them climbed the stairs, shoving and jostling each other.

'We saw a dog at the beach . . .' said Madeline breathlessly.

'It had wheels!' roared Leo, coming up behind her.

'Its back legs must have been run over by a car, they were all limp and pathetic, so it had wheels instead, and it dragged them behind it, and it went bump-bump over the rocks! It was withered!'

'The withered dog!' crowed Leo. He ran into the house, shouting, 'The withered dog! The withered dog!' The kids crowded round him, jigsaw forgotten, demanding an explanation. He stood at the kitchen counter, his hands shaking and fumbling over the ring-pull on a can of beer, and described the scene. 'Its owner was jogging and it was keeping up!'

Only Helen and Linda stayed at the coffee table, picking out the edge pieces from the box, fitting them neatly together. With their heads bent they looked like nuns.

The withered dog, within days, became a Shearer legend. Leo saw it again, and worked out when it would be most likely to be on the beach. It went running with its owner in the afternoons. He would take a posse of people down in the Kingswood to see it. They would find a place on the sand, spread their towels out, and sit there, watching the dunes until it appeared, ears flying, back legs rattling along on their little carriage. The whole family would watch, breathless, until it had disappeared from view.

Madeline and Helen spent one long afternoon drawing a roster for the shopping, the cooking and the washing-up.

Madeline sat back on her heels, Artline pen poised. 'I don't know if we'll ever get Leo to do his share,' she said.

'We'll make him,' said Helen, busily ruling a line. 'We'll nag him until he does what we say.'

'He'll just go down to the pub.'

The two women looked at each other, Madeline striving for an expression of detachment, Helen's eyes sharp and curious.

'Does it worry you?'

Madeline put the cap on the Artline, and cleared her throat. She had been asked this question before, with varying degrees of interest—by Leo's friends, kindly but fascinated, or one of their string of tenants. People wanted you to break down or declare war. They saw things from the outside only.

'Sorry,' said Helen quickly, feeling the pause. 'I didn't mean it was a problem or anything . . .'

'It's okay, I'm just not sure what to say. Everyone wonders if I notice that Leo likes to drink. I think they think I'm just sort of lovestruck.'

'Aren't you?' Helen blushed furiously as she spoke, and made her line thicker and blacker.

'I don't know. No. Do I seem like I am?'

'Sometimes.' Helen pressed harder into the cardboard.

'I don't get it.'

The words came out in a rush. 'You don't say anything, ever. You don't complain about him. You don't ever ask for advice. All my girlfriends talk to each other about their husbands. I wouldn't be able to survive without them.' Helen suddenly felt ridiculous. She was fifteen years older than Madeline but had the uncomfortable sensation that she was speaking to someone far beyond her in age. She reached for the box of textas and began to colour in the circles and triangles they had drawn, too embarrassed to say anything more.

Finally Madeline said, 'Look. Sometimes I worry about Leo drinking, but not . . .' she took a breath, ' . . . I mean, he never does what people are imagining. He never changes. He's not cruel to me. I only worry about it because he might die, and if he died I couldn't live. That's all.'

There was a pause. 'Tony is scared for him,' said Helen.

'Is he?'

'That he will do something stupid when he's drunk.'

'Like fall down the stairs.'

'Yes. Or . . . or . . .'

'Or have an affair.'

Helen felt her blood stop. Madeline had never shown any sign that she knew about Leo's infidelity. It was an open secret, not just in the family but at the pub, amongst their friends, and even at their parents' house in Coogee, but she had somehow, purposely or otherwise, sidestepped it.

Sometimes Helen had wanted to shake Madeline and shout, 'Stop being so happy! Everything is not right!' But looking at the younger woman she realised that Madeline was just talking—not about a possibility, but about someone else's world, where things like that happened. Her breathing was easy, her face was placid, her dark eyebrows were smooth.

'I'll look after him,' she said, 'but I'm not going to forbid him to drink. We aren't like that together. Do you know what I mean?'

Helen nodded, and a sliver of pain lodged itself in her heart.

The women finished their chart in amity, if not perfect accord. Helen made them her favourite drink, that Leo and Tony scoffed at for being too posh. The two of them were sitting together on the verandah, their feet up on the railings, sipping margaritas when the rest of the family came home.

Madeline managed to persuade Helen to come to one of Leo's shows. Helen had not been to see him play for years. He had gigs in Lismore, in Byron Bay and farther north, in Kingscliff and Southport, and he would spend a few weeks there after they left the Port Macquarie house, sleeping in a tent or on someone's floor.

On the morning of their second last day the ten of them piled into the two cars, heading for Byron. Annabel sat up front with Tony in the white Commodore, playing with the airconditioning and squealing with laughter at the jokes Daniel cracked from the back seat. Linda sat next to the window and looked out, her breath leaving no mark on the tinted glass, and beside her Marie bounced and jostled and read the map, shouting directions at her father.

Madeline drove the Kingswood, her chin only slightly higher than the big bus wheel, with Helen beside her. They talked in low voices about Tony, about his job, and whether he had enough time to spend with the kids. Leo dozed in the back between Mickey and Claire, who exchanged glances and stifled giggles when his head fell forward onto his chest and he began to mutter to himself in his sleep.

They arrived early and dropped Leo off at the pub. He climbed up the wide stone stairs with his back bent like a beetle's, dragging the black shells of his two guitars. As they watched, the doors of the pub split open and Sean, the drummer, appeared. He took one of the guitars and the two of them were swallowed up into the clicking, grumbling gloom of the lounge bar.

Madeline drove them through town to Tallow, with Tony right behind. It was past five, and only a few panel vans and motorbikes still sat in the shady, sandy clearing that led to the beach. They slipped out of the cars and, slinging towels across shoulders and stowing shoes in Helen's big string bag, headed down the path to the water.

The shell of the sky cracked open, revealing the beach as they came out from the cover of the trees. Its pale blue vastness gave way to the green water, which yielded in turn to the white, white sand, as though some giant had dipped three fingers in three colours and smeared them across an endless horizon. The sand and spray made a haze in the air. The sun warmed their faces, smoothing each into a smile of surprise and happiness. Far, far down the beach they could see some people, but beyond them, nothing but sand and water and sky.

'I forget,' said Madeline, 'Every time, I forget how beautiful it is.'

Silently everyone undressed and drifted down to the water. They waded until the sea caught at their legs and pulled them under, turned them over, held them down and brought them up, gasping for the sharp air, dazzled by the sun as it lowered itself in the sky, their skins cold and clean and edgy with life.

The water was clear and empty—if they stood in the shallows, they could see the sand puff and sigh around their feet. Three goats, their voices like seagulls on the salty wind, called from the cliffs. The sky turned lilac and the water grew heavy and cold.

They had dinner at the hippie cafe, where Annabel ate tofu and the twins demanded a hamburger. Madeline watched as Tony combed the menu to find them something real to eat, his big hand playing carelessly on Helen's knee. He made friends with the waitress—not as Leo would have, charming her with his hopelessness, allowing her to clean around him and bring him extra drinks—but asking her questions about Byron Bay, about the food, about what she did when she was not working. She made jewellery—her arms and legs, her neck, her ears and her nose were encrusted with it, bright silver with flashing coloured beads. She gave Marie one of her rings, a tiny one to wear on her little finger, and brought Tony a steak surrounded with chips.

'I'm too old for this,' Helen whispered to Madeline as they started up the steps of the pub, 'This shirt's wrong. Where will the kids go?'

'They can sit in the beer garden with Daniel and Linda,' said Madeline, smiling at Tony as he held the door open for them. 'And you look fine. It's Byron Bay, remember? You can wear what you like.'

Tony bought the kids a coke, handing Daniel and Linda a can of beer each with a complicitous grin that could have been his brother's, and sent them outside. He turned to Helen and Madeline. 'So . . . what'll it be?'

'Beer for me too, I think,' said Madeline.

'Where's Leo?' said Helen, peering into the depths of the pub. 'And where's the stage? Is this where he's playing?'

'He'll be out in the back bar. The stage's there. What are you going to drink, Helen?'

'Oh, I don't know. Is there something I'm supposed to drink? I don't want beer.'

'It doesn't matter,' Madeline laughed, 'have a gin and tonic. Have a double.'

Helen looked at Tony, 'Is that okay?'

'You're bloody mad, Helen,' he reached out and pulled her close, planting a kiss on her forehead. 'It hasn't been that long since we saw a band.'

He walked off, jangling the change in his pockets, and Madeline caught hold of Helen's arm. 'Come on, let's go out the back and see Leo,' she said.

They made their way out along a carpeted passage, its walls grey from the palms of people who had staggered down it. The only occupants of the back room sat in a circle around one of the high tables, their feet resting on the bar underneath it. Helen hovered at the door as Madeline stepped forward. Someone in the circle saw her and they all swung round.

'He-ey, Maddie!'

Nita slid down from her seat and came over, her arms wide to catch Madeline. The two women hugged and Helen caught sight, for a second, of Leo, his bright eyes flickering in the darkness. He was sitting next to a woman with long curling red hair who stared at Madeline as she swayed in Nita's embrace.

The others waited their turn to greet Madeline and Helen—Sean and his girlfriend Chris, Joel and Russell and the red-headed woman, who Madeline did not know.

Chris and Nita were really Leo's friends: hearty, cheerful women, their accents broad, their skin brown, their manner generous. As they became used to Madeline's continued presence by his side, they had quietly, without any encouragement, transferred their allegiance to her. She became one of them and they included her in their humorous diatribes against their men, assuming her agreement in matters of sex and fidelity. Secretly they wondered if she was a proper feminist, but publicly they claimed her and were loyal to her.

As a sign of this loyalty they had agreed never to tell Madeline about Leo's other women. It wouldn't be good for her. It would only make her unhappy. The responsibility of telling her was one that no-one wanted to take, for where is the line to be drawn between friendship and malice, between assistance and interference?

Madeline kissed Leo, sliding her hand around the back of his neck, introduced Helen to everyone, who had met them all before, and, coming to the redhead said, 'Sorry, have we met? I can't remember . . .'

'Natasha,' said Nita quickly.

Madeline put out her hand to shake Natasha's. The redhead's hand was cold and bony.

For Chris, for Nita, for Sean—in fact for everyone except Madeline and perhaps Leo—the atmosphere crackled and spat with tension. This was not the first time that Madeline had been in company with Leo and one of his lovers, but tonight Madeline had her other family around her. No-one could be sure that Helen would not take Madeline aside and point Natasha out to her, describe Leo's behaviour, and possibly implicate the rest of them. Helen herself shook with fear at the thought that Leo would be indiscreet, that he would lay a hand on this redheaded woman in front of Madeline and that the world would collapse around them.

Leo leaned forward to Helen who sat on the edge of the group, and said, 'Aren't you drinking, Helly?'

'Oh, yes, Tony's . . .' she swung round just as he came through the doorway, balancing their drinks. Leo leapt down from his stool and ran over to help his brother. Together they looked like a carthorse and a colt—Leo's long legs tripped him up so that he nearly spilt Helen's gin and tonic, but he caught himself in time and reached Helen's side with it. She took it and gulped gratefully at it, its cold perfume curling into her mouth.

Everyone was drunk by the time the band came on. Helen had been taken aside by Chris and engaged in a long conversation about sex. The women's openness—Nita joining in, raising her voice to be heard over the support band—both bewildered and fascinated her. They took her arm, smiled and talked directly at her and shared her drink, all without asking or needing to ask. Madeline watched them with a humorous light in her eye, happily nursing a beer and laughing at Tony's jokes, who sat beside her and shouted into her ear, bought beers for everyone and put a hand on Natasha's thigh. She pointedly removed it and stalked off to the bathroom.

After Leo's third song, Helen and Madeline went outside to check on the kids again. Each time they had gone into the beer garden the kids had made a new arrangement of themselves, like disciples changing places at the Last Supper. It was past twelve and Annabel was in Daniel's lap, her head heavy against his arm, fast asleep. The twins and Marie had made friends with some teenagers at the next table, and Linda sat beside Daniel, her back stiff with boredom.

'Who's that girl with the red hair?' said Helen to Madeline, her tongue made dangerous by gin and curiosity. 'Haven't I met her?'

'I don't think so. I've never seen her.' Madeline reached out and grabbed a handful of chips from the bowl on the table.

'She's attractive, isn't she,' said Helen daringly.

'You think so? Sort of thin, though. A bit witchy.' Madeline shoved another handful of chips into her mouth and Helen swallowed back more questions and the stale, sweet taste of tonic, marvelling at her ignorance.

'Is it time to go yet?' said Daniel, shifting Annabel so that her head leaned against his chest.

''Fraid not, Danny,' said Madeline in Leo's voice. He smiled and she went on, 'Why don't you come inside? Leo knows the guy on the door. He'll let you in.'

'But what about . . .?' he nodded down at Annabel.

'Here, give her to me.'

Annabel was too big to be carried, but Madeline stood up, lifting her into her arms and settling her legs around her waist. 'Let's go back in. Come on, Linda. The others'll be okay.'

They staggered inside again, ducking their heads under the wall of noise. Daniel took Linda's hand and dragged her down the front, where Tony was dancing uninhibitedly with Chris and Nita. Madeline and Helen made their way through the crowd to the back bar, where they climbed onto stools. Madeline leaned over her daughter's sleeping head to order a drink and, as she did, felt someone's gaze. It was Natasha, standing in the corner, her orangey eyes fixed on Madeline. Madeline smiled and waved, and Natasha looked quickly away.

They stayed at a hotel, and next morning Leo and Madeline woke early and drove down to the beach. The grass on the nature strip bristly-starred with dew. The dawn clouds were still clearing, bowing gracefully away, backing to the corners of the sky. The sun breathed warmly on them, but if they turned their heads, they could still feel the cold of night.

'Want to swim?' said Leo, drawing Madeline's arm around his waist.

'Mm.'

They wandered up the beach. A flock of black-backed gulls crooked their wings into sudden boomerangs. Two pelicans, standing feet-deep in the give and take of the tide, twisted their heads slowly as Leo and Madeline approached, cool black eyes following them. They raised their wings slightly, unsettled their feathers, but Leo and Madeline stopped. A silent group, watching each other.

The water was that muscular cold it always is in the morning. Washing their faces, holding fast to their arms and legs. Madeline swam a long way out, turning on her back, watching her feet tip in and out of the blue-green surf. The sun began to wheel higher in the sky. Tilting again towards the beach, she could see Leo sitting in the shallows, knees drawn up to his chest. She dived under and swam, eyes open against green ropes of light, feeling the roil and rush of water, straight towards him.

∞

Sean's friend's house was blue, made of wood, and always damp. You could see cracks of light in the splintered floorboards; through them, the dirt some two or three metres below. If you slept with your shoulder or back touching the wall you would wake in a puddle, the water soaking down your body and onto the mattress. It did not matter whether or not it was raining outside. The house had been built on stilts to save it from floods, but nothing could stop it from absorbing the moisture that sat heavily in the air, day after long, hot day.

Leo had a hangover. He climbed carefully out of bed, one hand uselessly gripping the sheet to stop himself from falling over, and stood up. Dizziness began in his chest, quickly rolling up so that his shoulders shook and his head whirled. He closed his eyes and tried to stand perfectly still. Slowly the movement subsided and, without looking back at Natasha, who slept with her body hunched away from him, deep in the bedclothes, he made his way out to the kitchen.

Sean was sitting at the table, building a shoddy joint with two papers. The tobacco was not mixed properly and kept sliding on to the plate in front of him. He looked up when Leo came in. They both nodded wearily—survivors of the night before. Leo sat down quickly in case he threw up.

'What's going on?' he said at length.

Sean finished the joint, clumsily folding a filter into it. He reached for the matches and lit it before he spoke. Squeakily, his throat thick with smoke, he said, 'Nothing.'

'Where's Chris?'

'Still asleep.'

Leo was too sick to look straight at Sean. He was having trouble containing even the scene before him—the kitchen with its pale-blue dirt-scarred walls, hung with saucepans and old photographs; its view onto the misty back paddock. A cow moved gently towards the house. He shivered slightly inside his damp clothes, waiting for the joint to be passed to him. Inexplicably, from a place deep inside his body, rose a terrible ache. It reached up and gripped his throat.

The floorboards in the next room creaked and there was a clank as something was dropped into the bath. Leo clutched the metal edges of his chair and felt his eyes fill with tears. The pain had become a cold knife behind his forehead.

Someone turned the shower on. Sean handed the joint over and Leo released one hand and took it, putting it to his mouth and snatching in the smoke. It was like the sudden smack of a fist on the back of his throat, and then the warmth of it filled his chest again and the pain dissolved, the tears that had formed disappeared.

The morning sun was a yellowish-grey behind the mist, which would clear later to a glittering light, and the day would be hot and would lose itself in the afternoon. No-one would see the sun set because they would be working, setting themselves up at the pub or club, taking drinks from their glasses of thin, cold beer, beginning the evening that would end once more in grey morning, in the damp blue house on the outskirts of town.

∞

Madeline woke suddenly in an utter vacuum of air and meaning. Pressing one hand to her empty throat, she scrambled to her knees and looked about her. She did not recognise the room. She could not think in what place the room might be. Fishing deeper, she realised that she did not know who she was or even what she was. Sleep hung cold and calm from the walls.

She choked, and did her best to breathe out, trying not to panic, and as the air cut into her lungs, began, with slow effort, to bring herself back, forming the ideas in a row in her mind. Person. Person—Madeline. A room. My room. Sydney. Our room. Leo.

She knelt unmoving for a while longer and the things around her gradually swelled with life and familiarity. But beside her in bed the sheets lay flat and hard, and the clothes strewn on the floor and hanging from the chest of drawers were hers only, giving out no added warmth or sweet smell.

Leo was still up north, and Madeline's tan no longer surprised her when she looked at herself in the mirror. Her flowered dresses were clean now, and cooler in their colours against her fading skin. Once Leo had rung, from a highway it seemed, from a background of rushing, roaring traffic, of clashing car doors and unrecognisable laughter.

Madeline tried to spend the endless waking hours painting or gardening, but mostly lay on the bed, feeling as though she was in a cardboard shroud of weariness and loneliness. People are places to send your emotions—without Leo, Madeline's had no destination. They floated instead, hanging about until they finally evaporated.

But in the afternoons Annabel came home from school. Madeline watched her walking slowly up their street.

An old milestone, uncovered by the layers of tar on the pavement, marked the distance from Parramatta and each day Annabel stopped to sit on it, unaware of her mother leaning over the fence. The house's aura, its spillage of talk and laughter, of food and homework and her mother's smell, did not reach as far as the milestone, and when Annabel sat on it she lived alone, tired but independent, thirteen miles from Parramatta.

Once she was in the envelope of home, the colours of the curtains grew brighter, the fridge started up, and the paintings in Madeline's studio showed doorways, entrances to change. It was hard to say who followed who—from room to room they went, and the floors and ceilings billowed with ideas. They began to make a collage. They cooked scones. With Fabien, who was living in the top room, they visited the old cemetery where the crumbling headstones, immersed in the afternoon sunlight, turned a rich gold; where people and their dogs trod happily through the grass or paused to talk at the entrance under the dark snakes' arms branches of the Moreton Bay fig.

Madeline had once run through the cemetery at night, dragged along by Leo. She could not remember whether they were being chased by someone or whether they were just in a hurry, nor could she remember whose idea it had been to take the shortcut, but she remembered scrambling to the top of the sandstone wall, which must have been ten feet high, pushing herself up from the graves that leant against it. It was farther to the ground on the other side, but Leo had dropped over without stopping, rolling away on the grass. It was too far—she had tried to grip the top of the wall with her hands but something cut into them, and the pain launched her forward so she landed with a shuddering thump on the hard ground, and fell over. Leo had picked her up and later, at home, she had looked at her torn, blood-clotted hands and thought of the row of broken bottles cemented into the top of the wall to keep away intruders. They healed, however, as hands will, in a matter of days, leaving no scars.

Without Leo, Madeline tripped and stumbled; she hit her head on the window sash as she leaned out, she smashed her toes against the bathroom door and crushed her fingers between the wall and the couch.

Meanwhile, on the long, sandy shore of Kingscliff beach or in the living room of the blue house, Leo danced and swung his way through the days, his feet made graceful by the disappearance of trust. There was nothing to trip over anymore. Natasha's skin turned the colour of topaz in the sun, and her eyes shone in her bare, spare face.

During the days alone, Madeline left her painting three or four times in an hour to look at herself in the mirror. Sometimes she undressed and tried on different clothes, dressing for outdoors while her head ached with the thick trance of hours spent inside. Her tan paled but her body did not change—stomach fitting into her palms, arms smooth and strong (the cup of her shoulder, where she could rest her face and smell Annabel), legs sturdy and covered with light hairs.

Sometimes she looked only at her eyes, but their colour could not be told in the dim light of the bedroom. She licked her fingers and smoothed back her eyebrows. She put lipstick on and took it off. And sometimes, wearing jeans that she had not worn for years, or with her hair caught up in a bun or wedged under a hat, she ventured out onto King Street. For ten or fifteen minutes she would walk from shop to shop, clutching her wallet, and then grow hot and uncomfortable in the unfamiliar clothes, and the exhaust from the trucks would make a dizzying mix with the heat and would shimmer the traffic all the way into town. She would see someone she knew and not be able to think of their name and she would walk quickly home with the sweat trickling down her calves and in her hand a bunch of grapes or a bag of oranges from the fruit shop.

Fabien's orange cat had been slender and sleek. He fed it fresh meat. It loved him; it forced its way into his lap while he was watching television, twined around his slender legs as he dressed in the morning, and was waiting for him on the verandah when he came home. But during the day it visited two or three other houses and demanded food, as though it was starving. It was beginning to grow fat and sluggish.

Sean had once scathingly described Madeline as 'a saint' after she'd failed to recognise a direct invitation to sleep with him. To the others she did seem to have the vacancy or imperturbability necessary for sainthood. Madeline could not understand when Chris or Nita, after describing some drunken night or fight, would add things like, 'But you'd never do that. You're so good.' The resentment made their voices sour. They did not see through her, could not hear the unoiled creak of her limbs as she moved, or know that she had spent many nights lying on her bed in a whirl of alcohol, enduring the clamorous echo of her own cruel, boastful or foolish words, shaking her head to try and knock loose her image of herself.

If the trees speak, if the traffic continues to roar and scream, if your daughter whispers in your ear and your loved one mutters and chuckles beside you, are you likely to hear anything else? Is this symphony or cacophony the right size for one mind?

Madeline did not hear the murmur beneath the noises that surrounded her, did not feel the reef underneath the urgent pull of the current. And Leo kept forgetting to call.

Natasha was long and graceful, her skirts reaching her ankles in an elegant swirl when she walked. Her legs did not dangle from the barstool. Her feet rested neatly on the crossbar and she held her beer in two cat-like hands. She was talking about her gallery. She sponsored young painters, and spoke as if she was not young herself. She was thirty. The other women had their feet curled around the bars of their stools. Sean sat with his legs crossed, and Leo perched next to Madeline.

Natasha leaned across to Madeline and said, 'Leo says you paint, Madeline.'

Madeline glanced at Leo and said, 'Just for myself, mostly.'

Natasha smiled. 'Are you any good?'

Madeline stared at her. She took a drink of her beer and Leo said, 'Oh, she's good, she just doesn't work hard enough.'

'Don't be mean, Leo!' said Natasha. 'I bet she works twice as hard as you. He spent all day sleeping, up north,' she added.

Madeline looked at Leo, and then away, and caught Chris' eye. The expression on Chris' face, the light of fear that glimmered there gave her a nasty, bewildering jolt, as though she had been accidentally elbowed in the face in a crowd. She quickly closed her eyes as the hurt spilt into them. The group of friends all stared shamefacedly into their drinks while Leo tipped his into his mouth, eyes tilted to the ceiling.

Leo said, 'Same again?' to the group and they jumped to agree, Russell fumbling in his pockets for change, Sean and Joel downing their beers to prepare for the next. Madeline opened her eyes and sat upright on her stool, keeping her head above water, feeling the ripple of the women's glances around her. Her ears were burning.

She watched Leo's set with her face still warm, clenching her ears and jaws tight against anything more. No more. Each time the beer began to flush sweetly into her veins she saw the look on Chris' face, her eyes shifting away, and she hooked her feet hard into her stool so that their joints ached. Other nights she had felt Leo's songs working their way across her mind. Tonight, nothing. She forced him away from her. The effort made her ears ring. The people in the pub were like cold sentinels, slowly drinking their beer and nodding their heads in time.

Leo took his shirt off and his pale body bent and twisted under the weight of the music. For a while Madeline stared at him, at his white chest, the lights washing blue and red over him, but he did not look at her once. People drifted in and she kept her eyes fixed on her hands. She heard Chris say, 'Are you okay, Madeline?' and lifted her head for long enough to smile and nod.

Leo finished his last set. The lights came on. Chris and Nita were red-faced and cheerful, calling for last drinks while the men packed up. Bracketed by them, Natasha was silent, a pale calm column, still delicately holding her oversized glass. Madeline climbed down from her stool, picking her way out through the tangle of people.

She stood outside, gathering breath for the walk home, away from the people lingering in cheerful groups against the tiled wall of the pub. Through the window she saw Leo lean over to the taps and fill his glass with beer, then swing around to where the women sat. Chris said something but he did not hear. He stooped forward so that his ear was next to her mouth, and Madeline saw Chris point to the door, and Leo look up, frowning. He caught sight of Madeline, nodded again when Chris spoke and, setting down his beer, pushed his way outside.

'What's up?' he said, taking Madeline by the arm and drawing her to one side.

'I think I might walk home,' she answered.

Leo said nothing.

'Why won't you look at me?'

'What? When? What do you mean?' he rubbed his hand nervously against the back of his neck.

'You just . . . oh, Jesus, Leo, you know what I mean.'

It was the fact that she had heard these words so many times before that surprised Madeline. As she and Leo stood under the yellow triangle of light on the pavement she was aware of a feeling of distance, of removal from the subject, even while the tears scratched under her eyelids. She could have been reading from one of the colourful women's magazines in the rack at the laundrette. Although she had never used them before the words came out already tasted and chewed.

'Well . . .' said Leo. His eyes kept straying to the dim interior of the pub where the band were packing up. They swarmed over the black boxes, they snatched and gulped at glasses of beer, they cracked jokes and shouted at the women, whose heads tilted towards each other as they talked. Watching his gaze drift past her shoulder Madeline could hear, silent inside her, the beginnings of one long continuous scream. Outside she stood still, arms folded tight across her stomach.

She looked around, trying to gather some sense from the thoughts that sang in her ears. 'Something's changed since you got back,' she said with an effort. 'I can't work it out, though. I can just . . . feel it.'

'Nothing's changed,' said Leo tiredly.

'Leo,' said Madeline, her face aching, 'there's a problem, isn't there?'

'I don't know,' he answered.

Without thinking, she went on, addressing the lights above their heads, 'There's a problem . . . and the problem is that I love you more than you love me.'

Leo looked straight at her and shrugged, and the breath kicked out of her chest. 'I love you more than you love me,' she repeated. The scream rose inside her and she turned away quickly and started to walk down the street.

'Maddie!'

She walked faster, wrapping her arms more firmly around her as the tide of tears began. The traffic rushed and shrieked on the black road and the streetlights glared.

'Maddie!' Leo caught up with her, grabbing her by the shoulders. She stopped, and he swung her round. She was shaking. She could barely see him.

'Where did this come from?' she said. 'When did this happen? Was I looking the other way? I don't understand.'

'There's nothing. It's nothing.'

'I'm going home.'

'Don't go.'

'I'm going home, Leo. I have to go home!' Her voice was

shrill with pain. Leo stood staring at her for a second. Her cheeks dripped with tears. He swallowed. He couldn't feel anything. He reached out and pulled her to him, pulled her close so that her face was squashed against his chest. She started to sob, howling wordlessly into his pale flesh, and his arms tightened around her—as though by crushing her he could somehow crush the misery, flatten it so that it slid neatly away. They stood like that for a long time, Madeline half-struggling to escape, as curious crowds from the pub pushed past them. A car full of boys honked and one leant out and yelled, 'She's heartbroken!'

Finally Madeline broke away. The lights dazzled her. Her T-shirt was soaked. 'I'm going.'

'I'll get you a cab.' Leo lifted his hand and straight away a cab nipped out of the traffic, pulling up beside them. He opened the door for her. She was dazed, staggering against Leo as he took her arm. 'Don't do anything, Maddie,' he said, glancing back down the street towards the pub. 'I'll be home soon. I've gotta pack up, then I'll be home.'

She nodded and climbed in, her knee crashing against the open door. Crunch. Kneecapped. She imagined someone swinging at her with an iron bar. She would crumple to the ground, bones bluntly broken.

'Are you going to be alright?' Leo stepped back as she turned her face up to his.

'I don't know,' she said.

'I'll see you later on.'

The cab driver did a U-turn, swinging right across King Street, and whisked Madeline towards home, where Annabel slept like a cat in front of the late movie and Fabien murmured to his friends over cups of chamomile tea.

Leo did not come home, that night or the next. He stayed at Natasha's. She took him to see a friend of hers, a clairvoyant, who read his palm and said there was great talent. In the mornings she slid out of bed and stood over him as he lay twisted in her clean white sheets, the blue light of early day making his face look sick and pale. Before the wild smile, the uneven teeth showed themselves, before he woke, Leo did not look like anyone. Asleep he was closed down.

In those moments Natasha didn't like him, didn't know what she was doing; hoped he would go. But she would dress holding her breath, not sure if too noisy an exhalation would wake him, bring him to life and make him remember where he was.

For the first day Madeline walked around smacking her rage from hand to hand like a sand bomb, packing it harder and harder, waiting for her moment to hurl it into Leo's face. But he did not ring or come home and she had nowhere to throw it. In the middle of the night she lay on the couch in the empty living room, the bomb of rage on her chest, and watched it crumble, right before her eyes.

When she moved now she felt her head held back, her spine forced rigidly upright, her stomach pressed flat so that she could not eat. She could not bend down, could not collapse into bed, could not cry through the feel of metal knuckling at her eyes, pushing against her throat. She cooked dinner for Annabel and Fabien, she put the garbage out, she sat on a chair in the kitchen and read the calendar on the opposite wall. And, at Annabel's insistence, she took her to a party at Chris' house.

The party was in the backyard. Leo was not there. For an hour Madeline sat on a rectangular chunk of sandstone and watched Annabel playing with the other kids. Someone had set up a trampoline for them. It was dark in her corner—the light from the barbecue was warm and red on the faces of the people standing around or moving in and out of it like dancers. Someone poured a beer across the hotplate, setting up a frightening hiss and spit, smoke and steam clouding around them. Madeline's thighs hurt. She felt like someone having a stroke in slow, slow motion.

She shifted her gaze to the little group who sat directly in front of her, clustered around their beer cans and cigarettes. She wanted a drink herself but was terrified that it would release a rush of sentiment, or even worse, desire. She could only bear to be awake if she was cold and sober. The group did not see her, and she did not recognise any of them. She bent her head towards them to hear what they were saying. Her throat began to close as she realised they were talking about music.

She waited for them to mention Leo. They had to. It was a game, surely; their moves were deliberate; they were circling but they would attack. When his name was mentioned she would stop being able to breathe. It would catch in her throat, she would not be able to swallow it. She felt the muscles in her neck and shoulders begin to clench.

A song of Leo's began playing on the stereo and one of the girls said, 'Leo Shearer . . .'

Madeline choked and tried to stand up. Someone swung round. *Breathe out*, she said to herself. *Breathe out*. Her legs would not work.

'Are you okay? Did you swallow something the wrong way?' The girl who had said Leo's name was looking at her, her cigarette prickling the darkness.

She shook her head and managed to get to her feet and her throat cleared, enough for one shot, two shots of air. She could hear herself making the low, growling noise the family had become so used to. The group of people looked curious and slightly repulsed. They had stopped talking and were all staring at her.

'Aren't you Madeline?' said one of them, 'Leo's . . .'

She stepped hastily, awkwardly over their legs and, breaking into a run, headed for the house. What was the point in being woken up for this? Better to have stayed asleep; better to have wound down like a clockwork doll than suffer this pain.

Someone said, as she brushed past them, that Leo was with a new woman.

Someone said that Leo was with a redhead.

Someone said, 'I bet he marries this one.'

She bumped blindly into Chris at the front door, who said, 'Maddie! Where you going?'

'I've got to go home,' she answered, head down.

'What about Annabel?'

'Oh.'

'Want me to get her? She's outside, I think.' Chris bent down to look into her face. 'Are you okay? Where's Leo?'

Madeline spoke in a voice screwed into a twist, a stifled shriek. 'Can you take Bella tonight? Do you mind?'

'No, of course not! I'll bring her home in the morning. But what about you? Are you alright?'

'Yes.' The word was a thin breath, slitting her throat.

'Okay. But call me, won't you, if you need me?'

'Yes.'

Madeline walked home fast, her shoulders down, pushing through the darkness. When a man whistled at her under a silvery streetlight she had just space enough to wonder, 'How can he even see me?'. She herself could only see the black pavement disappearing under her feet.

The party was held in a box of night. The sides of the box were papered with people, with the looming darkness of trees, with stars and, as Annabel bounced high into the air, with the orange flood of houselights over endless roofs.

The other kids fringed the trampoline, their heads moving up and down as they watched her jump. It couldn't be her turn for much longer. She had been jumping for ages already and she was sweaty, and her knees were beginning to ache. But with every bounce she went right over the heads of the people and she could see her mother, sitting safely still on her own on a big piece of rock.

Fairly soon her father would arrive. He might sing, or he might dance with her mother, and then they would go home. She would fall asleep in the car trying to tell by each sway and veer of the back seat (her head pressing uncomfortably against the vinyl-padded door) how close they were, and her mother might pick her up and carry her inside and she would listen to the two of them talking, they would say sweet incomprehensible things as her head drooped over her mother's shoulder. She would be asleep again before her body even touched the soft blue sheets.

Annabel began to gulp and cry with shock when Chris told her that Madeline had gone home without her. She was standing near the barbecue, surrounded by kids, who a second ago had been fun and friendly, and now were threatening, their mean interested faces devilish in the firelight. Where had her mother gone? Why hadn't she said anything? She tried to swallow her sobs.

'Hey, don't worry, sweetheart!' said Chris, taken aback. 'You can sleep in Zara's bed. Or you can sleep with me if you like, and in the morning we'll go and see Mum.'

Annabel was choking on her tears, unable to speak.

'Come on,' Chris took her hand, 'let's go inside and dance. You want to dance with me? Come on, sweetie. Your Mum said to tell you to be good.'

But Annabel was stricken with terror at the thought of spending the whole night with these wicked, laughing people, and although she followed Chris into the house and even allowed herself to be pushed and pulled around on the carpet in front of the stereo, she could not stop crying. She cried and blundered onto Chris' toes and watched the black frame of the front door until, rubbing one hand through his lion-coloured hair, his head thrown back in a roar of laughter, Leo appeared.

'Dad!' she shouted, snatching her hands out of Chris' and rushing towards him. His grin widened when he saw her and he dropped to his knees to catch her. 'Bella! Where've you been all this time?'

She giggled and swung back and forth in his arms.

'Where've *you* been?' she was just about to say, but then he beat her to it and said, 'I've had heaps of shows, sweetheart. Why you crying?'

The tears were forgotten; although her face was still wet, she could barely remember what she'd been crying for. She was too pleased to see him, but over her head Chris said (her voice suddenly leaden), 'Madeline was here, Leo, but she had to go home. She left Annabel with me.'

'Yeah?' Leo stood up, with Annabel's arms still twined about his neck. He heaved her onto his hip. 'D' you tell her I was coming?'

'I didn't say anything. I never know what you're going to do, anyway.'

Leo just stood there, jogging Annabel up and down.

'You're going to lose her, you know.'

Natasha slid in behind him, her hair a dazzling tangle under the hall light.

Chris folded her arms and tried not to look at Annabel, whose wide, inquiring eyes moved from one face to the other. No-one had seen Natasha.

'You're fucking hopeless, Leo! When the fuck are you going to grow up and realise that it's tacky and shitty and pathetic, and boring, and out-of-date to sleep with everyone who catches your eye? You're like a bloody fifteen year old! You've got a kid, remember?'

Natasha looked as though she had been slapped—the tears began to brighten Annabel's eyes again—and Leo bent his head and rested his face in the soapy soft hollow of his daughter's neck.

He drove Annabel home, leaving Natasha at the party. There was a knife-edged stillness in the house—not the stillness of sleep, but the sharp suggestion of someone frozen, awake. He carried Annabel into her room—she was already asleep, clinging round his neck like a koala—and put her into bed, pulling the sheets over her small form, still in its T-shirt and shorts.

He went slowly down the stairs, feeling his way in the dark. For once he did not count the steps as he was used to do (drunk, dazed, his mind turning circles) and thought he had an extra step to take. He thumped down heavily, awkwardly on the floor, making his teeth clash together painfully.

'Leo?' Madeline's voice cut through the ringing in his ears.

'Jesus.' He massaged his jaw with one hand and groped around for the light switch.

Madeline was sitting on the couch under the window, her knees drawn up to her chin. 'Are you okay?' she said automatically.

'Yeah, I missed a step.' Leo leaned against the doorjamb, watching her. She looked tiny in the big, spare room, her thick hair framing slow, dark eyes and a mouth that was tight with pain.

'Where've you been?'

He jerked one thumb towards the street. 'I was at Chris'. I brought Annabel home.'

'You didn't have to.'

'She was upset. You shouldn't . . .' He stopped himself short.

'I shouldn't have left her,' finished Madeline for him.

'Well . . .'

There was a long silence. Suddenly Leo felt a terrible weariness beginning to creep into his bones, and with it a rising tide of panic. His legs were weak.

'You want me to have a fight with you, I know . . .' His bottom lip shook with the sudden effort of controlling tears.

Madeline fixed him with her gaze, waiting for him to go on.

'I can't, though. I can't do it.' He wiped his eyes with the back of one hand, blinking furiously.

'I don't want to have a fight, I just want to *talk*, Leo! I just want to talk!'

But he cut her off, shouting, 'I won't fight with you, okay? Is that okay? Why do we have to shout at each other?'

'You won't fight with me . . . you won't listen to me . . . I can't say when I'm angry with you because you don't like it . . .' with each 'you' Madeline's voice tripped further down a rocky slope until she was sobbing, her chest heaving like a child's. Her anger felt as though it would smash open her rib cage. And Leo just stood there, his tears turning his eyes to jewels, his hands hanging, fingers curled, at his sides.

'Don't, Maddie, don't,' he pleaded.

'Leo! You're sleeping with someone else! What am I supposed to do? I don't understand . . .' she wept and wept, buried her face in her hands, and slid off the edge of the couch onto the floor. 'Am I supposed to not say anything? Is it normal to care about this sort of thing?'

Leo knelt down in front of her and tried to pull her hands away from her face. She resisted, pressing her wet fingers against her cheeks. He caught her wrists and tried that way, tugging at them until finally he broke her hold. Her face was wrung with red.

'I want you to care about it,' he said, swallowing the words. 'But you've gotta leave me alone.'

'I don't get it. I don't get you. Why do you want to sleep with her?'

Leo struggled with the words, 'I don't *like* her . . .'

'Don't say that, Leo. You can't say that. I have to keep loving you but if you say things like that I can't.' She fought to free her hands but he would not let her.

His fingers were digging into her as he said, 'I was just *trying* something.'

'You've been trying it for weeks,' she whispered.

'Just when I was on tour. I get lonely . . .'

'Where does she come from?'

'Randwick,' Leo loosened his grip on Madeline's wrists and she snatched her hands away. 'She went to uni with Joel.'

'Why haven't I ever seen her before?'

'I don't know. She's been around for a while.'

'Around where?' said Madeline.

'What?' said Leo.

'I said, around where?'

Leo blinked at her.

Madeline gritted her teeth. 'Chris never mentioned her. Nita never mentioned her.'

'She's just a girl,' Leo said. 'Maybe you weren't looking.'

There was a dull quiet, as though someone had just shut a window against the sounds of the street. When Madeline spoke, her voice was flattened, without air. 'You do this a lot, don't you? You sleep with other women when you leave town.'

Leo said nothing.

'And everybody knows, don't they?'

He looked away.

'And they think we have an open relationship because you're in a band and we live in Newtown and I'm too *cool* to care about that sort of thing . . .' she took a sharp breath, ' . . . and you thought that too and you thought everything was fine . . .' another breath, ' . . . but you know what? I never knew about it until right now. I never even suspected you. I never even thought about suspecting you. Not because of Annabel, either. Just because I thought we were in love. I must be stupid.'

'We are in love, Maddie,'

'Yes we are, but I am stupid, and you are different to me.'

Leo was caught. Her voice was so clear, so precise. He couldn't think. His mind felt thick with unhappiness. 'I just do it. They're there. I get drunk, and I just do it.'

'So do I get drunk. And when I get drunk I think about you and I can't wait for you to be with me.' Madeline was speaking without thought—the words were forming themselves on her tongue like crystals, glittering and sharp. 'But you won't wait for me. All this time I thought we were the same.'

'I'm sorry, baby. Please . . .' Leo held his arms out to her but she crunched herself further back into the couch, her body stiff.

'No. I'm not staying with you.'

'What are you going to do?'

'I'll go somewhere. I can't stay. I can't bear it. And I'll take Annabel.'

'But what about me?' He started crying again.

63

She stared at the wet slick of tears on his chest, disappearing into his shirt. 'You can stay here.'

'Is that all?'

'I don't know. You can't make me decide for you. You have to decide. I don't know what you're going to do.'

She got to her feet, and thought she felt her heart tearing with the effort. His head was bowed, and his thick, dirty hair flopped forward. She stepped past him and he caught at her thighs, pulling her close so that she stumbled and nearly fell. He pressed his face into her belly and bawled. But then he let her go and she climbed the stairs, finally crawling onto the bed next to Annabel, who slept in a little huddle of clothes against the wall.

∞

Chris made them up a bed in the sunroom, overlooking her long, wide backyard. Madeline sat on the back steps in the early morning, and detritus from the party—the foil from a champagne bottle, a piece of broken glass—winked and flashed at her in the sunlight. Annabel slept heavily at night, not moving, exhausted by long days at school and hours spent trying to get her mother's attention. She would tweak and tug at Madeline's hair, rub her back, bring her too-weak cups of tea, perform little dances and dumb shows in front of her stricken face. Madeline held her hand and squeezed back when Annabel squeezed, but could rarely be persuaded to speak or even move from her seat.

She sat on the back step, drinking tea and eating oranges, and when the children were asleep, Chris sat with her.

Madeline said, 'He's not coming to get me.'

Chris stayed still, holding her breath.

Conversationally, Madeline added, 'You know what I feel like? I feel homesick, only nowhere is home. I feel as though my home got up and walked away. I feel as though my father and mother have left me again. There is nowhere for me to go.'

'There is here. You can stay for as long as you like.'

Madeline smiled slightly, turning her mug between her hands.

'Yes, but this is your life. This is your place. I can't stay forever. Where will I go?'

'We can find you a new house,' said Chris. 'Nita and I will go out and look for you. We'll lend you the deposit.'

'I can't live anywhere,' Madeline looked away, her eyes blurring the dark backyard. 'I can't live. I don't want to live. What will I do?' She did not want to cry again.

'You'll be okay,' Chris slipped an arm around her waist that felt like a clamp.

'I think I am mad.'

'You're not.'

'I can hear voices.'

There was a pause.

'What do they say?' asked Chris.

'It's my voice, only about four different ways. They say, *What's wrong? what's wrong? you're going mad, you're going to die, what's wrong?* They ask me questions and they scream at me.'

Maybe there are degrees of madness. Madeline had always thought that to be mad meant to be utterly divorced from a once-solid reality—to live in a world peopled by nameless creatures, to be unable to understand the words they spoke, or to be careless of your own behaviour so that you committed unspeakable acts without conscience. But madness might be nothing more than a louder reality. Just because she could suddenly hear what went on below the surface—did this mean she was mad?

The world bleeds into you. She could not watch television. Someone was arranging meanings in the programmes to hurt her. She flinched as she passed their contained clamour, and was careful not to let any of the words make sense. Advertisements were not so bad, but the building society dragon was a gross distortion, a monster—it terrified and disgusted her. How could people invent such a thing. Evil dripped and collected in black reeking pools wherever she looked.

She was no longer certain if it was normal to walk down the street crying. The expressions on other people's faces were like

65

cars in traffic; they passed by, they replaced each other without reason, coming from nowhere, disappearing into nothingness. No-one was looking at her or reacting to her anymore. Everyone was traffic.

There was a photograph of Leo in her leather bag. There was also money for Chris, for the groceries. She took things down from supermarket shelves, handled them, put them back. *I won't eat that. Or that. Or that.* The only one left to spend money on was Annabel.

Somewhere down the sidestreets of her mind dodged the thought that she should take the photograph out and lay it flat on its face beside the bed, or bury it deep in the suitcase of clothes. Not tear it up, just put it where it could not be seen. It was impossible. As her fingers riffled through the notes and cards and coins they touched the photograph, but flicked past. To acknowledge it would mean too much pain.

It was bound to happen sometime. They were in Coles while the kids were at school, and Madeline found herself separated from Chris. She stood in front of the breakfast cereals and thought of Leo eating cornflakes in the middle of the afternoon. His mouth wide open as he chewed, talking to her, laughing, clean white milk on his chin. Annabel liked rice bubbles.

She herself could never eat breakfast, mornings being a time for thinking, for drinking tea, painting, moving around the house while Leo slept. Reading at the table for hours and sitting back, surprised, to find her shoulders aching.

She put a packet of rice bubbles under her arm and walked along the aisle, looking for Chris. Turned the corner and there she was, her back to Madeline, talking to Natasha.

As if she could not stop the movement once begun, Madeline continued towards them, even while Natasha looked up, her face suddenly stiff with fear.

'Chris,' said Madeline.

Chris turned around, and went red.

'Does Zara eat rice bubbles? I can't remember.' She was staring straight at Chris, finding that she could not look at Natasha. A streak of red hair in the corner of her eye, her dress brown or blue. She couldn't see her expression, didn't want to, couldn't bear to, but couldn't stop, went on, 'Bella loves them, but I won't get them if nobody else eats them.'

'It's fine,' said Chris, trying to swallow, 'Zara'll eat anything. Really.'

'You sure?'

'Sure. It's fine.'

'Okay,' and Madeline went walking past them, her neck cricked painfully sideways. She caught her foot on the wheel of someone's trolley, stumbled and nearly fell but held herself up, continuing round the corner into the next aisle.

Then, at the pool, Madeline saw Sean Penn. She was the only person who recognised him. He was one of those ordinary-looking famous people who could almost be lost in a crowd. He was sitting up against the wall with a friend, talking and gesturing (a slow handclap to emphasise something he was saying, which seemed particularly American), with his legs splayed like a frog's, looking common and confident.

Madeline swam twenty laps and lay on her stomach on the warm concrete, trying to breathe regularly. But even while she was swimming she'd felt it creeping up on her; panic beginning to nibble around the edges of the day. She sat up to try and free the air inside her, and looked around.

The pool, and the trees in the park surrounding it, and the people—their swimmers, and towels, and goggles—were beginning, subtly at first, to look angry. There was a gathering rage in the place that showed itself first in the chlorine blue of the water, vivid angry blue, shaking and jerking as it grew until everything was clamouring around her.

Out of the corner of her eye, calm in the quivering world, she saw Chris and the girls ambling towards her from the canteen, their faces soft with smiling. Chris reached down and kissed her on the mouth and she smiled back, feeling screams of rage behind her, and said, 'Did you see Sean Penn?'.

Chris looked and said it wasn't him at all, and Annabel said, 'Who's Sean Penn?' Chris pointed him out and explained.

'He looks like Dad,' Annabel said, and Chris sucked her breath in suddenly, eyes snapping to Madeline's to see her react. But Madeline was not looking at her anymore. The sunlight was glaring through her closed eyelids as she tried to curl away from the storm around her.

The afternoon turned the colour of burnished iron and the leaves on the trees were dark green. They rattled angrily in the new breeze. Thunder meandered through the heavy clouds—the sun lit the city in the distance, luminous gold columns, and a rainbow appeared, one foot in the north and one in the south.

The rain started suddenly, as though the sky had split open. It fell on the grass and on the concrete around the pool. It bounced and clashed off the hard blue surface of the water—thousands on thousands of bright glass marbles, and it fell on Madeline's upturned face, cooling her burnt shoulders and dry lips. She couldn't keep still any longer. She got to her feet and walked the length of the pool to the canteen, as everyone around her ran for cover or danced and shouted gleefully under the downpour. There was a big queue of people. She stood behind them, waiting her turn and feeling the tears slipping out of her eyes and sliding down her face. But the queue kept moving, and she bought herself a red iceblock, the water on her face like rain, dripping from her wet hair, and the anger of the place had calmed, and dulled, blurred with tears. The edges didn't seem so sharp anymore.

She walked back along the pool to Chris and Annabel and Zara, where they crouched under the shelter of the wall, gabbling and laughing with excitement, their teeth impossibly white against tanned skins.

It comes, and it goes.

Leo woke, confused, in a blue cage of moonlight. His arm was numb. Slowly he turned his head to look at it. It was trapped under Natasha who lay on her back, breathing softly and regularly. He eased it out, using the other hand, and bent it back and forward, rubbing his wrist, feeling it ache as his blood began to flow.

Everything was round, as though the room was at the bottom of a blue glass bowl. He lay still for a while, watching the ceiling, waiting to fall asleep again. When it became clear that sleep was not going to come he rolled his mind over and began to think about music. Usually the composition of a new song—its words and melody so clear in the dark liquid silence—could launch him on a tide of drowsiness, leaving him in the morning with a note, two notes that had been licked clean like pebbles in the surf. Tonight, though, the water did not stir. He grew hot, lying in the one position, and turned on his side. In a very short time his leg started to hurt. He turned again. Soon he felt as though the whole length of his body was slowly burning.

Defeated, he sat up and swung his legs over the side of the bed. His heels hit concrete and he stood up. Natasha did not move. He walked out, stepping over her spiky shoes and belts that lay strewn around the bed, ducking his head under the fringe of beads that hung over the doorframe. Natasha's house backed off her art gallery. It was part of a warehouse, its ceilings high, its floors bare and cold. He followed his feet across the wide open space to the table and chairs that fenced off the kitchen, and sat down, hands folded on the edge of the table, feet flat on the hard floor.

The fridge rattled suddenly into life. The light switch was in the corner. He couldn't decide whether or not to turn it on—it was no great distance from his chair, but a vast chasm of reasons yawned before him, between dark and light.

Stand up, step over, flick on; or sit still, turning colder and harder on the wooden seat?

The wise woman or man in the story who stands by the cradle and, laying a gentle hand upon the child's head, pronounces their fate, tells their life in accents slow and weighted with a thousand years of knowledge, had failed to appear at Leo's christening. Thus when the road down which he was travelling forked and he had to make a choice he was lost. He would proceed happily and at speed towards blind corners, take hills and hairpin bends with the same fearlessness and good cheer, but if asked to make a decision between one road and another he could only wait until someone or something appeared and shoved or coaxed him along his way.

He missed Madeline and Annabel badly but could not think how to set things to rights. He was not too proud to cry, to throw himself on his knees and beg for their forgiveness, but that was only one of a number of ideas that floated, weightless, in his mind. There was something to be fixed first; he could not pretend nothing had happened, he knew—but this was a thought only. The feeling was somewhere else, out of his reach, and this time there was no-one to get it down for him, no-one to trap it and put it, still warm, into his hands.

If he looked into the eyes of Chris, or Nita or another of the big-thighed, impossibly fertile-looking women who played pool at the pub and moved their lips to his songs, he could see righteous hurt and anger, as though they were the ones who had been betrayed. But it seemed to him as though they were hurt not because he had been unfaithful to Madeline, but because he had allowed her to find out about it. The crimes, as they were, were made public. Suddenly everyone had an opinion.

Late one night, when someone else's band was playing, he was sitting outside on the gutter, balancing an empty schooner glass between his two forefingers. There was no traffic. People drifted past in clumps, disappearing in darkness at the end of the street. Through the smoke, through the big tinted window, Chris saw Leo's lowered head, his rounded shoulders, and left the group to come out and sit beside him. She set her teeth against his offer of a last drink and began to talk to him carefully about what he had done, for just what sins he must do penance. She described

Madeline sitting on the back steps and watching the children bounce on the trampoline, her fingers endlessly unwinding the skin from countless oranges.

Leo dropped the glass into the gutter. It did not shatter, but rolled until he trapped it with the edge of his foot.

'You know what, Chris?' he said. 'I'm willing to be drunk. I am willing to be drunk for the rest of this long, long life. I'll just sit here, okay? You watch me, I'll sit here and I'll drink whatever you give me, okay? Hand me a drink and I'll drink it.'

'I'm not talking about you being drunk,' said Chris, 'I'm talking about . . .'

'See, I feel fine, you're the one with the problem. I'm drunk but you're unhappy. Get it?'

'Leo . . .'

Leo cut her off, 'You're trying to fix me up and you don't see that you need it, you need it. I'm fine, I'm drunk, I'm okay really so you don't need to worry.'

'You're not okay.'

'No, I am.' He sat back, throwing out his thin arms and flattening his palms on the black pavement behind him. 'Actually.'

The streetlight leaned closer to him, filling his eyes with gold. He smiled into it, hardly seeing the inky clouds of buildings crowding in. Somewhere behind them someone was smiling back at him, someone was waiting for him—whose face smiled he could not see, but she was there. He tilted his head so that the light spilled down his neck and soaked into his shirt.

Chris leant forward and fished the empty glass out of the gutter, setting it upright between them. 'She won't come back, Leo,' she said, but he answered, 'Oh she might,' not hearing her, not knowing her or understanding her, seeing nothing but the gold in his eyes and the faraway darkness of houses and vacant lots. *This is why we drink;* the thought dived across his mind, twisting and turning in the deep waters, hardly ruffling the surface. Everything is liquid. When I lean back the world leans with me. Up . . . back; up . . . back; he smiled and rocked himself like a child on a swing and Chris had no idea—she could watch him forever and she still would not see.

∞

Natasha raised her thin voice if Leo mentioned Madeline's name, and left the room if he talked about Annabel. She could not understand him. He gossiped about people she did not know, and easily dropped the names of his two women as though they were still around, as though he was not separated from them and she was not the cause of this.

What she did not see was that if he continued to pretend that they were still together, if he talked about Annabel's homework and Madeline's penchant for sleeping in the afternoon, Leo could trap reality. He carried it around with him like a container of light, pressing his face against its transparent sides, gazing in until everything else around him swirled and disappeared. He could continue to live in this way. It was too long looking up that hurt, looking into corners of wide, dark rooms where Madeline and Annabel did not stand, peering over the heads from the stage and seeing no-one at the back, perched behind the bar.

Leo had not moved for an hour. He sat at the table in the cave-lit kitchen of the warehouse, rubbing one finger along the A-string of his acoustic. It gave out a soft, slightly tortured hum. Natasha took down glasses and bottles—she opened the fridge and pulled out an icetray—she cracked the ice into the glasses, poured vodka on top of it, and then lime cordial. With one hand on the neck of the soda bottle, the other gripping the cap, she turned around.

'What's wrong?' she said at last.

'Nothing,' said Leo. His eyes were fixed on his finger as it slid up and down.

'Leo,' Natasha said, her voice heavy. He looked up. 'Shouldn't you be getting ready?'

'I am ready.'

Natasha opened the bottle. It let out a chilly hiss. She felt like a maiden aunt with someone else's child to stay. Couldn't she

72

ring Madeline and find out where Leo was meant to be? Was he late? Was he wearing the right clothes? She did not want to send him off feeling or looking wrong, uncared for.

'Do you want a drink?' she said, just as a tear slid out of Leo's eye and dropped onto the clear wood of the guitar. It sat there, quivering; she stared at it until he tilted the guitar and it slipped away. She gave a gasp as a whole series of tears dripped after it, on to his bare, bony knuckles.

Setting down the bottle, she knelt in front of him, taking one of his hands. 'Leo, what's wrong?'

He shook his head and salt water hit her in the face.

She swallowed, and said, 'Tell me. Tell me what's wrong.'

For a minute he said nothing but continued to cry, snuffling like a child. Then he said, 'It's hard, that's all. It's just . . . hard.'

'What?' said Natasha.

'This,' he gestured at the guitar, at the room, 'this whole thing. Everything.'

'You mean . . .' she searched her mind, not certain what she was looking for, 'You're worried that, maybe . . . you're worried . . .'

'I'm not worried,' Leo wrenched away from her and jammed the heels of both hands against his eyes, letting the guitar slither off his lap. It gave a disturbed echo as it hit the hard floor. Tears dripped down his wrists. 'I'm not worried, I'm not upset, it's just hard, and I get tired.'

'You want me to rub your back?'

'No!' he said. 'I don't want you to do anything! I'm just . . . it's not easy, okay? That's all it is!' He took his hands away and looked at her through bloodshot eyes. She was like a nurse, hovering with bandages and syringes. 'I'm not trying to make you feel sorry for me. You don't have to do things all the time. You can just let them be, you know?'

'That's not fair,' said Natasha. 'You scared me. I thought I'd done something wrong. How am I supposed to know?'

He took a deep, shivering breath, and blinked until his eyes stung. 'Forget it. There's no drama. I'm alright.' He nodded again. 'Yes.'

'What?'

'A drink. A drink'd be good.'

She narrowed her eyes at him.

'Please.'

Still she did not move.

'What,' he said.

She said nothing.

'What?' he almost shouted.

'Now you expect me to wait on you?'

'Oh, God,' the word was a snort of disgust, 'what is it? You were making us a drink, now you won't? Fucking Jesus bloody Christ, Natasha, I'm not fucking oppressing you, okay?' His tears had dried, leaving his face stiff. 'Jesus Jesus Jesus. I just want a drink. If you don't want to pass it to me, I'll get it myself.'

Leo got to his feet and pushed past her, snatching up one of the glasses, ice melting into the vodka. Awkwardly, he topped it up with soda. Natasha stepped away and sat in his chair.

'Do you want one?' he said to her, about to put the glass to his lips.

'Yes,' she said. The chair was still warm.

'Okay,' he said severely, and pouring soda into the second glass, handed it to her. 'There you go.'

Natasha was having an exhibition at her gallery, a set of frighteningly elegant cubist paintings on canvases the size of a paperback. Only one was different—a great starburst of a picture, covering nearly the whole of one artificial wall, its fierce reds and lime-green yelling for your instant attention.

She was giving a private, informal showing for her circle of friends some days before the opening. Like Natasha herself, her friends were serious people, closer to Leo's age than Madeline. Their adolescent enthusiasms for pub bands, for socialism and an old but still angry Gough Whitlam had slowly settled as the years disappeared, and they had become quiet-voiced, humourless advocates of domestic recycling and health food. Their concerns, having once been universal, were now personal—and perhaps, would complete the cycle and turn back to the universal again one day.

It was an uncharacteristically grey day, still and humid, and Leo had not left the warehouse once. He'd read the papers painstakingly, forcing interest in even the business section, until the bed was damp with sweat. Outside a lost koel bird, far too late with its spring song, called relentlessly, dropping its cold single note into the early afternoon. Eventually, after making himself a meal that he did not really want to eat, he collapsed on to the sofa to dull himself with television.

When Natasha and her group arrived—the gallery suddenly a-clatter with feet and voices—he froze, his heart thumping stupidly, and wondered if he should run back to the bedroom and dive under the sheets. Foolish. His heart slowed and he stood up, flicking the remote control onto mute, and went out to the gallery. The group was clustered under the big canvas, their voices merging harmoniously as they discussed it.

'Leo!' said Natasha as he came in. Her face was taut with false surprise. She held out one hand to him which he did not take, smiling and bobbing his head at her friends instead, looking like some caricature of a medieval serf. His hair was greasy and his torn, sleeveless shirt showed slim, hard-muscled but awkward arms, dangling at his sides.

Natasha introduced him to each friend in turn. He took their hands and shook them but said little. His eyes slid around the wide, bare room until they came to rest on the glasses and bottles of wine and mineral water that Natasha had set out. Unobtrusively, he made his way over and helped himself to a glass of wine which he downed in one gulp. He poured another, took a sip and began to walk around the room, giving each painting a portion of his attention.

One friend detached himself from the group and easily

caught up with Leo, who stood in front of a work entitled 'Vernacular #4'.

'What do you think?' the friend said to Leo.

'I don't know,' said Leo. 'Vernacular. Does he mean—is he saying it's slang?'

'Dialect, maybe,' said the friend, allowing his eyes to settle on the canvas. 'Shorthand, perhaps. Colloquialism.'

'It doesn't look colloquial,' said Leo.

'Yeah,' said the friend, 'but maybe within the confines of the cubist discourse . . .'

'The language,' said Leo.

'The language,' agreed the friend, 'Perhaps within those boundaries . . .'

'I like landscapes.' said Leo.

'Do you,' said the friend, slightly nettled.

'Water. Tidal waves, you know, and coastal stuff.'

'It would be coastal, if it was water, wouldn't it,' said the friend quietly.

'Mm.' Leo continued to look up at the painting and Natasha, careful to drift rather than stride, came towards them.

'Like it, Leo?' she said brittlely.

'He prefers landscapes,' said the friend.

Natasha stiffened as the friend went on, 'Whose? Whose work do you like?'

Leo turned to them. 'Van Gogh,' he said, 'I've got a friend . . . Madel . . . my gir . . .' He suddenly caught Natasha's eye, saw the tightening of her facial muscles and understanding rushed into him, chilling him to the core. He blundered on, however, not knowing how to turn back, 'Madeline paints mostly landscapes. Sometimes she takes her stuff down to Maroubra. Her work's good. It's sort of . . .' he was gasping for air, each word freezing in his mouth, ' . . . she loves Van Gogh, nobody would buy his work but he kept going.'

There was a silence.

'Well, you can't argue about Van Gogh, can you,' said Natasha bravely. She raised a hand. 'He's up there. He's just . . . he's Shakespeare, you know?'

Her friend, surprised, looked as though he was about to disagree, but changed his mind. 'Probably,' he said meaninglessly, looking into his glass of mineral water.

By tacit consent the little group broke up, leaving Leo still standing under 'Vernacular #4'. The green blocks of the tiny painting glowed under the light.

Later, as they all sat around the wooden table in Natasha's kitchen, Leo was silently drunk, his bare feet slipping uselessly on the polished floor as he tried to keep himself upright on his chair. During a heated conversation about films, the friend who had asked him about the painting leaned forward. Leo was abandonedly pouring himself more wine.

The friend said, 'You won't find any answers in that glass, you know.'

Leo's gaze swung onto his face like a trapeze artist making a successful landing. There was an endless moment and then he spoke. 'Mate, I'm not asking it any questions.'

On the afternoon of the opening, Leo wandered into the gallery where Natasha stood agonising over the placing of the paintings, fingertips in her small bright mouth.

She heard his footsteps, turned to him and said, 'What do you think? Do you think it'll go okay?'

He dipped his shoulders and laughed and said nothing, and quickly left the room. She did not see him again until the first visitors were arriving. He had been tuning his guitar in the concrete backyard, under the dark and spreading fingers of the fig tree, waiting for someone to arrive and get between them.

Later, when she sat on the floor against the wall with her long, booted legs drawn up to her chest and Leo had come home from his gig, she asked him whether he loved her.

Leo did not stop in his tracks but grinned to himself, grinned desperately to himself and tried to keep his mind wheeling ahead. If he moved fast enough such moments could be passed, rolled over—if only someone would come in, or a painting would fall off the wall. He swung round to stare at the starburst canvas and laughed out loud, throwing his head back. For a second the sound drowned out everything else and the colour flooded his eyes. But then the silence began to steep in and he was left with the words, still and silver, shining beneath the surface, 'Do you love me?'

'Ooh, that's a hard one, Tasha,' he said to the painting.

'Do you still love Madeline?'

Leo shook his head, hoping she hadn't said that, trying to dislodge her, trying to dislodge the image of Madeline . . .

'Leo!'

He took a deep breath and wished he had drunk more. 'I've gotta go, Tasha. Really . . .'

He started towards the big, barred door, not looking at her, trying not to break into a run as he heard her get to her feet. She caught up to him and stood in front of him before he could pull the door open. The bars were just for show.

'Come on,' she hissed at him. 'Say what you think.'

He hung his head, and in a second that surprised them both, Natasha pulled back her hand and smashed it into his face, palm outward, so that his tongue caught between his teeth and was split open. He put a hand up to his mouth, horrified. Then, touching his bleeding tongue with his fingers, he managed to speak.

'I don't love you,' he said, his voice thick with blood, 'you can't . . . how could you think I would. I don't even know you. All I know is that,' he swallowed, trying to go on, 'all I know is your hair and your eyes. And what you do. *You* wanted to fuck *me*.'

'I thought you were interested . . .'

'But it was your idea. You asked.'

'You,' Natasha's voice dropped to a whisper, her eyes wide with disbelief, 'you, oh God, you absolute bastard.'

'It's not me,' Leo choked, and spat into his hand. 'It's everyone else. Not me.'

'How can you say that?' Natasha did not have enough breath for expression. Her words came out tied together, rattling, beads on a string. 'What about Madeline? What about your daughter? How can you say it's not you and then leave them, how can you?'

'They left me.'

'They . . . left . . . you.' she repeated slowly. Then, 'You are really amazing. Something amazing. I think you believe that you can do anything, anything you like. You don't have to work like the rest of us. We're all working for you, that's what you think.'

'I don't know what you mean,' Leo gave his hand one violent shake, and a mixture of blood and saliva spattered across the concrete floor.

'You don't want to do the everyday stuff. You just want to be on stage all the time. Never had a real job.'

This was a phrase he'd heard before, in jest and in earnest, but this time it caught in his flesh like a rusty hook, poisoning him.

Natasha stepped aside and pulled the big door open. 'Go home,' she said, not looking at him.

He slithered past her and didn't say a word, and didn't start to run until he was round the corner and well out of her sight.

∞

Zara, Chris' daughter, had an expression that surprised and fascinated Annabel. When Annabel could not finish a sentence, she ended it with, '. . . and all that jazz.' Leo would have said, 'Blah blah blah.' Zara, however, said, '. . . and all that shit.'

Zara was freckled and tough; she wore dark blue, terry-towelling shorts that creased over her thin belly, and thongs instead of sandals. She could turn backflips on the trampoline, and was not always interested in coming in for dinner. When Annabel suggested that they play at being horses—wild brumbies whose hooves were sure and knew every rock and gully in the whole outback (she could do this to perfection, throwing back her head and snorting, galloping forwards with her eyes never straying to the ground)—Zara had laughed raucously and told the kids next-door and anyone who came over to play what a dag Annabel was. Annabel could not think about it without a blush and a small shiver of humiliation. And when she hovered around Madeline, waiting to be asked what was wrong so she could tell the story and shed her shame, her mother, for once, failed to play her part and she had to nurse her embarrassment alone.

One evening Annabel and Zara had a fight, an argument over the television, and Zara punched Annabel in the stomach with a hard, hot fist. For the first time in her life Annabel was winded. She couldn't speak. She stood in Chris' horrible living room with her hands clutched over her stomach, the burning, terrified tears rising in her eyes, wanting Leo so much that for a moment it seemed he would appear in front of them and snatch her away.

He didn't, though, and Chris' anger at her daughter was not the anger of someone who has seen a loved one hurt. Chris was ashamed of Zara, angry with Madeline and Annabel for staying on so long, and angry with herself for wanting them to go. The hand with which she held Annabel's heaving shoulders was rigid, bruising.

'Where's Mum,' gasped Annabel.

'She's in bed. She's . . . go on, get out of here!' Chris turned on Zara, who ducked out of the room, sick with guilt and fear.

'Well, where's Dad then?' Annabel went on, beginning to weep, the pain in her stomach suddenly releasing the words she had so carefully held back.

'I don't know,' said Chris, setting her teeth.

'I hate you,' Annabel was sobbing now, doubled over, with Chris kneeling beside her as she crunched onto the floor. 'Where's Dad?'

She cried and cried, and in the sunroom Madeline lay stiff and straight in bed, listening but not moving. She could not even lift her hands to cover her ears.

The next day, a heavy, hot Sunday morning, Madeline rang Helen to ask about Leo. Helen arrived and packed Annabel's books and bags into the Commodore. Apologetically, efficiently, Chris folded Madeline's clothes and put them into her suitcase.

'Where are we going?' said Annabel, leaning over from the back seat.

'We're going back to Newtown,' said Helen. She pulled out into the road.

'Yay!' shouted Annabel. She collapsed onto the seat. 'When's Dad coming?'

Madeline turned weary eyes on Helen. 'Have you seen Leo?'

Helen's mouth went tight and her gaze flicked to the rear-vision mirror, a blur of colour as Annabel bounced and rolled in the back. 'He came over yesterday.'

'What, to Balmain?'

'No. We were at Coogee. Having a barbecue with William and Lily and the kids.'

Madeline bit her lip. 'Did he have Natasha with him?'

Helen shook her head, and swung the car expertly onto King Street. Annabel was leaning out of the window now, her eyes screwed tight against the acrid engine smell, the hot late-summer wind. Madeline relaxed, her face losing its aching stiffness. She stayed silent as they inched through the midday traffic. People drifted up and down the pavement, their talk unintelligible under the roar of cars.

Fabien's orange cat came out to greet them as they climbed out of the Commodore, running importantly down the front steps with its tail up, pencil-straight. Annabel bent down to it and it leapt heavily into her arms, clambering over them until it was curled around her shoulders. Madeline and Helen could hear it purring as they followed Annabel into the house, hauling the bags.

'Fabien! Fabien! We're home!' shouted Annabel, disappearing down the dark hallway.

'Up here!' he called from the top room.

Annabel thundered up the stairs, leaving the two women standing in the hall with the bags around them.

'Let's have a cup of tea,' said Helen, 'then we'll fix this stuff up.'

They sat on milk crates in the dark green-shaded courtyard, mugs beside them on the damp cool bricks. Helen crossed her legs neatly and arranged her flowered skirt over them. Her forearms, Madeline noticed, were still hard, still brown from their holiday and from working in the garden, but her legs were pale. She had once told Madeline that after she reached forty they stopped tanning. Madeline lifted her eyes to Helen's face, waiting to be talked to. She trawled idly through the advice she had already been given.

You must rise above this.

You must never see him again.

You must forgive him.

Helen said nothing, and finally Madeline said, 'How is Leo?'

Helen cleared her throat. 'He's thoughtful.'

'Ha!' Madeline choked slightly. 'What is he thinking about?'

'He wants to start again.' Helen grimaced at the taste of the hackneyed words.

'At the same place? It doesn't exist anymore. Everything's changed.' Madeline's face was fierce, her breathing quickened.

Helen said nothing.

Madeline said, 'What do you think Leo will say if I ask him why he sleeps around?'

Helen answered, 'He'll say, "It doesn't mean anything. You're the one I love".'

'And if I say, "But if you love me why do you need to sleep with other people?". '

'Then he'll say, "I don't know". They do know, though. That's the thing.' Helen picked up her mug and rested it on her knees, swirling the tea gently.

'You think so?' said Madeline.

Helen paused, and took a sip. 'I think it makes them feel defiant. They're fighting for their *freedom*.' She swallowed. 'It's like being in a battle for something you never wanted. Something you never asked for.'

Madeline stared at her. 'When did Tony . . .'

'All the time. Once I thought . . . he and you . . .'

'Helen!' Madeline tried to recall Tony's laughing face, tried to remember a salacious glint in his eyes. 'I couldn't. I mean, he never . . .'

'No, I know,' Helen cut her off, 'but at Christmases, on holidays, the way he looks at you. He gets *festive*.' She bowed her head, looking down at her softly-shod feet. She waited for Madeline to say something more, to ask questions—*when? how?*—but the younger woman did not speak, and so she had to finish the story herself, she had to tell it as though it had an ending. 'It's not that bad,' she said, her throat aching.

The tree fern shivered as a silver-eye landed in it. They watched as it flicked towards them, along a leaf that lowered itself to the cool bricks. With a prrrt! it was beside them. Its beak and face were grey-green, its eye bright.

'What will you do?' said Madeline and Helen at the same moment. They laughed, embarrassed.

'I don't know,' said Helen at last. 'You think you'll never take them back. You think you couldn't forgive them, that your love's too strong and good to be ruined by their stupidity. On paper it looks easy, doesn't it? You just leave. You don't put up with it.'

Madeline shook her head, letting out a shh of breath.

'Or you find a lover yourself,' Helen tried to catch Madeline's eye but couldn't. She sighed, and went on, 'Sometimes I think I can't leave because of Tony, because it's not fair to him. As though I have to stay around and help him. Then I think I can't leave because of me, because I don't want to be without him.'

'I feel sick,' said Madeline.

'Don't. We aren't alone, you know. There's a million other women . . .'

'Oh, God!' Madeline jerked to her feet and the silver-eye flipped out of sight. 'I'm not thinking about a million other

83

women. That's why I feel sick. Don't you see what's happening? Don't you see? I can't bear being a part of this stupid sisterhood where we all sit around and whine and say "Isn't it terrible? Aren't they mean to us?". '

Helen stared suspiciously at her, drawing her pale legs back against the milk crate.

'I'm with Leo, Helen, not with Chris or you or . . . or the other women. I can't make my life alongside everybody else, I'm trying to make it with Leo. He's the person I love,' Madeline's voice changed as she began to cry, 'I want to be with him and Annabel. I have to be with them.' She stood against the dark leaves, her blue shirt a sudden handful of colour.

Helen's voice was hard with shock, 'But Leo's the person who betrayed you,' she said. 'He's the one who's made you like this. Who has dragged you this low.'

'But you can only be betrayed by someone you love or who loves you. There's no-one else who could do that to me. There are no women who could betray me, and no other men.'

'You hate women,' said Helen, mortified.

'I don't!'

Helen folded her arms, trying to control the shaking that had suddenly overcome her. 'You're like those women who are only interested in men and ignore other women if there are men around.'

'That's not true,' Madeline's tears covered her cheeks. She wiped them away with the back of one hand. 'You know it's not.'

But Helen was suddenly frighteningly angry, 'If you can say those things, it must be. You don't like us.'

Madeline folded her own arms, in unconscious imitation of Helen.

'It's unnatural, thinking you can exist on your own.'

'Please, Helen,' said Madeline quietly.

'I am not surprised that you think like this. I've never under-stood you. No wonder you're alone now.'

'Please. You don't want to say this.'

'How do *you* know what I want to say?' Helen spat. She felt possessed.

'I didn't mean that I don't like women. It's not even . . . it's not even a question of that. I *am* women. I'm the same. That's the whole thing. I can't love what I am . . . I just am it.'

'What do you mean? You're not like me.'

'Not completely, but . . . I mean, I love difference, you see? Like Leo. He's . . .'

'He's hopeless!'

'Helen!'

'He's bloody hopeless! And you are too! Wasting your lives. You think you're an island, you think you're so different . . .' Helen was incoherent, spluttering. She was on her feet now. She could not remember where the argument had started, or if she was having an argument. She was so angry that her whole body screamed with it. She hated Madeline and she hated Leo. If Madeline had taken a step towards her now she would have hit her, as hard as she could, not caring how much damage she did.

'You deserve to feel like this!' she shrieked. 'You deserve someone who cheats on you!'

'Don't, Helen!' begged Madeline. 'We're friends. You can't take this kind of thing back.'

'You just said you don't want anyone but Leo! You don't care about *me!*'

'You're wrong. You weren't listening.' Madeline suddenly put out a hand as if to hold off a blow and then sat down, both hands screening her face. Her sharp, jerky breaths disappeared into the shadowy thickness of leaves, into the dark curve of her arms.

Helen stood very still, feeling out of place—ridiculous—like a gargoyle, twisted and misshapen with rage in the quiet greenness of the courtyard. She was not sure if she could move her arms and legs, if they were made of stone.

A scrape on the step made them both look up. It was Annabel, still enfolded in the huge orange cat.

'Mum!' she said, seeing Madeline. She took a step forward. 'What's wrong now?'

Madeline held out her arms—they could see tears shining on her face—and Annabel walked into them, the orange cat making a sideways leap for safety. It landed with a clatter on a milk crate.

'She keeps crying,' Annabel said into Madeline's shoulder.

Helen straightened, smoothing down her flowered skirt with stiff hands. Her mouth would not work. Phrases sat in it, cold, heavy pebbles. *I'm sorry. I'm going home. I hate you.*

'Will you see Aunty Helen out, Bella?' said Madeline after a moment.

The two women did not look at each other. The tree fern distributed its green light onto the bricks and in the distance a train battled and rattled its way through the city.

Madeline slept for hours after Helen had left, waking to the sound of a currawong outside her window. It squeezed and sighed, bubbled and gurgled, gently, thoughtfully. She sat up and looked out over their verandah, at a darkening sky, and the trees turning greener. It was going to rain.

Leo and Madeline lie head to head on the grass in the park. It is Annabel's birthday, her fifth. She is in town with her grandmother Lily. They are going to the top of David Jones where the dresses are on tiny bandstands and in the restaurant the rich old women's voices grate through the clinking of silver and coffee cups.

The May sunlight is lovely, lemony. Their conversation feels like a Sunday afternoon; when you leave the house with someone you love and decide to walk around the streets of your suburb. There are houses you knew were there but never saw. You can't think why. The houses are new-painted, bright sky colours, the gardens swish with scented breeze, and from open doors comes the sound of children rolling toys up wooden halls.

'Mum?' Annabel was at the door. 'Fabien wants to know if you want some dinner.'

'Oh . . .'

'I could bring it out to you. You could have it in bed.'

'Okay. Thanks.'

Annabel turned and ran back out to the kitchen. Fabien was unwrapping foil from around an enormous fish. The steamy smell of ginger filled the air. He smiled at Annabel as she set out three plates and cutlery.

'Does she want some, then?' he asked.

'I'm going to take it to her. She doesn't feel very well.'

Fabien lifted the fish carefully out of its wrapper and laid it on a long dish.

'Dad loves fish,' said Annabel after a second.

He glanced at her. 'I know.'

'He caught a shark when we were in Port Macquarie.'

'You told me.'

'It was huge . . . with teeth. He threw it back.'

Fabien took the lid off a saucepan and meticulously began to serve the beans. He did not know what to say.

Annabel took Madeline's plate, holding it firmly in two hands. Fabien put seven green beans, a piece of fish and a potato on it. He watched her as she tightrope-walked, one foot in front of the other, back out into the hall.

He heard them whispering in the next room as the sky suddenly collapsed into the garden.

Later, when Annabel was asleep, Tony turned up at the house. Madeline was sitting on her bed, listening to the rain, when she heard a footfall inside the house that made her swing around. She thought for one dizzying, sickening moment that Tony was Leo. Though heavier and darker, his shoulders rose and fell when he walked in just the same way. The room was dark; she could not see clearly; she thought it was Leo and her whole body rushed to meet him while she sat perfectly still, watching him approach.

'Hi,' he said, his face suddenly appearing in the gloom.

She couldn't speak; she followed him with her eyes as he stepped through the door into the room and stopped in front of the dressing-table.

'Came to see how you were going,' he offered.

She watched him, the breath still caught in her throat; he wore black trousers and a red shirt, smelling faintly of sweat and smoke. It was as though someone had moulded clay around the wire figure that was Leo—added cheeks, strong thighs, heavy arms.

'So . . . how *are* you going?'

She found her voice, surprised by its lightness, 'I don't know.'

'No, well . . .' he kicked at the wooden floor with one shiny toe, 'I saw Leo. He asked me to come over.'

'Where is he?'

'Coogee.'

'Where's Helen?' she asked carefully.

'Home, I suppose. I've been out.'

'Why doesn't Leo come over himself?'

'Because he's a dickhead.' Tony answered.

The wind was flinging a cloak of rain against the window. 'Did you know?' said Madeline.

'That he was a dickhead?' said Tony, laughing awkwardly.

When Madeline said nothing, he shoved his hands deep in his pockets and cleared his throat, a caricature of confusion. 'Yeah,' he said, not looking at her.

'Well, fuck you,' said Madeline. The words were a handful of black dirt, chucked straight in his face.

Tony shook his head, blinking, and then spoke. 'You wouldn't have listened, Madeline. You wouldn't have wanted to know.'

'If I'd known everything would be different. It wouldn't have gone this far. I could have *fixed* it.' Her voice shook.

'How?'

'Somehow.'

'Look . . .' Tony took a breath, and pushed his hands deeper into his pockets. 'You couldn't have done anything. I'm telling you the truth. It's just one of those . . . situations.'

Madeline's voice was bitterly sarcastic. 'Some sort of natural disaster, you mean,' she said, 'like a volcano.'

This time Tony did not flinch. 'May-be,' he said, halving the word neatly. He paused, and went on, 'It doesn't make any difference, you know. He loves you. He doesn't love anyone like he loves you. Not any girl, not Mum, not Dad, not me . . .'

'But he still did it. You want me to be like everyone else wants me to be, you want me to say it's okay, this is just life, this happens, we'll get over it. I'll get over it. Oh . . .' Madeline made an exclamation of pain, wrapping her arms around herself, clamping down.

He exhaled loudly. 'Jesus, Madeline, it's not the fucking movies. It's not an epic. This is ordinary. The shitty stuff, the nasty stuff. He's sorry, okay? He wants you back.'

Madeline glared at him.

'Don't tell me you never slept with anyone else. You must've. Everybody does.'

She said nothing.

'For Christ's sake! Give it up! Are you going to take him back or are you going to lose him? He's Annabel's father. And I thought he was the love of your life.'

Madeline's eyes glittered. 'Of course I'm going to take him back. Of course I love him. But he did this. He did this, you know? It's happened, it's been happening. I can't just turn it over like a page in a calendar. It hurts.' She hunched back against the wall, pressing down harder with her arms.

Feeling divided itself for Tony, like a river split by rocks. He felt contemptuous of Madeline, and angry with her, and slightly bored—but shaken at the same time. He wavered for a moment, thinking of Helen, and then sighed and said, 'Well, it's up to you. Leo's at Coogee if you want to see him. I agree that it's pathetic of him not to call you himself, but you know what he's like. You can't expect him to change all of a sudden.'

'I know.' said Madeline.

'I better go. I told Helen I was just having one drink.'

'Okay. Goodbye.'

'Yeah.' He shuffled his feet, and then turned to leave. There was a second when she thought he would stop, stop in the doorway and swing around to deliver some last pithy advice. But this was not the movies. She heard his feet disappearing up the hall and the careful clunk of the front door as he pulled it to.

Annabel woke early and made her own vegemite sandwiches, folding them awkwardly in greaseproof paper and putting them at the bottom of her backpack. She tiptoed into the living room and turned on the television, the sound only just forcing its way through the screen. She sat close to it, flooded in changing light, until her eyes were sore and the rest of the room was as dark as a ghost train. The rain had stopped in the middle of the night and the morning was building to bright sunshine, the mynahs already twittering and dancing in the courtyard.

Hours later, she looked up, startled, to find her mother standing over her, hands on her hips.

'It's time for school,' she said.

She seemed huge, and the sun dazzled and danced behind her, blinding Annabel. Her mouth was dry, and her arms and legs ached with concentration.

A small thing becomes big and a big thing small, depending on the time of day, the light, and the way you come at it.

Leo had once said to Annabel (after he had caught her lying on her back in the bath, face under, desperate bubbles escaping to the surface) that *a baby could drown in a drop of water*. He meant, *not very much water*, but Annabel was impressed. Just one drop, it could go up a baby's nose, and bang. Dead.

He told her that she was *as mad as a meataxe* and she imagined a *meetax* to be a small black creature with staring eyes and a red blaze of a mouth, like a Tasmanian devil.

He had once had a disagreement with Madeline and afterwards had lain on their bed with a pillow pressed over his face in shame, not moving when Annabel stood at the door and called to him. She had nightmares about it all the time.

The small things become big. But the big thing loomed so close over her that she could barely see it—her mother's tears in floods, her father's absence an enormous valley down which they flowed. Later, perhaps, when these things dwindled with distance, their strangeness, their magnitude would be apparent.

Leo sat on the verandah of his parents' place and watched the blue sea swell. It rolled and shifted as though some great animal arched its back under the water, arched its back and then stretched itself out flat. The sun lay thick and brilliant on the paintwork, smoothing its brightness over the enamelled chairs, hurting his eyes.

A movement in the garden below—colour slipping onto the rectangle of buffalo grass—made him get to his feet and look down. Madeline was there. She stood, shading her eyes from the light, her face tilted up to see him.

'Maddie,' he said weakly, his hands closing over the sun-hot railing. 'Wait a sec.'

He went downstairs, his knees shaking. His parents, listening to his footsteps, sat quietly in the kitchen. They poured themselves cups of tea without clinking spoons, and sipped them with pursed lips.

Madeline was standing at the edge of the garden, and she did not know what to do with her arms and legs. When Leo appeared at the laundry door she crossed her arms, uncrossed them, and looked around her. An old tin watering-can lay on its side against the fence. She picked it up, and, holding it to her mouth, sang into it, 'He-ey, Leo'.

Her voice still boomed sweetly inside it as he came forward and took it out of her hands. He laid the echo on the buffalo grass and curled his hands around her hips, pulling her closer to him.

∞

Touching someone you love when you know they have been touching someone else. It's a freezing feeling, a clutching pain in your stomach as though you have suddenly swallowed a handful of ice.

Wait for it to melt.

∞

'There's a difference. I didn't realise what it was.' said Leo.

Fabien leaned over the marigold and pinched off a dying flower. 'How do you mean?' he said.

'People think they're responsible for you.'

Fabien tipped the watering-can and showered the marigold. The water dripped through the slats of wood and onto the courtyard below.

'Madeline's never been that way,' Leo continued.

Fabien tore the leaf from a silk-soft geranium and handed it to Leo. 'Smell this,' he said.

Leo held it to his nose.

'Maybe you act like you want people to be responsible for you,' said Fabien.

There was a long pause. Leo breathed in. The leaf smelled like peppermint; sharp and fragrant. From the street came the sound of the gate creaking, steps on the path, and the clank as it was pulled to. Someone pushed a key into the lock of the door.

'What a loser, eh,' he said at last.

∞

A long dawn in Newtown. The church spire is the orange-pink of shells, the roofs are dark, the sky is breathing its slow way back to light. Someone is playing their radio softly. The words and music slide and tumble down the sloping corrugated iron, dropping into the bricked gardens. The pigeons in the park coo their morning notes, up, down, up, down.

Leo sits up. The bed shakes slightly. The iron creaks. Madeline turns over. Leo watches her face, now tilted to the ceiling. She coughs.

Which moments are the moments when we are truly alive? We use nets of words to try and trap time but it swims past in its flickering, flashing shoals, darting and dodging away from us. Only now and then does some dark shape blunder into our net and there it struggles for a while, caught, until it turns on us or breaks away, leaving a great and gaping hole.

That hole takes so long to mend.

If I love you should I let you swim forward with the rest of time or should I try and wrap my net around you?

∞

'This is what's happening,' said Madeline to Chris. They were sitting on a bench at the park in Mort Bay, watching the water.

Madeline held up forefinger and thumb. 'See, if these are both sides of my windpipe . . .' she pressed them together, 'well, they're sort of sticky. Mucus, I think. When you breathe normally they come in and out, but sometimes when I breathe they just stick together. So they close off the air.'

'Full-on.' Chris shook her head. 'Can't you do anything about it?'

'Yeah, I just breathe out. I breathe out, instead of trying to breathe in.'

'No, I mean, can't you do anything to stop it happening in the first place?'

'Like what?' Madeline stood up and went to the edge of the water, peering into it.

'I don't know—antibiotics.'

'It's not infected. It's fine. I'm used to it, really. It doesn't happen all the time. Look!'

Chris got up to join her. The translucent green water contained the pale circles of jellyfish. They drifted past in a gentle chain.

Late February, late afternoon. A new chill in the air. Zara and Annabel, Sean, Leo, and Mickey were playing touch football behind them, taking up great swathes of the yellowing grass with their game. The cool water soaked up the sharp, bright sound of their voices, deepening it. The currawongs made liquid noises like angels swinging in the trees. The boats veered slowly around with the tide, chains clanking as they moved, and, over all, the sun flooded the water and the trees, warm and gold, occasionally flashing in the window of a building or glancing off some edge of metal or glass on one of the boats.

'Are you happy again?' said Chris.

The afternoon seemed hung with an elegant filigree of cold. For Madeline, the knowledge of power—that she was the one wronged—glittered in the air. There are moments when you think you might sacrifice the noisy, comforting solidity of love, of companionship for that perfect feeling of isolation. Just me in this stillness of weather, in this sun, in this heartbreakingly beautiful promise of winter.

She looked up, her face drenched in honey-coloured light. 'I don't know.' She smiled and closed her eyes. A small dog scuttered past them, its breath coming in harsh little gasps.

Leo wanted to go back to Tony's and Helen's at Mort Street, but Madeline was unwilling. She hadn't seen Helen since the scene in the courtyard at Newtown.

'Come on, baby,' he said, flinging his long white arms around her waist. Sweat made her cheek slip on his bare chest, sweat too new to smell of anything. She pulled him closer, slipping her hands into the back of his jeans. Mickey panted up behind him, with Annabel and Zara in pursuit.

'Mum's making bouillabaisse,' he gasped, 'she said to ask you to tea.'

Mussels, and prawns—the briny soup like seawater. Madeline shook her head, keeping her ear against the fast thud of Leo's heart, and heard his voice boom inside, 'Fantastic'.

He pulled her to one side as the girls came running towards them, swinging her easily off her feet.

'I hate bouillabaisse,' she said petulantly.

'I can't even say it,' said Leo. 'What is it?'

'Seafood.'

'Great. Fish. Shark. I hope there's heaps, I'm fuckin' starving.'
He let go of Madeline. 'You coming, Chris? Sean?'

'Are we invited?' said Sean.

'"Course,' said Leo, 'Let's go.'

They started across the grass up to Mort Street, the kids
trailing behind with the football. Mickey held it high above the
girls' heads—they pranced and leapt around him like puppies,
trying to snatch it out of his hand.

'Leo!' Madeline called. He didn't turn round but lifted a hand,
airily, to show her that he'd heard. 'Leo!' she called again. 'I'm
not coming!'

Chris and Sean kept walking but Leo stopped and, dodging
the kids, came back towards her. 'Are you okay, baby?' he said.

Madeline smiled. He held out his hand to her. 'Come on.
Don't you want to come?'

She shook her head. His face was soft, his mouth slightly open
as he grinned uncertainly at her. 'Are you angry with me?'

'No, oh no,' she shook her head again, seeing the place below
his shoulder where her cheek fitted so beautifully, where she
could hear the echo of his voice and the steady march of his
heart, and she said, 'I'll see you later. I'll see you at home.'

'Okay, Maddie. If you're sure.'

'Sure.' They kissed and he breathed in sharply, lips half-open
a second, a second longer, and then he turned away.

Annabel stood behind him, staring back at her mother,
trapped.

Madeline laughed. 'Whatcha going to do, Bella? You want to
have dinner at Mickey's?'

'I don't know,' said Annabel, her voice slightly shrill.

'Or go with Mum?' said Leo.

'I might walk around to the oval first,' offered Madeline.

Annabel's gaze swung wildly between them.

'Fish?' said Leo, 'Shark?'

'Or toasted cheese in front of the telly?'

'The Kingswood?' said Leo, his grin splitting his face.

'Or the bus?' said Madeline.

Annabel's mouth started to open in a wail, her eyes screwed up, and Leo and Madeline, instantly regretful, both made a jump for her. Mickey, trying to spin the football on the tip of one finger, watched as they hugged and kissed her, smoothing her hair and wiping away her rush of tears, picking her up and holding her high in the air. Finally she started to smile, to grin like Leo and he lowered her to the ground and let her go. He set off again towards Mort Street, followed by Mickey, leaving Annabel and Madeline behind, leaving them to walk hand in hand as he chased after Chris and Zara and Sean, shouting their names, his voice rolling and bouncing across the short dry grass.

Madeline lifted her head to take a breath. The air was becoming heavier. She felt like a seal, trapped in an ocean of cool, thick water, her face breaking the surface now and again so that she could breathe.

Some of us will leave our lives till the last minute, and then some. Madeline thought that she must have been imagining the weight she felt. Everyone else walked with their heads high and straight. She stopped near the top of the stone stairs and leant back, gasping.

'Breathe out, Mum,' said Annabel, catching at her hand to pull her up the last step.

Madeline nodded. It sounded easy, but it was terrifying. With your whole body shouting for air, it was very difficult to give up your last breath.

From the top of the stairs they could see all of Mort Bay, the water like a board game with the boats moving in and out of position. If Annabel stood on tiptoe she could catch sight of the dark green roof of Mickey's house, and watch her father threading his way up the street. He drifted from one side of the road to the other, tailed by the smaller figures of Mickey and Zara.

∞

The big house in Mort Street was like a barrel of noise, voices, footsteps, the scrape and clatter of chairs echoing against the polished wooden floors and high sculpted ceilings. They came in shouting and laughing. Tony threw the football into one corner of the living room and everyone followed him out to the kitchen where Helen was slicing bread at the table.

She glanced up, her gaze shuffling them like a pack of cards, looking for Madeline.

'Beer?' said Tony, going over to the fridge.

'Cool!' said Leo, but Helen stopped them, putting down the knife and the bread.

'Don't have beer,' she said, 'there's all that wine we bought.' It was a wine Madeline had once said she liked, during one of their slow evenings on the verandah at Port Macquarie.

'Okay.' Tony reached into the fridge and handed Helen the first bottle. She found the corkscrew and began to open it.

'Remember that old ad?' said Leo, settling down at the table. He motioned to Chris and Sean to join him, while the kids ranged over the kitchen, tasting the soup, grabbing pieces of bread and shoving them into their mouths.

'You make us smile, Dr Lindeman's . . .'

'Smile, Dr Lindeman's . . .' sang Tony, nodding.

'Smile, Dr Lindeman's . . . smile!' Leo threw his arms wide, gracefully accepting a glass of wine as part of his finale.

'Dinner's ready.' said Helen.

'I always thought it was *got* the Lindeman's,' said Chris, taking a sip.

'You make us smile, *got* the Lindeman's?' said Leo.

'Yeah.'

He shook his head, grinning, 'Jesus you're dumb, Chris.'

'Get fucked!' She laughed, and kicked him under the table.

'A sentence . . . right . . . a sentence has got to have a . . . um . . . a subject and an object. He was trying not to laugh, holding forth as though behind a lectern. Get it? So . . . *you* make us smile . . . well, who's making them smile? Not *got*, mate. It's Dr Lindeman who's making 'em smile.' He lifted his glass to his lips, about to take a gulp.

'It's a fucking ad, Leo,' said Sean, accepting a plate of bouillabaisse from Helen.

He put the glass down. 'Don't knock it, Seanie. Some of those guys are very well educated. They don't make mistakes, you know.'

'They will if it doesn't fit the music.'

'Yeah, but *got the* and *doctor* . . .'

'Leo!' Helen was holding the bread out to him. 'Take this, will you?'

'And shut up!' said Tony.

Leo laughed and stuffed his mouth full of bread. The others began to talk, kids reaching over the table for more, while he sat eating and grinning to himself.

Before they had all finished the phone rang. Helen got up to answer it, swinging her legs carefully from under the table, one hand on Tony's shoulder as she stood up. The kids were crammed up one end of the long table, fighting for Leo's and Sean's attention.

'I can play the tabla,' boasted Mickey, leaning over to help himself to bread, 'it's a Middle Eastern drum.'

Sean grinned nervously and Daniel shouted, 'Bullshit!' and Leo said, 'I know, mate, I've heard you. You're excellent.'

'What? Are you sure?' said Helen.

'Do you play the tabla?' said Mickey to Sean. He was not quite old enough to be embarrassed to ask such a question, but Daniel grimaced and tried to give him a dead-leg under the table.

''Course he does!' Leo laughed. 'Sean can play anything!' He started to drum on the wood with his spoon and fork.

'Not really,' said Sean.

'When?' said Helen. 'Where?'

'More white?' said Tony, holding the bottle up and smiling at Chris.

Helen hung up. 'That was the hospital,' she said.

'More, more!' said Leo, holding out his glass.

'Fabulous drop,' said Sean, draining his.

'Mickey couldn't drum his way out of a wet paper bag!' burst out Claire, remembering an expression she had heard at school.

'What, Mum?' said Marie, catching sight of her mother's face. It suddenly looked as though her skin was too tight for it.

'That was the hospital,' Helen repeated.

They all stared at her.

'What's up?' said Tony, getting to his feet. 'Is it Dad?'

'Leo,' said Helen.

Who will decide how these things are to be said? Words are paltry, leaking vessels, never solid enough to contain all their meaning.

'What?' said Leo. 'What? Bella?'

She shook her head.

Leo set down his glass and put one hand out, palm flat, like a celebrity deflecting the bright snap and glare of a camera. 'Don't, Helen,' he said. 'Not now.'

The rest of the family turned to look at him, their minds caught in the sudden thud of shock, the moment when everyone knows but no-one can say, not even to themselves.

'It was that breathing thing,' said Helen, 'she couldn't breathe. She died at the hospital.'

Tony came forward and took her hands. She did not sway, or stagger, but stood upright, her eyes clear and dry, watching Leo. Chris, who was sitting next to him, moved closer and put an arm across his shoulders. His shirt fell open and she slipped her hand inside it, pressing it against his cold chest.

'No way,' he said thickly.

'They tried to revive her,' said Helen.

Claire and Marie began to cry, small sobs like the first licks of flame on something set alight.

'What about Annabel?' said Mickey.

A death will never, never leave the living alone. If you are loved, you need no headstone, no plaque, no yearly service or biography. If your bones do not fertilise the earth under the trees, their blossoms will still speak of you. Each year the jasmine will murmur your name, its sweet scent stealing into the sleep of the ones left behind. The flowering gum will shout of days by the beach, of light, bright gatherings around tables in beer gardens, of laughter and weariness. And the bare branches of the liquid-ambar and the oak, the claret ash and the once golden, golden elm will be bare—sometimes—because of you.

Leo was not used to Maroubra. 'Can't we go to Bondi?' he said to Annabel, 'Or Coogee at least? We might see someone we know and then I'll have someone to talk to while you're swimming.'

'I want you to swim with me,' Annabel said, and Leo sighed.

He did not stand much of a chance against the surf. It savaged him, it bent his back and took bites out of his arms and legs. He would lie on the sand for hours until he was way past burning, until his skin was the colour of Annabel's leather sandals, and only ever venture as far as the edge where the silvery waves advanced and retreated politely on the flat, giving way to each other, crossing each other in formation, as slow and careful as dancers in a minuet.

Maroubra was a beach without reason—no cliffs to clasp it, no rolling, bowing dunes—only miles and miles of sand and behind it the rifle range where all day the guns popped and echoed over the grumble of the surf. It was not safe to swim at Maroubra—two steps into the water and you were deep in a gully that stretched all the way along the beach—so close to the shore and to safety, but you could drown in the rip and tear of blue if you lost your footing. If you had courage and strength you could fight your way out past the gully, struggle up onto the sandbank and be like Jesus, walking on the water, your body rising from the waves.

The bus took ages from Anzac Parade but it went right down to the beach and the water yelled blue behind the surf club. Annabel ran awkwardly down to the shore, her small ankles sinking and turning in the yellow sand, and Leo followed her, winding their towels around his shoulders. There were, as usual, hours to be filled. Annabel skipped along the edge of the water, kicking up exclamations of spray, commas and flying full stops and quotes! Punctuation! She chose them a spot way down the south end, past the puny red-and-yellow flags, past the people. It was a weekday. There was hardly anyone there. The surf club, its showers and toilets, its iceblocks and sausage rolls and chocolate bars, its cross-armed, impassive lifesavers and deep brown, wrinkled old men and women, was left far behind.

Leo's head ached with boredom as he watched Annabel in the water. The autumn sun, so pale and harmless on the streets at home, seemed to be holding its hot, hot hands to his temples, pressing into them. He wished he had a watch. If he had a watch he could look at it and say, 'Time to go,' and Annabel would have to agree. He would be the boss with the watch and she would trail home after him where they could make something to eat and sit in front of the TV.

They had been there for hours, he was sure. He had tried to read the paper but the sand slid and rattled in its folds, flicking up into his eyes when he turned the pages, and the stories that looked so interesting over coffee in the kitchen were packed with facts, nothing to really see or think about.

Finally he got to his feet and, anchoring the newspaper and their towels with his sandals, made his way down to the water's edge. Annabel was standing knee-deep on the sandbank beyond the gully, expertly leaning into the waves as they rose and fell. She was watching and counting each wave, for while Leo had been reading or turning angrily in the sun she had seen something happen.

Instead of running side by side or politely giving way to each other, the waves about twenty metres past the sandbank were marching towards each other and colliding with a crash! of surf. Every seventh or eighth wave the water would be flung high, high into the air. If you swam out to just the right point and waited, treading water, you would be thrown up with it and the sea would still be holding out its white hands to catch you when you came down.

'Bella!' Leo shouted, and took one step into the water. It plucked shyly at his ankles. Annabel did not hear him. She began to move farther out, bracing her legs against the current. He saw the marching and meeting of the waves, the spring of spray. She was moving closer to it.

'Annabel!' he shouted again, but she did not turn round. She was swimming now, her small, strong arms pulling the water away, inching forward, and all the while the waves waltzed and crashed, waltzed and crashed.

Leo took another step and the water joyfully wrapped its hands around his calves and tugged him forward, nearly toppling him over. He fought for a foothold in the sliding, slipping sand. Annabel edged her way across the bombora just as the seventh waves thundered towards each other. As Leo lost his balance and pitched forward into the blue gully they collided and, catching her up, threw her high into the sky where she turned and tumbled, her eyes shut tight against the scudding, stinging spray.

THE CHIMING OF LIGHT

'Morning, and more
Than morning, crosses the floor.
Have I been wrong, to think the breath
That sharpens life is life itself, not death?'

From 'At the chiming of light upon sleep'
Philip Larkin, 1946

Captain's Flat (Burning Off)

The fire burned and pitied. Sam hooked one leg under the wooden rung of the chair, shifted against the hard, sore back of it. The black dog watched him from the corner, its eyes like bright glass. Without furniture the room felt wider and deeper. Half-filled boxes lined the walls, and outside the night was a page of deepest black, unturned, and still with cold.

The fire becomes so hot that it begins to eat wood, barely chewing the handfuls shoved into its liquid red mouth. It warms the eyes, makes the lips soft, receptive, brings tears.

Finally, the sound of a car pulling up outside the house. He got to his feet and went to the door, feeling a rush of blood at the back of his neck. Pulled the door open, so the headlights swept over him and the cold barged into the room. Stood there, one hand over his eyes, squinting outwards.

Rachel was the first out of the car. She came up the steps, arms held awkwardly halfway out as though she was not sure whether to touch him. Over her shoulder he could see the empty fields and the few lights of the town, glimmering like a ship anchored in the distance.

'Good drive?' he said.

'Okay,' she answered. She took one of his hands.

There would have to be a moment when they mentioned it, but the thought made him choke, desperate.

Frank and Vince appeared behind Rachel.

'It's *freezing*!' said Frank.

They moved up and in, so they were all standing around him; Rachel still holding his hand, Frank and Vince, eyebrows lowered, watching him. Their breath congregated around them like an audience of ghosts.

Nobody spoke. They could hear the fire muttering inside. Then,

'You must feel like shit,' said Vince.

Sam nodded and swallowed.

'Has she been back at all?' asked Rachel.

'No.'

A crumpled rattle as Frank pulled his tobacco out of his jacket.

'She'll probably come tomorrow, pick up the rest of her stuff.'

'So we've just got tonight and tomorrow to get through,' Rachel said, and Sam tried not to shudder. 'It'll be good, having you back in town.'

'Yeah,' Sam managed a grin, 'I can't wait.'

'Well.' Frank stepped back, lighting his cigarette, and spoke through a stream of smoke, 'Let's go to the pub.'

It was Saturday night, and there was a queue for the pub's single bathroom that wound past the pool table. Sam stood there a second, peered to one end, then, shrugging his shoulders, pushed past and out the wooden door at the back. Outside it was deep night. You could walk along the wide, empty street in darkness and be lost until you appeared under the clear silver of a streetlight. Hands in his pockets, the cold biting at his face, Sam crossed and went behind the post office. It was suddenly quiet, the noise from the pub like a radio in a distant room. The silence filling his ears, the voices in his head began again.

The conversation—the argument—the discussion he'd had with Florence when she'd said she was going to leave replayed itself over and over whenever he was alone. These last three nights he had been plagued with it, body twitching with wakefulness as he lay on his back on their hard mattress. Where did it start?

It was morning, they had been in bed talking and she had just gotten up to make the tea, and then turned —

'I can't live with you anymore.' She in her flannel pyjamas, standing at the door of the bedroom, head down.

He wasn't sure he'd heard her. 'What?'

'I said, I can't live with you anymore.'

'Why not?'

'Because you don't do anything.'

He'd dragged himself up in bed, holding the quilt around his bare chest. 'I don't understand what you mean.'

'You just live. You don't *do* anything. It's driving me crazy.'

There was a long moment—him looking at her, her looking at the carpet.

'What sort of thing . . . ' he'd spoken carefully, slowly, as though he had just caught sight of the ice below him and realised it was transparent, 'what sort of thing would you want me to do?'

'I don't know.'

And she, shamefaced, had slid down in the doorway, pulling her long legs against her chest, watching him. She could have left—she could have walked out at that moment, put a coat over her pyjamas, her boots on, climbed into the ute and driven away. Instead she sat and watched, waited for him to speak.

All day they'd been there, as the sun rose, as it warmed the valley. The call of cows, the snap and fizz of the electric fence. The dog scuffling against the door. And him growing colder and colder under the quilt and her just sitting there and them talking and talking and talking.

Sam unzipped his jeans and pissed, staring down at the steam that rose in the darkness. He hadn't remembered to say, 'This is not like shopping. You didn't buy me for what I could or couldn't do.'

And it had grown dark and finally, with tears reddening her

107

face, her lips bee-stung with unhappiness, she'd gone. Changed into her cold black jeans, put on a blue sweater and boots, and gone. Leaving him still in bed, the taste of no food in his mouth, no water on his lips, his body cramping, aching, the night falling.

The pub was woodsmoky, dim; noisy with the black mass of the crowd. Everyone seemed to know Sam. Rachel had been to the bar, and found herself wedged against a table, cut off from the three boys. She could see Sam's cheeks turning pink in the warmth of beer and people.

She held her glass of beer in two hands. If it had not been so close—thighs shifting steadily against hers—she would have fallen down. Her knees and ankles shook. Three, four people away Sam was talking to a woman with smooth brown hair and liver-coloured lips. They were laughing. His whole body curved over her.

'Here's to Jimmy . . . ' said the man next to her.

She turned around. He was tall and thin, elaborately bearded. About her age. He held up his glass, oily with vodka, and tossed it back.

'Who's Jimmy?' said Rachel.

'Old friend. He's . . . ' he made a slitting movement across his throat.

'What did he die of?'

'Threw himself out of a seventh-storey window. Must be two years ago now.' As he moved Rachel could see past his shoulder: Sam reaching one hand to the table, hooking it around the neck of another bottle of beer. Stepping away from the brown-haired woman, towards Frank and Vince.

'Makes you wonder. You know, why they do it.' The man was holding a cigarette in the corner of his mouth; it moved when he spoke.

Rachel breathed in a heavy mix of smoke and dim air. 'Everybody wants to sometimes. Just some people get caught between wanting to and changing their mind, I suppose.' She felt one knee begin to give.

Sam and Frank and Vince stood together next to the wall, Frank with one arm propped against a shelf. Turning his head to the side every time he took a drag of his cigarette.

'I'm glad you came down,' said Sam, taking a drink of beer, staring into the crowd.

'Well . . . ' began Vince.

'We were thinking there must be something we could get out of it,' Frank cut him off, 'I don't know—whitegoods or something? The TV? Who gets the TV?'

Sam laughed. Frank's face was serious—he put down his cigarette for a moment, using both hands to tuck his long hair behind his ears.

'And we had nothing better to do,' Vince added.

'So—don't worry about it.'

There was a pause.

'I keep wondering if she's with someone else,' said Sam, hesitating.

Vince sighed and looked out the window but Frank, grinding his cigarette out with his boot, said, 'Listen. It doesn't make any difference anymore. Who she's with. What she's doing. You know that?'

Sam winced.

'You've got to think about it like that, otherwise you'll go fucking nuts. From now on she's always going to be with someone else. *Always.*'

'Frank . . . ' said Vince.

'I'm not trying to hurt your feelings . . . '

Sam broke in, 'I know, I know. You're right. I know you're not. It's okay. It's going to take a while, that's all. Jesus, Frank, it's only been two weeks.'

'Yeah. Sorry.'

'No. It's okay. It's okay.'

They faced each other, embarrassed, the crowd milling past their backs, and Frank said, 'Want another drink?'

'Yeah. Sure.'

Midnight, and people were being vomited out the doors of the pub, clustering together, clouds of smoke and breath mingling above them.

The stars were like spattered milk. Rachel was drunk; she leant backwards to see them; overbalanced, but staggering, managed to stop herself from falling. Sam caught her under the elbow.

'See the Saucepan?' she said, tilting back her head again. It was the only constellation she could remember. The sky was so black. She found she couldn't tell the Saucepan from the other stars.

Sam said nothing. Again, an image of Florence flickered across his mind. What was she doing now? Who was she with? He shook his head and, holding Rachel's arm, pulled her closer to him. She bumped clumsily against his chest; he cupped a hand around the back of her head and buried his face in her neck, the tangle of her hair. The smell of her, and smoke, and beer. Perfume.

Vince and Frank appeared behind her, Frank cursing and stamping his feet, arms wound tightly around his narrow chest. Sam let go of Rachel and, shivering, they crossed to the car. The cold seared through their shoes and made their eyes sting with tears.

'Is the bottle shop open?' said Vince, as Sam unlocked the car.

'Closes at twelve.'

They got in—Rachel in the middle, crushed between Sam and Vince. She leaned over to the dashboard and pushed the heater on. It started with a roar of air.

'Do we want any more to drink?' Frank said from the back seat.

'There's nothing open.' Sam revved the engine.

'What about at home? What've you got at home?'

'There might be a cask in the fridge.'

'Shouldn't we go and buy some?'

Sam swung round, his shoulders looking suddenly broad as he leaned over the seat to look at Frank. 'The only place open's in Canberra. It's an hour's drive. It's not worth it, Frank.'

'Well . . . ' Frank held up his hands.

'Let's go home,' said Rachel. Her eyes were chilled and her feet on the floor of the car were like blocks, despite the rushing heater. She pulled her thighs in tighter, away from Sam and Vince.

'Vince?' said Sam.

He was looking out the window, his breath marking the glass. 'Let's go,' he said.

'Big day tomorrow,' agreed Sam, and swung the car out into the street.

Frank collapsed into the back with a groan of disgust.

They slept tribally, as Frank put it—the four of them on two mattresses in front of the fire, with the dog shifting and snuffling in the corner. At a freezing hour some time after dawn Rachel woke, the air like liquid hydrogen on her cheeks and nose. Vince and Frank woke soon afterwards. They left Sam sleeping at the far end of the room, black eyes hidden beneath weary lids, and went for a walk. A thick fog enveloped the house.

Green-grey grass, and the sun a pale disc behind the fog. As they walked things appeared quite suddenly—to their right a tumble of moss-covered rocks—straight ahead, the three concrete pillars of the landlord's folly. The black dog scudded in and out of view, emerging once from the mist with a long, greasy yellow bone in its mouth.

'It looks like Wuthering Heights,' said Rachel as they reached the folly.

'I'm Heathcliff, then,' said Frank, 'Vince'll have to be Edgar.'
'What do I do?'

'He died, I think,' said Rachel.

'Didn't everybody?' said Vince.

'They all just kind of dwindled,' said Frank, taking out his tobacco. 'Life ebbed out of them.'

The three of them stepped under the pointed iron roof. The dog cracked the bone loudly between its jaws.

'Actually, Sam would have to be Edgar. He was kind of pathetic, wasn't he?'

111

'Frank!' said Rachel, punching him on the shoulder.

He glanced at her. Her skin, the curve of her cheek, looked like an apricot's, a faint blush of pink as it turned towards her ear. He put out one finger, pressed it gently, as if for ripeness. 'Well. You know.'

'He's in *shock*.' said Rachel.

'Fine diagnosis, Dr Waters. It's as though he's found out he's got something terminal. And we're the ambulance.'

'You really are a fuckwit,' said Rachel.

'He's not a fuckwit.' Vince said. They turned to him in surprise. He shrugged. 'It's not the end of the world. Sam'll come back to Sydney, forget about Florence, meet someone else. He'll get over it.'

'I think you're both wrong,' said Rachel.

'That's because you're a girl,' said Frank, lighting a cigarette.

'It's because I'm smarter than you are,' answered Rachel, and Frank laughed. 'No, look . . . I just mean that things are different now. You choose people for a reason. It's not random anymore. I really think Sam meant to be with Florence for the rest of his life.'

'Oh, please,' said Frank.

'He'll find someone else, Rachel,' said Vince again.

'And who cares if he doesn't? Surely you're not going to be up nights worrying about it. If you say you are you're lying,' Frank added quickly. He pulled at Rachel's leg, making her sit down next to him. Vince sat down too.

'That's not the point . . . '

Frank broke in. 'Anyway, I was just saying that he's kind of changed. He's weak.'

'Well, so would you be,' returned Rachel.

Frank slid a hand down the back of her jeans and dragged her towards him. He could feel her teetering on the border of a truth or some sort of challenge, directed at him. As though too nervous to speak plainly.

Peering through the fog, Vince said, 'How long has it been now?'

'What?' said Frank.

'That you two've been sleeping together.'

There was an audible intake of breath from the other two, then Frank laughed. Vince was perhaps the only person who was allowed to cross this line.

'A few months,' said Rachel carefully.

Frank took a long drag on his cigarette. Rachel could feel his hand, warm against her back.

'Who knows what'll happen?' said Vince.

Rachel leaned towards Frank.

'Very insightful, Vincent' he said.

Vince nodded, as if accepting a compliment, and continued to stare out into the fog.

They sat there until the morning cleared and the house was visible across the paddock. It was dark green and cream; federation colours. It was pretty, but even from the folly they could see the bags and boxes piled along the verandah. A sudden bright blue in the doorway as Sam came out from the kitchen.

As they watched, a white ute entered the scene from the right, dragging its dust cloud along the road. It pulled up outside the house. The tall, straight figure that unfolded itself from the front seat was Florence.

The blue dodged and disappeared into the black rectangle of the doorway.

Frank whistled up the dog and they started back down the hill, the gentle slope forcing them into a run.

The faded wood of the verandah almost shone in the sunlight. It resounded with the thud of boots as Sam carried load after load out of the house. Florence sat with her long legs dangling, quivering slightly as Sam dumped each armful behind her. She smiled—grimaced—at Rachel, Vince and Frank. Vince split from the group to hug her. Wide, strong-knit shoulders enveloped the thin, bony ones.

Sam would not stop moving. He came back out onto the verandah, holding two pillows, their slips flowered in red and purple. 'Flo . . . do you want these?'

Florence twisted around to look at him, still holding Vince's hand. 'Oh . . . God . . . what do you think?'

'I don't know. Where do they come from?'

'Mum and Dad gave them to us.'

Sam hovered for a moment, clutching the red and purple to his chest. Florence said nothing, watching him.

'Do you want them?' he said again. His face was unreadable.

'It doesn't matter. I've got some in . . . ' Florence gestured out towards the unknown, where she would be without Sam. Sam chucked the pillows down on the boxes that stood against the wall and went back into the house.

'Jesus,' said Florence, staring out towards the paddock. They all looked at her. There was a great clang of saucepans from the kitchen.

'Who's taking the dog?' said Vince.

Rachel climbed the steps onto the verandah and went inside the house. Sam was on his knees, wrapping an iron frying pan in newspaper. He had crammed a beanie over his black, matted hair. His blue T-shirt was ringed with sweat.

'Want some help?'

'No,' he said.

Rachel squatted beside him. 'Want a cup of tea?'

He shook his head.

'Hey,' she said.

'I'm okay. I've just got to get this finished.' He put the frying pan into a cardboard box and pulled a pile of plates towards him. 'Why the *fuck* don't you all go?'

Suddenly desperate to be alone, Rachel volunteered to drive Sam's car back to Sydney. He could not keep the dog at his mother's house because of her aged Siamese, so Rachel was going to take it for the time being.

It sat on the seat beside her. There was no room for anyone

else; the tiny car was crammed with belongings and the dog kept trying, frustrated, to climb into the back. On the unsealed road, whose crests appeared to lead nowhere—peaks sheering off into blue space—she swerved and skidded, pulling the dog by the collar into the front seat. It grunted angrily, and settled with its nose on her thigh, paws splayed across the gearstick. Every time she changed down, her elbow hit its hard, slick forehead.

Sam, Vince and Frank drove back in Vince's father's Gemini. It was green. Frank told the story about how he'd overheard two teenage boys on the train talking about cars. One of them said, *If my first car was a Gemini, I'd kill myself.*

It was a clean car, the carpeted floors free of leaves and sand and newspaper.

'Guys,' said Vince.

Frank was asleep. Sam turned to look at him, eyes dulled by the landscape. 'What?' he said.

'My finger's hurting.'

'So?'

'No, it's really hurting.' He held up a hand for Sam to look at it. Bent, the knuckles dry, fingernails rimmed with dirt.

'Looks okay to me.'

'It fuckin' hurts.'

'Want me to drive?'

'Nup.'

They drove on, Vince flexing his index finger, the other hand resting on the wheel. Freeway, a fringe of scrub and struggling trees, from the dark green background a cough of smoke.

'Look,' said Vince, using the finger to point. 'Bushfire.'

'They're just burning off.'

'Oh.'

There was a tortured squeak as Frank turned over on the sweaty vinyl of the back seat.

Parramatta River

The first words you speak at school are a foundation stone for the rest of your time there. A lie discovered, an uncertainty revealed make the ground beneath you like quicksand. The more you flounder about trying to make things right (fix your story) the deeper you sink.

Sam and Vince, both nine years old and new to the school, had already told stories about their families. Vince said little. Mother, father, no sisters or brothers. The other boys ranged around him like wolves, not liking or trusting his silence, his tell-nothing eyes, but there was nothing they could do. He was already half-a-head taller than everyone else. He had hands like a grown-up's; wide-knuckled and competent, never quite clean.

Sam told about his mum and the river at the end of their backyard. The next-door neighbours' speedboat. And the cockatoo (its black plastic eye sliding open out of a grey web, its voice pensive as it cracked sunflower seeds). But he never mentioned his sister.

It must have been three-thirty, or closer to four when they reached Sam's house (the two of them taking the long way home by the water, passing through the sudden dinosaur cold under the bridge). The house was bigger than Vince's—he tilted his head back to see the wood that curled over the roof like piped ice-cream, sharp against the blue sky.

They came out into the backyard, mouths and hands full of

Sara Lee chocolate cake. There was the cockatoo on its perch and a woman lying on the grass with a book. Beside her was a pram—a chair—with an oversized baby in it.

'Who's that?' said Vince.

'Jane,' said Sam. 'The babysitter.'

Vince opened his mouth to ask more, then shut it.

Jane looked up at them, smiled and beckoned them over. 'Homework, Sam?' she said pleasantly. She had streaky yellow hair and a round face.

'Nuh,' said Sam, shoving more cake into his mouth.

'Spelling,' said Vince nervously, and Sam elbowed him in the stomach. He could not take his eyes off the huge baby in the chair. He couldn't tell if it was a boy or a girl.

'Who's this?' asked Jane, turning her smile on him.

'Vince. From school.'

'Have you met Nina, Vince?'

Vince glanced at Sam. 'No–o . . . '

'Sam's sister. Come and say hello.'

Vince advanced across the grass and Sam went back into the kitchen to get a drink. The baby—but she was four or five, too big, too skinny for a baby—slid down in her chair, kicking at the footrest, and then suddenly pulled herself upright, drunk flower's head drooping on her stalky neck. Vince came closer, but not too close. Her eyes, which looked as though someone had used their thumbs to press them deeper into her head, were fringed with black. They blinked, bluely, blearily at him.

'What happened to her?' he said. She reached out a hand and he pulled back quickly.

'When she was born. An accident.'

He stared at her and she stared somewhere past him. Her body never stopped moving. Like an octopus in a harness, sticky skin trapped by straps, her arms and legs waved and rippled and scraped at the air.

Vince and Sam walk alongside the school. Five pm, the only echo of screaming kids in the occasional squawk of a galah. No-one around. Empty chip packets and sandwich wrappers scuttle across the playground, harried by the breeze.

They're carrying sticks, running them along the heavy wire fence of the school, b'dom, b'dom, and chanting 'Tonight's the Night'.

'Tonight's the night for what?' says Sam, turning suddenly to Vince. His knees and face are grimy, his school shirt ripped at the collar.

Vince nearly crashes into him, but stops, his stick dangling from one hand. 'You know,' he says, looking at his feet.

'No.' says Sam wickedly. 'What?'

'They're gonna . . . fuck.' Vince is red, his face aching.

'How do you know that? Does he say it?'

'I suppose so.'

'Bet you he doesn't.' Sam turns back and starts walking and singing again, dragging his stick, and Vince runs to catch up.

First form. Vince makes a mixture of gin, Bacardi, scotch and vodka in Sam's drink bottle. He slips it under his shirt and meets Sam at the corner. They run down to the wharf, leaping and shouting. Their sandshoes thump on the cold, knobbled tar and the people watering their gardens or setting the potatoes to boil hear them, a sound that tears the afternoon quiet, leaving it gaping.

The water is ruffled—the wind skates and trips across its surface, smacking into boats so they swing wildly around, giving off a panicked clatter of chains. The sun is obscured behind the grey arc of the bridge, its rays scorch on either side. The boys have to hold their hands in front of their faces, warding them off.

They settle behind the brick columns of the bus shelter, and Vince brings out the drink bottle. 'You first,' he says, holding it out to Sam.

Sam snatches it and throws it against his lips, taking a burning, horrible gulp. 'Aah . . . ' he gasps and hands the bottle back to Vince, wiping his medicine-sweetened lips.

Vince gulps too—he can't swallow it—his gorge rises and he turns away to throw up, but holds it back.

The sun bleeds gold below the bridge.

Sam drinks. Vince drinks. And again.

'Nothing's happening.' Sam says.

Vince gives him the bottle. 'Stand up,' he says.

Sam does, his back scraping against the rough bricks. He turns round to look into the sun, which swings now under the bridge, a ball of bright yellow, he does not need to blink, this sun is kind, sweet. It shines lovingly into his eyes.

A shuffle, and Vince is standing beside him.

'Fuck!'

The oily sun.

They begin to laugh.

Sam says, 'Walk in a straight line,' and Vince tries, and he can, but it's too funny and he collapses in a welter of legs and gasps. Laughter chokes him, he's pointing at Sam, saying, 'You . . . you . . . you . . . '

Anaesthetised air caught in his chest.

They bumble against each other underneath the iron roof, tripping, giggling, singing, as the sun sinks below the water. It leaves a choppy pool of blood that shrinks and disappears. For a short time the apartment buildings on the other side of the bridge are clear and clean against the cooling sky, but as their lights are kindled their frames disappear.

Now Vince and Sam are crouching against the brick columns in the bus shelter, where the bus never comes because the hill is too steep and its turning circle is not small enough. Vince's bare arms are prickling in the new chill. He is giggling into his chest.

Sam is looking out at the bridge and hearing the fat mosquito croon of cars across its wide crescent. Up there the wind blows dark and sharp.

The boats clink and turn.

Sam's mother looks at her watch and takes the chops out of the fridge.

∞

All that time, Rachel lived so close, down on the peninsula, and never once ran into Sam or Vince. Even though they were a few years apart they must have been to one or two of the same parties.

Although it's possible Rachel never went. Her bedroom, high in the corner of the huge, crumbling house, framed by a willow tree that licked its green tongues on the window in the summer wind. She slept best when her parents were having parties; the sound of her mother's voice rising above the clatter of plates and laughter, and at the end of the night her father playing the piano, big hands covering chords, underwater voice that made her think of whales. When he was a child he had been able to see whales from his bedroom window by the beach, or he said he had, or said he could have if he'd been there at the right time. It was hard to remember.

The morning she begged her mother to let her stay home from school. She had, with that frightening suddenness of childhood, become unpopular, and all her friends gigglingly ignored her in the playground, punching or kicking her if she got too close to them, picking her last, with exaggerated sighs of disgust, for the softball team. One morning before school she cried and said she couldn't stand it, would her mother let her stay home one day, just one day? Rachel was horrified when her mother started to cry too, softly, and said that she could.

Still, the free day stretched before her, gloriously warm and hung with cloudy blossoms, and she went outside to play. The street was dappled with shifting sunlight under the liquidambars. There was no-one around. She strapped on her roller-skates, and started to skate back and forth in front of the house.

At first she went fast, panting and sweating, but gradually the day overwhelmed her, the warm, close, slowness of it, and she found herself staring at the road, its dips and divots and the moving pattern of the shadows. There was a great chunk out of the lumpy tarmac, about the size of a soup tureen, and it was filled with water. Someone was hosing off their driveway and the water sped down the gutter in a ribboning stream.

She edged forward on her skates so she was standing in the puddle. The water barely covered the wheels. With their tractor tread they looked like the tyres of a jeep. They pushed through the puddle like a four-wheel drive through a great lake. She was in Africa. A tall, beautiful redhead drove one jeep—her right foot, always slightly ahead—and the redhead's lover, a faceless but intrepid man, drove the other. They were exploring.

The water in the gutter—splashing around the wheels, wetting Rachel's sandshoes—became a rushing river, almost impossible to ford. She clomped onto the nature strip and the sharp buffalo grass was treacherous undergrowth in the jungle. The swaying trees overhead she dismissed—they were too vast to be part of this continent. But at foot level the street was hers to discover.

When her mother called her in for lunch she sat down to take her skates off, and walking down the path, her feet felt as light as air.

Things change.

She was thirteen, alone in the house on a Saturday afternoon, standing in the upstairs bathroom with a towel wrapped around her, watching her reflection in the mirror. The way her breasts overflowed, silky and thick like cream, when she pressed her arms inwards. The skin on her face soft and downy.

Downstairs, the sound of footsteps on the path, the creak as someone lifted the doorknocker and the crash of it against the splitting wood of the old door. She tucked her hair behind her ears and ran down to answer it, leaving the reflection behind.

It was one of her brother's friends—she knew him by sight, but couldn't remember his name. He stood on the doorstep, grinning at her.

'Hi,' she said. 'Patrick isn't home. He's at the park.'

'With Jeff?' The boy was small and smart like a jockey—he seemed to swagger even when standing still.

'Yeah. I think so.'

'He knows I'm coming over. I might wait, if that's okay.'

'Sure.' Unselfconsciously, she held the door open.

He stepped in, and she said, 'You'll have to listen to the radio or something. I was just getting changed.'

'Can I watch?'

'What?' She would have done a classic double take if she had understood what he was saying.

He laughed at the blank look on her face. 'I said, can I watch?'

'*No!*'

His smile felt like it was chasing her up the stairs—her feet hardly touching them, her whole body stinging as though it had been slapped. And a grin of her own, making her face ache with delight.

∞

And Frank. Youngest child of a large family, all boys, and still the smallest even when they were all grown. Spending his life watching doors and windows for escape routes, planning and building elaborate hide-outs, away from his brothers. He was so small, and so quick of tongue, *a little smart-arse*, that they could not stop themselves punching him, pushing him around.

How the world looks through a sheet; lying flat as he could in his parents' bed, sheets over his face. The dark, shifting shadow of a brother above him. His heart hurting with the effort of keeping still.

There were five of them: Paul, Tom, Steven, Warwick and Frank. Alliances formed early in life, partnerships falling neatly into place. Frank was born too late to fit into either gang— the car-driving, smoking, staying-out-late gang of Tom and Steven; the studying hard, having steady girlfriends, helping-Mum-round-the-house gang of Paul and Warwick. His mother was in her worn-out mid-forties when he was born. Frank was *an accident.*

He could remember the moment when he first began to realise he had an opinion of his own, when everything he thought was not an echo of or reaction to his brothers. He was sitting in Tom's car outside the fish and chip shop, waiting for Tom and his friends, who were buying potato scallops, swigging soft drinks in the greasy steam at the counter.

A tape was playing, a man was singing in a rusty voice, a song about riding through the desert on a horse with no name.

He was ten. He thought—tasting the swearword in his mouth, enjoying it—what a *fuckin'* stupid song.

Sports carnival, the grass on the oval yellow and rustling with heat. Warwick is the second-last of the Lynch boys at the high school. He's in sixth form. He is tall, with blond hair that will not fall anywhere except into a neat part. His long legs and arms are muscular but pale.

He has been training for months for this, and has already soared over the high jump, landed past the pit in the long jump and finished first, red-faced, his hair still tidy, in the 100, 200 and 800 metres.

He is preparing for the shot-put, his greatest challenge. His limbs are fleet but not used to bearing weight. The Lynch boys are all thin, rangy. Warwick drops the shot-put from hand to hand and stands alternately on one leg, then the other. He shakes them professionally, looking as though he is trying to kick them loose.

Half the school is watching. His youngest brother, Frank, is one of them. He crouches out of the line of teacher-sight, under the flickering shade of a gum sapling with two of his first form cronies, holding a cigarette between sweaty finger and thumb. He has walked the compulsory 1000 metre race with them, although in the last stretch they couldn't contain themselves and burst into a run, shouting, shoving each other aside. He came last.

Warwick's turn is up. He jogs to the circle, closes his eyes, takes a deep breath, and bends to throw. You can feel the silence. He stands still a second. He gulps, does the shot-putting whirl (careful to keep his feet inside the line) and flings the shot-put as hard and fast as he can, giving out a strangled yell. The faces are upturned, watching it, the muttering already beginning as it flies through the air.

And lands, in a sad puff of dust, way to the left, yards and yards from the rest of the field.

Frank's friends shriek with laughter and push each other, knocking Frank over. He lies on his back, feeling the cigarette burning his fingers, while his friends scuffle over him. He can hear the shouts of derision from the crowd. He stares at the sky until it becomes too bright and he shuts his eyes against it, white light immersing him.

The Rocks

Frank liked to quote the catchphrase from a show that had once been on TV, called 'Chance or Coincidence'. After you'd seen some story about a celebrity communing with their dead bodyguard or an alien landing in a whirlpool of blue and green lights, the voice-over man would say, 'Chance—or coincidence?'

The sticky-thread web of chance or coincidence joined them like this.

Frank and Rachel met at university, in a class about film theory. He sat next to her in the first class (everyone finding seats with their heads down, the clatter and scrape of chairs, bumping against each other) and then the second, and the third. In those early weeks Rachel did not have the courage to look up, even at the tutor. Her only impression had been of arms, and the stretched-out legs of the other students. A plethora of boots, the occasional set of bare feet (black from the dirty, hot tar on Broadway).

Frank's hands perpetually screwing and unscrewing the lid from his seldom-used pen.

Their tutor was American, his accent sugary, Californian. One day he was conducting a discussion about the gaze (these indistinct nouns inexplicably become concrete; the *gaze*, the *other*) and an unusually intelligent, energetic student put forward a new idea. The tutor nodded, thoughtful, and said, 'That's a very suave concept.'

He pronounced it *swave*: Rachel, jerked out of the familiar half-sleep, had to sit up to swallow a mouthful of laughter. There was a small splutter beside her. She glanced at him. Frank's face was warm with smiling. Their eyes met; he kicked her with one booted foot and she put a hand across her lips, feeling suddenly wide awake.

By tacit agreement they walked to the lifts together after class, introduced themselves, stood next to each other in the cramped space, trying not to touch. They stopped in the echoing concrete hall next to Broadway. Rachel talked too fast, her hands slipping and fumbling with her books, and Frank, calm and amused, asked her if she wanted to come for a drink.

Rachel will always remember, embarrassed, thinking, *Will this be my boyfriend?*

She said no, regretting it as she spoke, and tried to catch at it, breathless, 'Maybe . . . maybe tomorrow.'

'Come now. What've you got to do?'

She followed him down to the bar and he bought her a beer, liquid slopping out onto the greasy plastic table. He offered her a cigarette.

It was hard not to enjoy the conspiracy of laughter that grew between them. It felt like real youth, the kind you are too frightened to properly enjoy at high school—freedom tempered with just the right amount of authority. Sometimes Rachel saw the look on the face of a justly irritated tutor and it only made her laugh more.

They left lectures early to play pool in the bar, they went to movies together, they danced at parties and wove home through jasmine-scented streets, singing and shouting to the dark canopy of fig trees and their furred jewellery of bats.

Frank was three years older than Rachel. He'd spent the years between school and university travelling, living in huge, shared houses up north, squats in London, an edgy existence that finally propelled him back to Sydney.

Rachel had come straight from school. Round, soft-skinned.

Her clothes startled Frank; skirts just covering her backside, hair three colours, heavy shoes and tight T-shirts, her mouth a red bite of lipstick. What would resolve itself into her particular, abrupt speech was then, at seventeen, a kaleidoscope of words. Once begun, once teased by Frank into speaking she couldn't stop.

Before they moved in together to the house in Stanmore, when she still lived with her parents, they spoke on the phone every night. Rachel's mother would pass the lino-tiled corridor where she sat, her legs locked like a safety pin, the cord of the phone swinging quietly from the wall. She was muttering, whispering, giggling.

Frank and Rachel; sometimes flatmates, always friends, never lovers.

The movement, the transformation from friend to lover is, to all honest people, a difficult one. There is nothing else in life that so admirably illustrates the difference between—what? Thought and feeling? Between what you know and what you feel.

You love your friend. You are gratified by their obvious affection for you. You spend a lot of time with them, and you play that deliberate, frightening game of discussing other lovers with your friend. You are absolutely straightforward about your lovers, with whom you are often not straightforward at all. There is both certainty and uncertainty in the friendship—the certainty of affection, the uncertainty of attraction not consummated.

In this time you come to know all the things that so regularly destroy the hearts of your friend's lovers. You know them so well, you are warned by them, you would recognise the pattern anywhere. You think you know everything.

Some are happy to keep it that way, happy to keep the friendship in place, but many reach the point where the head begins to race, the heart to thump with possibilities. When you are with your friend you suddenly realise there is only the most gossamer of barriers between you, and you can't help wondering whether you should just reach out and tear that barrier down.

Rachel, Frank, Sam and Vince came together for the first time at the deserted warehouses in The Rocks. Rachel was twenty. The boys were older. They'd been to an all-night party there and the dawn had broken while they were still inside. On the street the morning light was blue and chill—a garbage truck rumbled somewhere in the distance, a train clattered over the Bridge, and Rachel and Frank burst into the clean air, blinking dazzled eyes, ears ringing still from the music.

Sam and Vince were leaning on a car. Weary and hazy with drugs, they fell to talking, finding (as people always will in Sydney) that they shared some vague acquaintance, a university friend who had studied with Sam for a while. Sam was doing the writing course that neither Frank nor Rachel had been able to get into. Vince was just finishing his first degree.

The four of them stood there a while, chatting idly. Everyone was dazed, leaving sentences unfinished, feeling the easy, instant liking that comes from exhaustion. Eventually the conversation slowed and died and, saying goodbye, Sam and Vince lurched away.

Frank sat down in the gutter and began to roll himself a cigarette, but Rachel watched them walk down the long, wide, empty street, the Bridge spanning the distance, slowly making their way towards the water. She watched them until she could no longer hear their voices, until they were nearly out of sight under the Bridge. They paused a second, and Sam suddenly jumped onto Vince's back. They staggered away like that, silent tiny figures, beetling along the bright horizon of new light.

They found Frank's car, cold and still in the backstreet where they had left it. When Frank started the engine the radio exploded with music, the two of them grabbing for the volume control at the same instant.

They pulled out into the road.

'I don't want to go home,' said Rachel, leaning her head against the seat.

Frank changed into third. 'Okay. Where? More to drink?'

'No. Breakfast.'

'The Cross?'

'Yeah.'

They swung round through The Rocks, past street cleaners and early joggers. Coming up George Street they saw Sam and Vince, ambling along the pavement.

Frank drove alongside them. 'Need a lift?' he called over Rachel.

Sam said, 'Sure!'

Vince said, 'Where you going?'

'Up to the Cross for something to eat. Want to come?'

Frank leaned over to unlock the back door and the two boys climbed in. The smell of sweat and booze filled the car.

Up through the city, Frank taking red lights on the empty streets, fiddling with the radio. As they rounded Hyde Park, the morning sun suddenly burst over the buildings. It flooded the valley of William Street with a rounded, gorgeous light, washing over their faces, pooling into the car and warming their sore bodies. It was glorious, like heaven's path, an endless tide of gold.

'Jesus,' said Vince.

'Beautiful,' said Rachel softly.

They drove into it, torrent of brilliance, up towards the Coke sign.

A party in Surry Hills. Rachel was meeting Frank. She had been disinclined to go, lying on her bed at home with a book, but at eleven or closer to twelve Frank rang and demanded to know where she was. She dressed quickly and caught a bus up Parramatta Road; bought some beer at a pub on Cleveland Street and drank a bottle before she arrived, hoping to find some kind of enthusiasm.

Stepped over rows of people at the front door, sitting on the carpet with their backs against the wall. Found the kitchen, cursing Frank inwardly for dragging her into this.

He was sitting at the kitchen table with a girl she didn't know, under the impolite blue of a fluorescent light. He looked up and grinned when he saw her; reached out, grabbing her skirt, and made her sit down next to him.

Rachel said nothing for a while, listening to Frank talking to the girl. Her name was Lucy—she had short hair, big dark eyes, a pink shirt. Frank's voice was like a smoothing hand on a cat's back; Lucy preened under it, a got-the-cream grin spread over her face.

Rachel had the uncomfortable, familiar feeling that Frank was practising. Filling in time.

He turned to her. 'We're talking about us,' he said, waving at Lucy with his cigarette. 'How we're a lost generation.'

'Well,' said Lucy. She arched her shoulders slightly.

'Are we?' said Rachel, uninterested.

There was a flat quiet, while Lucy tried to work out Rachel's relationship to Frank, while Rachel wished she had stayed home, while Frank tilted his eyes towards the window, looking for something new to amuse.

'Have you got to get up early?' he said to Rachel.

'I doubt it,' she answered. They were on holidays, surviving on AUSTUDY back pay, sleeping late and going to the beach in the afternoons.

'Good. I feel like staying out.'

'Frank . . . '

'What?'

'I don't know. What'll we do?'

Frank was getting to his feet, his eyes fixed on the window. 'Wait a sec.' He climbed over her and went into the backyard.

Rachel smiled at Lucy, looked away, felt in Frank's discarded jacket for cigarettes, not wanting one. A silence stretched between them—thinner and thinner. Rachel lit a cigarette and opened her mouth to speak, to snap the silence, just as Lucy did, the two of them simultaneously saying, 'So what do you do?'.

They both blushed, and before they could continue, Frank reappeared at the back door. They turned their faces gratefully to his.

He was grinning. 'Look who's here!'

Sam and Vince were behind him. Vince in a big striped T-shirt, sneakers, baggy jeans, his eyes nearly hidden behind a curling fall of dark hair. He kept his hands in his pockets. Sam was different, looking around, used to being watched. Smooth brown face dark at the jaw with stubble. He was carrying a bottle—seeing Rachel, he lifted it in a salute.

'Hey!' she said, pleased, trying to get up. She was wedged between the wall and the table.

'How's it going?' Sam stepped past Frank and held out a hand, helping her to her feet.

Lucy bridled and smiled, 'Hi Sam,' she said.

'Oh, hi.' He kept hold of Rachel's hand as she clambered across Frank's legs. 'Do you know Rachel? And Vince. And this is Frank.'

Lucy looked at Frank. 'Yeah, we just met.'

The stereo in the next room suddenly burst into speaker-splitting music, and everyone at the table roared.

Fucking hell!

Turn it down!

There were shouts of laughter, the peal of smashing glass and the sound was halved. Frank said to Lucy, 'Aren't you a photographer? Or something?'

Sam was tugging at Rachel's hand; she turned to him, and he held his bottle in front of her face. 'Look what I found in the cupboard!'

It was Cinzano, the clear kind. Bianco.

'Horrible,' said Rachel, shaking her head.

'I know, but it's free.' Sam was unscrewing the lid, looking around for glasses.

'Don't you need some kind of mixer? You're supposed to have it with lemonade.'

'And an umbrella,' said Vince. He took the bottle from Sam and put it to his lips. Swallowed and handed it to Rachel.

Rachel gulped and made a face. 'It's so sweet! Like that stuff we used to drink at the youth centre.'

'What stuff?' Sam took the bottle back from her.

'Brandy something. Brandivino. Stronger than wine but not as strong as spirits.' She could still smell it. Taste it; syrupy, like sultanas. Sitting on a boy's knee under the dark chill of the fig trees.

'Vince and me used to drink Southern Comfort.'

'Fuckin awful.' said Rachel.

'I know. We drank it with Coke.'

'At pubs?' Rachel caught the Cinzano bottle by the neck.

'After a while.'

'Jesus.'

1983. Waiting till their parents had gone out. She remembered crouching in front of the chipboard liquor cabinet at Cathy O'Dwyer's house, licking sticky-sweet creme de menthe off her lips and wondering if she would get drunk or be sick before it happened.

The Balmain Leagues Club. Toohey's Old—thick, brown beer like liquefied leather. The old men at the bar, their voices curdling the air.

Rachel is standing in front of the brightly lit mirrors in the toilets at the Leagues Club with Cathy and her face is staring, staring wide-eyed and thick with mascara and her pink lipstick has worn off and she is talking to Cathy and giggling, and reeling a little, against the white laminex counter. She turns away to say something to Cathy but then she catches sight of her white, smudged face again and she has to fix her lipstick. She leans into the mirror, laughing, lipstick extended in one hand, and applies it very, very carefully. And slowly. So carefully and slowly that when she turns around—shaken back to earth, suddenly—Cathy has gone. She twitches her skirt into place and follows, walking in a straight line in her high heels.

The three of them went into the backyard, leaving Frank with Lucy, but he was out in minutes, eyes gleaming.

'Look what I got,' he said, putting a hand into his top pocket. He brought out three tablets.

'What is it?' said Vince.

'Acid. That girl gave it to me.'

'Fuck you're smooth!' laughed Sam.

'Jeez, Frank . . . ' said Rachel.

'What?'

'I don't know. I don't want to visit hell.'

'You'll be fine. Look, I've only got three. Someone'll share one with you.'

Sam and Vince looked at each other.

'I don't mind,' said Vince. 'I wasn't really on for a big one.'

'Good.' Frank handed one of the tablets to Sam, one to Vince, and put the other in his mouth, swallowing it dry. 'It'll be fun, you'll see.'

It sharpened everything. And Rachel could hear the sound of grinding as she turned to look at things.

The other girls had long hair. Hers was shorter, thick and brown—it twisted into curls at the nape of her neck. The other girls all looked somehow delicate—fragility in their white arms, curving pink lips, luminous, thick-lashed eyes. Rachel stood against the wall, shifted so that one knee dropped forward, pulled her shirt closer about her. It had started to rain in the dark backyard.

The distance is unfathomable. Frank stood so close his nose almost touched hers—when he turned away the lightprint of his face remained some seconds behind her eyes.

There was a silvery edge to everything. The rain clacked and smacked onto the roof. Somebody lit a candle beside Rachel, on a ledge at the level of her shoulder. It did not seem to burn so much as snap. Orange. Off.

When she turned to look for Sam or Vince a sudden row of

blue lights crossed her vision. Four blue lights. They faded and disappeared.

Time unreeled around them. On summer afternoons they lay in the park and drank beer, and played 'how much would you charge?' It was a game that could easily take all day. Trying to put a price on humiliation. Frank could always have you squirming and raising the stakes.

'How much would you charge,' fixing an eye on Rachel, 'to sleep with Vince?'

Vince laughing and Rachel trying to. 'Nothing! It'd be a pleasure!'

'No, come on. How much?'

'How much would *you* charge to sleep with him?'

Frank grinning. 'You couldn't afford it.'

Sam always went for the ones it was easier to pay. How much to walk into the pub wearing nothing but a pair of platforms and a wig? How much to stop someone on the street and ask them—straight out—if they'd fuck you? How much to eat your own shit?

Vince was the worst at it. He was too serious; he could never name a sum, always worried he'd got it wrong, hadn't quantified the humiliation properly. Where the others would demand millions for sleeping with Michael Jackson or eating nothing but Kentucky Fried Chicken for six weeks, he would agonise, trying, always, to play fair.

They seemed joined so easily, laughter and talk and endless idleness rocking them, cradling them. The trees and sky feeling loose on their moorings.

It was a year at least before Sam met Florence. She was tall, womanly and calm, with the kind of face that veered wildly from heart-stopping beauty to strangeness. Beside her, Rachel felt the need to hold her breath. She learnt not to look around when they stepped into a room of people together—the faces like streetlights flickering on as they saw Florence.

Florence openly disapproved of Frank, although she liked him.

For the others, the beginning of a good night came when the two would swing towards the bar together, slender shoulders bumping, when they looked at each other and smiled. Frank called Florence *spaghetti legs*, and if Florence was in the mood she thought it was funny.

Once Sam saw her reach out and flatten the palm of her hand against Frank's face, covering mouth and nose to shut him up. He found himself wishing she would act that way to him—or really, wishing she would act every way to him. He was not satisfied being just Sam to her. He wanted to see every kind of light reflected in her eyes.

Aracena, Ayamonte (Spain)

Each Christmas, Easter and family birthday the Lynch boys gathered unwillingly at the house to be fed by their mother and sickened by their father.

Mr Lynch was a tall, spare, bad-tempered man who held onto life with a furious, knuckle-whitening grip. His opinions could have been blasted in flame across the walls of the house; his stance on women's lib, on spoiling the *bloody* dog by feeding it at the table, on commercial television, and most of all (and forever) that *bloody bugger* Malcolm Fraser. His constant and angry disappointment with the boys had driven them all from home at the first opportunity.

Now he was old, fiercely retired, and drinking heavily. He could feel his grip weakening, fingers being pried loose by time. He demanded that his sons *respect their mother* by turning up for each occasion.

Mrs Lynch moved amongst them like a waitress; grey-haired, forever wrapped in an apron. She had aged faster than her husband who seemed, despite the whisky, to still have power behind his punch, to still have authority. Paul and Warwick, the good boys, sat in the kitchen with their mother while she prepared celebration meals, listening painstakingly to her conversation. They were kind enough to respond to her enquiries about their lives, listing their achievements, leaving out the detail, so she could tell her friends about them later.

Frank, however, stood drinking in the garden with Steven or (if Steven had brought his wife) lounged angrily from room to room in the enormous house, picking things up to look at them, putting them down, slipping quickly through the door if he heard his father approaching. It made his heart beat too fast—the empty rooms with carpets smelling of disuse, the family dog once full of barking life collapsed like a split cushion at the foot of the stairs. More often than not he would pick up the phone in one of the many connections, in a cold, distant bedroom and call Rachel. Or Sam, or Vince.

Tom had not been home since high school. He had been working since then; first as a builder's apprentice, then running his own business. He'd left for Europe five or six years later, still working, still with his high school girlfriend Angela, moving from place to place.

It was March, the entrancing leaf-drift days of early autumn, and the air was a woven blanket of warmth, shot through with chill. Sam was living in Captain's Flat with Florence. Frank was still with Rachel at Stanmore, Vince was in Glebe.

One cold morning Frank opened the front door onto the street. It had been raining all night—the road was still drying, leaves in damp clumps caught in the gutter. His car was wet. Coin-sized drops sat on the bonnet.

He looked up at the sky. It was clear. Looked at his watch. Nine o'clock. He shivered, thinking about the next few days. He wasn't working at the pub until next week.

He lit a cigarette, and the prospect of doing nothing began to nauseate him. It was too cold to go to the beach, too expensive to go to the movies, too sickening to think about writing. He looked at the sky again, and felt a sudden rush of decision, dizzying, pleasing.

It took him four hours to reach Captain's Flat, and when he came bumping along the paddock road that led to the house he could see Sam lying on his back in the squared-off sunlight of the verandah. The black dog came barking along the track and bit at his wheels until he pulled up outside the house.

He got out of the car.

'What are you doing here?' Sam sat up, grinning widely, shading his eyes.

Frank shrugged his stiff shoulders. 'Felt like a drive.'

Sam stood up. 'Fucking hell. This is great. *Fuck!*' He came forward, jumped off the edge of the verandah. His hand went down to the dog which leapt and wagged around him. 'Come and have a beer!'

It was cold inside the house but Sam took a longneck from the fridge and led Frank back out to the verandah. They sat in the afternoon sun, drinking from small, inadequate glasses. They smoked Frank's cigarettes, flinging fragments of tobacco onto the drying grass.

'Why don't you move down here?' said Sam. He was leaning against a wooden pillar, sunlight in his face. He looked well.

Frank laughed. 'Getting desperate?'

'No. It'd be good though.'

'What would I do?'

'Write.'

Frank stared down at the grass, swinging under his dangling boots. 'I'm not ready yet. I've got to do something first. It feels like being retired down here.'

'It's not like that.' Sam took a drag on his cigarette, coughed. He never smoked on his own. 'This is life, as much as anywhere else.'

'I don't know.'

The radio was playing in the kitchen; a mist of music that dissolved in the cooling air.

'You could get a job in Canberra, like Flo.'

'Get fucked!'

'She likes it.'

'Yeah, well . . . ' Frank jammed out his cigarette, finished his beer. 'Come on. Let's go to town.'

They drove out to Braidwood, some forty kilometres away, a small, wildly pretty town filled with people in their twenties and thirties. There was a knot of them in the pub, matted, dirty, healthy in heavy knitted jumpers and beanies. There was a vacant table next to them. Sam and Frank sat down.

'Beer?' said Sam.

Frank felt in his pockets, brought out a handful of coins, flattening them on the table. 'I'm a bit low.'

'Don't worry about it. I'm flush. Nothing to spend my money on.'

'Okay.'

Sam came back from the bar with two schooners and two shots. Frank raised his eyebrows, said nothing, knocked back the tequila and pulled his beer towards him.

Sam sat down, did the same. The tequila felt like it drenched his whole body with warmth. He grinned stupidly at Frank.

'What?' said Frank.

'I don't know. It's good you came down. What about Rache? What's she up to?'

'Looking for work.'

Sam winced. 'What a waste of time.'

'We've got to do something.'

'Do we?' said Sam.

'Well, what's the alternative?' Frank, too, could feel the tequila heating his veins. He felt convinced suddenly—articulate. The gang beside them were leaning into a circle. One of them got up to put something on the jukebox. Jimi Hendrix. 'You're gonna end up in a beanie down here.'

Sam laughed and ran a hand over his black hair, cut close to his skull.

'Really! I mean, are you happy?'

'Of course!'

Frank snorted, looked around, took out his cigarettes. 'It's like some fuckin' refuge in this place. A refuge for morons. For fucking brain-dead, middle-class losers. Vegetarians.'

'Yeah, but you think everyone's a moron. Things aren't easy, you know. It's not like there's a whole lot of work around. This is an okay place to be if you're unemployed.'

Frank lit a cigarette.

'We didn't get such a great deal. People our age. We're sort of nowhere.'

'Fuck that!'

Sam grinned again, taking a long drink of beer. 'You got a problem?'

'Jesus,' said Frank. 'It's pathetic. I mean, who started this bullshit about *our generation*, that we're lost? As if no other generation was lost when they were our age. It's only afterwards that everything looks like it has some sort of form or structure. It makes me think of that 60s stuff, how they're supposed to have changed the world for us. Get fucked! They were wandering around like a bunch of fucking retards, no fucking idea what they were doing. It's just later you can tie it up in this neat little we-changed-the-world package.'

'What's your point?'

Frank sighed. 'No point. It's just . . . shit, I can hear what we'll be saying in twenty years, that we *made* something out of being lost. We turned the world green, saved the forests, whatever. But now, right now, it doesn't look like we're doing anything. It doesn't feel like we're doing anything.'

Sam was laughing now, spluttering into his beer. 'Mate, you need a hobby. Or a challenge.'

The beanies shifted and murmured. The tangle of guitars filled the pub.

Frank smiled reluctantly, giving in. 'Maybe I should go bushwalking.'

'Find your goddess.'

'Do guys have goddesses too, or just gods? I want to know. And I want to be able to choose my god. I don't want some pussy god—the god of being nice or something. *I want Thor*!'

Frank banged his glass on the table, and Sam let his head drop forward. He laughed and laughed.

∞

It happened so easily, Frank began to wonder whether he should start believing in order, in a planned universe. In a grand scheme that held a scheme just for him.

The night he got home from four days with Sam and Florence (four days watching them; the way when Florence ate, Sam's mouth moved in sympathy, chewing with her) he was lying on his bed. Worn out by the drive, but his mind ticking endlessly, unable to sleep. He heard the phone ring downstairs and reached behind him for his pillow, pulling it over his face.

Rachel came thumping up the stairs and stood in the doorway, slightly out of breath. 'It's for you. It's long distance.'

Frank took the pillow away and looked at her. 'Who is it?'

'I don't know. A guy.'

He followed her down and picked up the phone. 'Hello?'

'Frank!'

'Who's this?'

'It's Tom, dickhead.'

The surprise made him gasp, made him sit down on the couch with his legs and chest feeling stupid.

It was a good line; they could have been a suburb away from each other. Tom was in Spain.

He had a job just outside a small town in the south, building a swimming pool at a guesthouse. The construction was over and there was just the prettifying to be done, the icing on the cake, Tom called it, but he couldn't finish it. He'd had enough. He was coming home. He and Angela wanted to get married.

'I thought you might want to come over and finish the job for me.'

Rachel, trying to be busy in the kitchen, heard Frank's voice go high with pleasure.

'How would I get there? I haven't got any money.'

'Borrow some from Mum. It's fantastic pay, you'll make it back in a month. And you don't need to be here for that long. Few months maybe.'

'Shit. I'd *love* to.'

'Do it then. It's a good place. The people are nice. They're English, but they're nice.'

Frank felt his weariness dropping away. 'What made you think of me?'

'I don't know. I thought you might be at a bit of a loose end. It seemed like a good idea.'

For just a moment, a bright-coloured moment, Frank caught a flash of himself as others might see him. He closed his eyes, let the image fade, took a sharp breath.

He had no doubts, none at all. Rachel, Vince, his job at the pub—they were landscape. He could leave them. It was perfect.

Rachel had made and drunk a cup of tea by the time the conversation was over. She came back into the front room, hands in her back pockets, feeling as though she was walking through syrup. Everything slowed.

Frank was sitting on the couch, staring out at nothing, his eyes actually shining. He didn't say anything. She watched him for a moment, and then stepped over and switched on the TV.

Frank on the plane, his forehead resting on the cold window. The red-caked roofs of Sydney describe a long, sweet arc and he feels the air humping the plane from underneath like a whale under a boat. The plane gets up, it gathers speed, the air pushing it, the land swirling away, the sudden height making him breathless.

Rachel had been looking for work—flicking through the paper every morning with a cold feeling in her throat, half-terrified she would find something she could do. Things had changed, though, since she started university. Where once there had been twelve, thirteen pages of jobs in the Saturday papers there were now only two or three.

Vince was living in Glebe and doing his honours year. When Frank left he took over his job at the pub. Met Rachel nearly every night for last drinks. One evening as she was sitting at the bar, bumping the toes of her boots against the hard, brown wood, he leaned over to her and said, 'There's another job going, you know.'

Rachel felt that sudden, screaming feeling of being trapped, forced it down and said, 'Yeah?'

'Somebody just quit. You should grab it.'

She was doing nothing with her days, she was living on the dole, she was bored to the point of violence, and still she hesitated. 'I don't know how, though.'

''S easy. I'll show you.' Vince demonstrated, pulling a neat schooner. 'See. Bang it on the tray, like this.'

'Do you think they'll take me?'

'Of course. It'd be good. We'd be working together.'

She shrugged. 'I suppose so.'

'Well, don't do me any favours.'

'Vince! I'm sorry, okay? I'm a loser. I don't even know how to have a job anymore. It's been fucking months.'

'I know. And this'll make a big difference, I'm telling you.'

He was right, of course, and soon Rachel began to take pleasure in the new quickness of her hands as she pulled a beer, swung a bottle of spirits over a seven-ounce glass, flicked money off the counter. She listened to herself being tough with the customers. She turned down many offers of sex.

Frank wrote to her, after only two months, and asked her to come and see him in Spain. Rachel could not remember a single instance—in all the years that had dripped away—of Frank asking her to do something. He had demanded or ordered or claimed that he didn't care what the hell she did. She began to feel, for better or worse, as though she was filling up. For the first time.

She gave all her hours and days to saving money. She took on all the extra shifts, falling into bed at night with sore feet and shoulders, sleeping late, spending nothing, seeing only Vince. He teased her about her dedication, suggesting she take a management course, but she only laughed and kept on working. She felt flooded with love.

Head down, she served and wiped and poured and cleaned and tried not to think about it.

Travelling on the train from the French border to Madrid, Rachel started a conversation with a Spanish woman, a city woman some five or six years older than she was. They could only exchange the simplest of sentiments. They agreed that it was a long way, and that there was need of rain. The desert that ran past them was orange-brown and splitting in the sun. The woman said that she did not like Spanish films; they were too difficult to understand. She preferred films from Hollywood.

She told Rachel that she was travelling from the border where she had been staying with her boyfriend, who was French. Every weekend she took the train north to see him. He didn't like the city, and would not come to Madrid.

The woman pushed her hair back, a shining streak of brown, and looked out of the window. They were leaning against the bar drinking thin, yellow beer. Rachel looked out too and tried to think of something else to say. He will not take the train for me, the woman had said. The carriage was thick with smoke and Spanish and laughter.

At the station in Madrid Rachel waited in line for two hours to buy her ticket to Seville, only to learn that she had been waiting in the wrong place. There was a row of slot-machines behind her that sold ice-creams, chocolates, chips, tins of olives and nuts, and San Miguel beer. Ten pesetas. She found the coin and pressed it into the slot. A can of beer clunked into the trough. It was freezing cold.

It sang in her throat, not yellow but gold. She downed half

the can thirstily. Her fear was extinguished in the ever-bursting bubbles.

Rachel's fat, heavy leather jacket had to be folded and fought into her bag every new day. She had worn it in London, feeling sweat run down her shoulders and gather under her breasts. She could smell a series of old parties in it; smoke, and whisky down one cuff. The smell did not disappear—rather, it matured. It stayed on her skin when she took the jacket off. She lay stiff and straight on a high camp bed in the hostel and the dowdy, dusty mustiness of other displaced women was lost in the tough, brown scent of the leather.

Filling time in the markets at Madrid she bought Frank a jacket just like it; black, square-cut, almost knee-length, with pointed Edwardian collars and purple satin lining. He was slender to the point of fragility—he would look like an elegant highwayman in it. She could not fit both jackets into her bag. It was forty-two degrees. Her hair was greasy with heat. She wore jeans, boots, a singlet and her own jacket, and still her bag was almost bursting.

She reached Seville at midday. It was like being the only outsider at a vast family gathering. Rachel stood in the scurrying centre of the station, her bag a stiff heap at her feet, and felt tears aching in her eyes. She put her hands in the pockets of her jacket to stop them from shaking. Sweat trickled down her palms. When she moved, she could not hear her jacket creaking—the noise of the city was too great. A group of girls her own age, their slender, brown waists displayed between bright shirts and cool, swirling skirts, passed her on their way to the Metro entrance. They were laughing as they disappeared down the steps.

Rachel kicked her bag across the dusty concrete towards the telephone booths, feeling in her top pocket for Frank's phone number. She fed pesetas into the slot, not knowing if they would be enough.

An English woman answered the phone.

'Hello?' said Rachel, 'It's Rachel Waters. Frank's friend. Is Frank there?'

145

'Rachel! We were wondering when you'd call. It's Margaret here. Where are you?'

'Seville. The station. Is Frank there?'

'You've missed him. He's gone into Los Marines to do the shopping. He said you'd be on the three o'clock bus.'

'Yes, but . . . I was . . .'

'Terminal 3. Or sometimes 4. It's the one that stops at San Lucar, not Valverde. The Valverde one doesn't go any further. You've got a couple of hours to wait, though. Maybe you should go into town. There's lots to see.'

'Actually, I was . . . I was going to ask Frank if he could come down and pick me up.'

'What for?'

'I don't know. I'm a bit . . .'

Margaret laughed. 'He's not on holiday yet! We can't spare him or the car, Rachel. Catch the Aracena bus, it's easy. Some-one'll meet you in Aracena at about six.'

'But . . .'

'Don't miss it, there isn't another one till Monday. We'll see you later on.'

'Okay.'

'Okay?'

'Bye.'

'Bye, Rachel. Looking forward to meeting you.'

They hung up, and Rachel shoved her bag out of the way. Two men stood behind her. They jangled the coins in their hands.

The girl beside her on the bus was from San Lucar. Her arms and neck were draped with cheap gold chains. She smelt strongly of sweat. She read a local paper, and drew Rachel a map of the area.

'*San Lucar, aquí—Aracena, aquí*,' she said, pointing. A blue biro line, leaning to the left.

When she got off, Rachel was desperate to follow her. The girl held up a hand, palm towards her, and smiled. 'Then— Aracena,' she said.

146

The bus climbed a tar road that was grey with dust and heat, through cork plantations, fields of grapevines and desertous ranges of crumbling dirt. Rachel had not eaten since Paris. Her stomach clenched at the thought.

She tried to see herself, a pale reflection in the window at her elbow. Her face was blotched. Her hair clung to the sides of her head. She ran a hand through it, and her leather jacket groaned.

The sign that said *Aracena—Ciudad* was white, outlined in blue. Restricted and creaking, Rachel got up and pulled her bag down from the rack. It thumped at her feet and she was thrown backwards as the bus twisted like a snake into the first pebble-paved street of Aracena.

It pulled up in a small, dusty square. Rachel and her bag fell out onto the road. The sunlight was blinding. The other passengers split and disappeared down backstreets that curved out of sight.

She looked around, her heart leaping crazily in her chest.

Frank was standing under the scattered shade of a eucalyptus tree, over at the edge of the square. He was wearing a white shirt; King Gees and boots. His brownish, straight hair had grown down his neck, against his shoulders. His legs were still skinny, but so tanned they looked dirty.

They saw each other. Neither moved, and they smiled. It suddenly seemed ridiculous. There was Frank.

'Rachel.'

Tears started in her eyes and laughter began to gurgle in her throat as he came towards her. His arms wide to catch her. They went round her neck, pulling her tight, and she wound herself into his body, legs tangled, hands inside his shirt. Swaying in the dust. Crying now, and laughing.

The whole of their lives in Sydney whistling and singing and shouting between them, and around them the silent square, the eucalyptus trees, the clear, cruising sky.

'The value of friendship . . . ' They were back at the house, by the pool, and Frank was lying on his back, one foot propped on a deckchair, one hand around a bottle of beer.

Rachel let her head tilt to look at him, feeling the beginnings of a great relaxation. Her back pressed into the warm flagstones. Her hair had dried in minutes.

'What I mean,' she said, 'is . . . well, do you think we've come to the end of making new friends? Like the top of a learning curve.'

'I don't know.'

'And then I wonder sometimes if we keep the friends we have just out of laziness. It might be too difficult to get someone new used to your . . . '

'Weirdnesses,' supplied Frank.

'Yeah.' Rachel sat up so she could see the house, bringing her feet round to trail in the pool's blue water. It was pink, frosted with white windows and verandahs, sitting comfortably on the side of a mountain. The pool was further up the mountain, looking down on it—to reach it you had to climb a large, winding driveway.

Each level of the house gave a wide view of the valley and the mountains beyond it—they were dark green, uncut by roads, shimmering under the pitiless eye of the sky. Unpacking in Frank's bedroom she had heard donkeys braying, and the house workers grumbling to each other underneath the cork trees. During the day and the early evening swallows wheeled and ducked over the eaves, made sheer dives along the flat-paned windows. Sometimes in the distance a hawk appeared, suspended, swinging slightly over the valley.

Frank did not move, except to tip the last of his beer down his throat. As Rachel sat there, the loosening in her body continued. The evening descended in silence, hot and almost entirely still. From the valley, a swallow suddenly swooped up and sped across the surface of the pool, picking up a bright ribbon of water in its beak. A breeze turned her thoughts slowly as a windmill. Frank fell asleep.

She was swimming silent, drunken laps—trying not to splash Frank—when Margaret's husband, Gil, appeared. He was big, his bare chest brown and hairy, his belly hanging over drawstring shorts. He stood at the side of the pool, waiting for Rachel to notice him.

'Rachel?' he said.

She pulled up, shaking the water from her ears and hair.

'It is Rachel?'

'Yeah.' Rachel looked over at Frank, who seemed to be still asleep. His ribs cast an intricate shadow on his chest. 'Is there anything I can do? Help you with dinner or something?'

'No, no.' Gil's accent was suddenly more British. 'You're on holiday. I just wanted Frank.'

'Frank!'

'God, he can sleep,' said Gil turning to Rachel, 'can't he?'

She shook her head and swung at the water with her fist. Balls of water sprang up, hitting Frank. He sat suddenly upright, wide awake.

They had one more day before they left, and Frank had to work until the last minute. Rachel swam, tried not to follow him around, and got taken into the town by Gil and Margaret. Every second day they made the trip to buy more food for their guests. It was mid-summer, and they sometimes had six or seven people at once in the upstairs rooms.

Their rich English accents filled and rounded their Spanish—their voices reverberated across the sun-blasted plaza. People greeted them—to each one they introduced Rachel and then left her standing, a smile aching on her face, as they talked.

Gil took her into the supermarket, long, cool and dark, an ancient fan whirring in the dust-grimed ceiling. Together they walked down the aisles.

Rachel picked up a round of soft cheese from the barely-working refrigerator. 'Cheese?' she said to Gil.

He nodded, '*Queso*.'

They put it in Gil's basket.

'Meat?'

'*Carne*. We'll get it from the butcher.'

'*Carne*,' repeated Rachel.

'Not so much of an accent. It's not like Italian—it's flatter. Less rrromantic.' Gil rolled the 'r'.

'*Carne*,' said Rachel in broad Australian.

Gil laughed. 'Better!'

The meat—sausages, pigs' knuckles wrapped in plastic—smelled cold, sweet, of rosemary and thyme. They walked past it to the breakfast cereals, where the bright-coloured exclamations, the have-a-brand-new-day faces of the people on the boxes, looked far more ridiculous than they did at home. As though this was a toy culture, one that had not progressed beyond a kind of 1950s innocence or ignorance.

'In Spanish, cornflakes?' asked Rachel.

'*Cornflakes*,' said Gil, somehow making the word sound exotic.

They moved through the supermarket, seeing no other customers, talking in low voices. Gil held up each new product and Rachel repeated its name after him. After they had paid they stepped onto the threshold of the building, under the slanting shade of the roof, and looked out into the blinding sun and the people in the plaza hiding under umbrellas and trees.

'How's Frank's Spanish?' said Rachel, lifting one arm to shield her eyes.

'Pretty good. It took him a little while. He's clever, though.' There was a pause. 'Have you two been friends for a long time, then?'

Rachel looked up at the sky, its deep blue almost purple. 'I suppose so. Maybe four years.'

Gil nodded, and they stepped out into the brilliant sunlight.

Margaret was at the fishmarket, her heavy-skinned arms hung with baskets. She looked up as they approached and bellowed 'Gil! Come over here! Look at the price of these!'.

She was standing over a gravelly bed of fish, their open throats bleeding red onto the ice below them.

Rachel kept behind Gil as he strode up, shouting something in Spanish at Margaret and the shopkeeper. The market was a huge, brightly lit shed, no windows, no fans. The cold of the ice and the heat that rose to the roof met somewhere near eye-level, or nose-level, where the smell was intense. The place was full of people—children ran and shrieked around their knees.

Margaret and Gil kept up what seemed to be a cheerful argument with the black-haired shopkeeper, though the volume of their voices hurt Rachel's ears. With one arm she held a sheaf of gladioli that she had bought for Margaret. She could actually see them wilting. As though they had been dyed with some inferior colour, red leaked out of them. Water dripped like hot sweat from their thick stems. Her other arm was laden with plastic bags full of food.

Margaret and Gil bought the fish, still shouting at the man as they left the market. They made their way to the car, parked in one of the sandy sidestreets. Rachel watched them as their big, comfortable bodies collided, listened to them talk.

They packed the car, and Rachel stepped forward with her flowers.

Margaret said, 'Oh, your poor glads! You can't get good flowers for love or money in Aracena!'.

Siesta, and Rachel lay on the middle of the double bed, star-shape, feeling the sweat collecting damply under her arms and legs. Outside her window a tiny cement-mixer mumbled ceaselessly. Frank was down there, shirtless, shovelling wet cement into a wheelbarrow that was balanced by one of the English house workers. They were laying a new path to the swimming pool.

Sexual tension. The expression made Rachel feel sick. It was always an issue, she supposed, between friends; probably always had been between her and Frank. But never approached, never addressed. And now she was here, lying on his bed while he worked downstairs, and trying to stop her mind charging like a bull at the time they were about to have together. The two of them, alone, in a place where they knew no-one else.

It was impossible to know what might happen if they moved closer together.

When Sam had begun seeing Florence, it had made an effective and necessary split in the group. Before that, they had been spending all their time together. Even Sam stopped noticing women noticing him. Frank, of course, continued to make frequent and entirely private forays over the borders of sex. If he was seeing anyone she very rarely appeared amongst them.

Some centrifugal force pulled them all together nearly every night; the pub, the movies, someone's house to watch TV and drink cups and cups of tea. Any woman of Frank's who found herself dragged inwards by this would be insulted and offended by their lack of attention to her. They hated Rachel, tolerated Vince (thinking he was too stupid to try and impress) and lusted secretly after Sam, whose beautiful face was made only more so by lack of sleep and too much alcohol.

It was different with Florence, who appeared unaffected by their opinion of her. This secured their respect and liking. She cut through Sam's uncertainty, claiming him as though there was no doubt about her right to him. She wasn't scared of his good looks, threatened by his close friendship with Rachel, annoyed by the presence of Frank and Vince. When she got the job in Canberra they relinquished him easily, each secretly pleased by the idea that, through Sam, they were finally beginning to change. They had all wondered when their lives would cease to be so interdependent. Sam leaving for Captain's Flat seemed to be the first move towards separation.

And so Rachel lay on Frank's bed in the unbearable heat, trying to decide whether her attraction for him would cause some kind of implosion, whether it was real or brought about only by loneliness and habit, by the difference of their surroundings, by fear.

Whether she could stop herself from showing it.

'Frank,' she said, her mind breaking onto open ground.

The cement-mixer turned and turned.

'Frank!' said Rachel, louder.

'Care-ful!' said the English boy, his voice framed by the window.

Rachel got off the bed and went to look out. Cement was slopping out of the wheelbarrow onto the path—Frank held the shovel against its lip, trying to control the flow.

'Frank?' said Rachel, leaning out.

'Just a sec! . . . Hold it . . . ' he said to the boy, 'Stop, that's it!'

The boy dragged the wheelbarrow back, snatching up a shovel and starting, with Frank, to push the new cement into place. Sweat dripped from them both. Their bare legs were caked with white dust. The cement-mixer chewed its mouthful over and over again.

'Can you come up,' said Rachel in a low voice. Frank used his forearm to wipe sweat from his face. She left the windowsill and went back to the bed, sitting down on its edge. The mattress dipped so that her feet were flat on the floor. Her diary, its pages crushed, was at the top of her unzipped bag. Her leather jacket hung on the back of a chair.

They left the next morning. It was already about thirty-five degrees.

Rachel stood in the courtyard while Frank took last minute directions from Gil. A split log—grey with sun and age—sat on a stone just outside the door. It was laden with halved tomatoes, drying and curling in the heat, each covered in a thick layer of rock salt. There had been dried tomatoes on the table the night before, acrid and sweet at the same time. Fried almonds, and avocado—great slabs of fish with coriander, and glasses and glasses of Spanish rosé.

They drove south in Gil and Margaret's old brown Peugeot, Frank at the wheel, on the left-hand side of the car. Frank had not been to the beach once in the three months he had been in Spain. They planned to spend a week by the water and the next two driving across country.

Their first stop was in a small town with empty streets and the usual blocks of low, white buildings. They pulled up in the square. It was siesta time and there was no-one around. Rachel had never been so thirsty.

A dark doorway flickered with strips of coloured plastic.

'Here?' said Rachel.

'Tapas is over, but we can still get a drink.'

He shooed her in. The bar was cool, dim, its floor littered with tiny white screws of paper, its walls covered in fading posters of bullfights. It was empty. There was a television on in one corner.

'*Hola!*'

Someone moved at the darker end of the bar—a man got slowly to his feet and came towards them. He nodded at Frank.

'*Dos cervezas,*' said Frank, holding up two fingers. 'You hungry?' he said, turning to Rachel. She put one hand to her throat, shaking her head.

The man crashed two open bottles of San Miguel onto the counter, scraped up Frank's coins and disappeared.

A warm breeze blew; three strips of plastic lifted into the room, and the paper twists scuttled towards them along the stone floor. Frank began to roll a cigarette.

'Do they have breath-testing here?' said Rachel, taking a cold gulp of beer.

'I don't know,' he lit the cigarette, 'that's something I never asked. I drive back from town pissed quite often.'

'Up that mountain?'

'You get used to it.'

'Who do you get pissed with?'

'Gil, mostly. He's pretty good to talk to. He's a writer.'

'Really?' Rachel prepared herself to feel jealous.

'Yeah, but he hasn't finished anything in about ten years.'

'Oh.' A pause. 'Sounds like us.'

'Ye-ah.'

They looked at each other. Neither of them had yet crossed

the point where they considered themselves to be actually writing something. Frank had hardly touched his work since coming to Spain. And Rachel had written a series of poems; poems whose clumsiness made her dizzy and sick.

(A poem as a balancing act; herself trying to clear her mind, move steadily and precisely ahead, follow an idea to its tightrope's end without wobbling and tripping. It was hard to stop trying to balance, to ignore the rope completely, allow the eyes and mind to wander at will.)

'Why doesn't Gil keep writing?' asked Rachel. She reached over, taking Frank's cigarette and putting it to her lips.

'He says he's got too much to do.'

'Well . . . '

'It's not true. In winter hardly anyone comes to stay, and anyway you've never got too much to do. To work. It's something else.' He held out his hand for his cigarette.

'It's embarrassment,' said Rachel, giving it to him.

'Exactly!' Frank laughed.

'You have to *write your way past embarrassment*,' intoned Rachel.

The words came from a tutor at university, a phrase that had appealed to them both.

'I don't know,' said Frank, 'I can't ever see it happening. Fuck it. Do you want to get drunk?'

They stayed until late afternoon, when the bar started to fill up again. It was still dark and cool inside, the hot day a rectangle of bright brass light at the doorway. When Rachel looked around she could see people's teeth gleaming in the dimness. Frank watched her, held her knees between his under the table. He could feel himself swaying towards her; she was, after all, someone he loved. Her bare arms brown and soft.

That swaying, so lovely, so dangerous.

'Have you met anyone nice here?' said Rachel recklessly.

Frank laughed. 'We've only been here a few hours!'

'Come on. Give.'

'Couple of girls from the village. They're not really into it, though.'

'They won't sleep with you, you mean.' Rachel tried not to listen to herself, winced, hearing a ringing in her ears.

'They're Catholic.'

'So are you.'

Frank shook his head, drank. 'It's not that, anyway.' He looked at her. 'I'm getting sick of trying. And the thing is,' testing the words on his tongue, feeling their slow tumble from thought to sound, 'I feel like I'm never going to find someone who hasn't been with someone before. No-one comes to you just themselves, you know? It's like the odds are stacked against you already. All their history.'

'So . . .'

'So you're always having to hear stories about past boyfriends, about how they've been hurt before. Every girl I meet has always been a girlfriend already. You don't even have to go through with it, you know how it's going to happen, how it's going to end. They anticipate everything.'

Rachel pointed the neck of her bottle at him. 'Just like you.'

Frank stared at her. 'Yeah.'

They came out into the glare of the afternoon hand-in-hand, weaving towards the car.

'Can you drive?' asked Rachel, grinning.

''Course.'

'What if we die on the road?'

'Then we'll just be statistics.'

Frank let go of Rachel, went round the side of the car, and opened the door. 'Come on! We've got to get to the beach!'

It was easy. They drove for the rest of the day. When they had headaches they stopped and bought a big bottle of Coke. The airconditioning did not work, and there was no radio. They talked and sang at first and then relapsed into silence. Rachel stared out at the drying landscape, trying to keep Frank's arm out of her line of sight. Each town rose into view like the opening scenes of a western—a dusty sign, a road with one or two dogs asleep in the heat, a line of shuttered shops. They reached Ayamonte, on the Portuguese border, in the early evening.

Their room in Ayamonte was big enough to fit a bed and their bags, nothing more. They had to stand on the bed to use the sink. The window opened onto a concrete courtyard and the backs of other people's apartments. Someone—Rachel imagined him to be a boy, about fifteen, although she had no way of knowing—was playing a tape when they arrived. On one side was Madonna, on the other a pastiche of Spanish dance hits. Songs that she had heard in Sydney had been re-recorded with faster, shriller drum-beats and Spanish lyrics. The boy played his tape over and over again, so loudly that Rachel could not be annoyed. It was ludicrous. It woke her at eight o'clock in the morning. He never played anything else. He was mad.

They spent their time at a beach called Isla Cristina, packing in the morning two bottles of water that would be warm by eleven o'clock, some fruit and bread, and their books. The sand was so hot that they could not lie on their towels—a leg or arm over-lapping its edges would be blistered. They stood in the shallows to keep cool.

The days were clear enough to see Africa from the water; a yellowish, thin line of mist along the horizon. It was interesting, and they were turning very brown in the sun, but it was not like any beach they had seen before. There were no waves, and the water, despite the blue sky, stayed the colour of a cattle dog.

Rachel practised being shot.

'See,' standing thigh-deep in the water, 'if I was shot in the face I'd fall back like this.'

She leapt up and crashed backwards, arms outspread, sending up a wash of white spray.

'Or,' getting to her feet, shaking the water out of her eyes, 'if you shot me in the back I might die like this.' She stopped suddenly, a stricken look on her face, clapped her hands against her chest and toppled slowly forward. Under the water she found herself laughing and laughing. A rush of bubbles went up her nose and she struggled to stand. Through blurred eyes, and still choking on her own joke, she saw Frank watching her, grinning, holding a lit cigarette just above the surface.

In the afternoon they would come home, skins sore from the sun, and fall asleep on the narrow bed until it was time to eat. Then they would dress and walk through the streets to the Plaza Mayor where they sat and talked, eating *churros* and ice-cream, drinking beer from the freezing slot-machines that lined the square. The evening fell like a stage curtain in a dream, a dusty shade of lavender, so slowly that you did not notice it was dark until you couldn't see your hand in front of you.

By the fourth day Rachel was feeling words gathering and clattering behind her clenched teeth. Frank smelled so beautiful, of salt water and sweat. Their skins touched coldly in the narrow bed. She thought—she couldn't decide, her shoulders hurt—she thought if she could not sleep with him she would go mad.

But the fourth day was fiesta, the town's annual feast of the Virgin. The streets were closed off. Men were hanging banners and streamers across the eucalyptus trees. A line of coloured light globes was slung along the railings that fenced off the plaza from the main street.

They'd been to the beach and strolled, heat-dazed, into town. Rachel wore her good dress. She could feel it swinging between her knees as she walked. Her mind felt like a carnival, seen and heard through thick glass. The colours of the last few days swirled together; she could hear her voice, her cheerful, constant voice, trying to keep Frank amused and interested.

Frank didn't notice. He loved Rachel. He walked beside her in her pretty green dress. Sometimes he let her move a little ahead so he could see the shape of her backside. He thought they'd probably sleep together soon.

There were metal tables outside the bar on the main street, covered in sea-anemone clusters of people. They found an empty one and sat down. Rachel started to sing one of the songs that the boy at the apartment played. They finished their first beer quickly and Frank ordered another, and two shots of vodka. It was Spanish vodka—impossibly cheap, smelling like the turpentine her mother used to wash paintbrushes. They drank it quickly.

The word 'evening' began to gather meaning. The day's heat lessened, became reasonable, and the pale-blue scream of the sky became a whisper. The street was filling slowly with people who took the seats around them. Bottles of wine appeared on tables. The air was soft.

'Are we dressed right?' said Rachel.

Two women, their hair piled high on mantillas, passed the table. Black lace dragged along the ground.

'Put some lipstick on,' Frank said.

She looked at him narrowly. The beer, third or fourth, was beginning to sweeten, separate, dissolve her thoughts.

They ordered another drink. Something was happening. From somewhere, the sound of a band turning corners, slowly approaching—the thump and roll of drums, the shriek of a trumpet. The crowd around them shifted and muttered, as though wind had passed through trees. Rachel stood up and was pulled down immediately by Frank. He jerked his thumb at the people behind them—a clot of old women in black, their eyes and jewels glittering alike.

The band appeared, winding their way right past the table. Drum majorettes, Rachel thought drunkenly, not quite sure what the words meant. Young boys in suits and girls in short, white skirts. The trombonist's arms shook with effort as she tried to pull deep, convincing notes from the yellow metal. Priests in heavy white robes, holding crosses. And finally, lumbering like an elephant—its carriers men of different heights—the bier of lilies that held the statue of the Virgin.

The sky behind her was the blue of eggshells—clear, barely a colour at all. The waxy, white lilies stood stiff against her stone skirts. Her face was small and pinched, her hands cradling the

159

head of a dying Jesus, her robes lined with gold. She leaned over Rachel; or so it seemed. There was a ripple of prayer from the crowd.

Rachel reached for her glass of beer, and gulped. A rush of light in her throat, and the Virgin passed on, followed by pairs of women in blues, reds, purples, their mantillas coloured to match, their dark glossy lips closed and firm.

∞

The bed is barely wide enough for two people. The darkness in the room has become soft, like flesh—their shoulders brush the cool walls, shins against the warm edges of the bed. They do not turn the light on. The boy in the next apartment is playing his tape; it sings on the rivers of night air. Their faces bump gently together—Frank's hands in Rachel's dress, buttons loose, the dress falls down her arms. Her face fits easily in the half-moon of his neck. He smells of sweat. The bed opens to take them. The night murmurs to itself.

∞

They took two days driving north through Andalusia to Toledo, an old, old city riding atop a great chunk of orange rock. In the late afternoon they climbed a winding road into the town, through big gates, and parked where the view was wide, clear blue, intense, over a river and a huge sweep of land. They followed the signs through dark, high-walled streets to the Plaza Zocodover. It was fringed with people and bars, silver chairs, wasted-looking trees. Its cobbled expanse, however, was empty.

Frank bought them a couple of beers, coming back to their table with the goldy glasses and a packet of chips. He settled easily by Rachel. The feeling of an occupied seat beside her.

'Weird, isn't it,' he said, nodding out at the Plaza. 'It's the kind of place you could see a mob just appearing.'

'With bulls,' said Rachel.

'It'll be packed out in a couple of hours.' He tore the purple packet open with his teeth.

'Where're we going to stay?'

'We'll find somewhere.' Frank forced a handful of chips into his mouth and slid back in his seat, making it creak and scrape on the cobbles.

A woman had approached Rachel in the street in Cordoba, telling her in angry, broken English that her dress was too short and all the men were looking at her (she pointed at the row of black-hatted *hombres* on benches by the mosque) she'd grinned, apologised, and waited for Frank to come back from the chemist to describe the scene to him. He'd laughed and put one hand on her backside, pushing her gently along in front of him. Her sandals caught on the uneven road and laughter dragged them both back to the *pension*.

Rachel did not mind where they went. There was heat and humour in Frank's voice when he spoke Spanish. The Spanish men were hardly bigger than him. They were broader, their brown skins oiled and muscular (they glanced sideways at his long hair and skinny body inside filthy T-shirts)—but never taller, never imposing. He smiled gently and waited for people to finish talking. He was different. He was there all the time.

Salamanca; the sandstone heart of the town, radiant in the infinite sunlight. They found the information centre and a map of its streets. There was a pool, a small square of blue on the shiny paper. They spent the middle of the day there, taking their siesta in battered sunglasses and swimmers, their legs touching on the warm concrete.

The afternoons, when sleep is like a weight dropped from aching arms. They woke by the pool with the heat still wrapping them, the taste of bread in their mouths, the only cool coming from the sweat that lined their bodies.

Frank let the tip of one finger fall on Rachel's thigh. 'Rachel?'

'Mmm?' Sleep filling her mouth, warm in her nostrils, pressing against her eyes.

'Are you asleep?'

'Mm.'

'Hot, isn't it?'

Rachel shifted on her towel.

'I was thinking about Sydney.'

'How do you mean?' She didn't open her eyes, but felt on the ground beside her for Frank's cigarettes. There was one already rolled. She lit it, let the smoke sit in a hot blanket on her face.

'You know. Coming home.' His hand slid easily down the brown gully of her thigh.

A column of warmth began to build inside her, a smile leaking out of her shut eyes. 'Go on,' she said.

'I don't know yet.' His stomach gurgling.

'Come home with me?' Letting sleep cover the question in her voice.

'I was thinking about it,' he repeated, and inside the words began to ball up into a knot, a screaming tangle of *what am I saying? what am I saying? what am I saying?*

There was a shriek as a small boy hurtled past them, crashing into the blue water. The cold drops made them flinch. Rachel sat up and opened her eyes.

The castle of Almodovar del Rio, in the province of Extremadura, stood on a perversely craggy mountain of rock in the middle of a plain. Birds hung heavily in the air around its crumbling turrets, and one or two houses knelt in the dust at a respectful distance from its foundations. The sky as blue and startling as a lizard's tongue.

Frank pulled up and they got out of the car, slamming the doors, Rachel shouldering her backpack.

'Got any water?' said Frank.

'Run out,' answered Rachel.

They started up the steep climb to the castle.

Halfway, Rachel stopped, her face bursting with heat. Sweat coursed down the back of her knees and neck. Frank kept walking, wiry legs eating the rocky slope.

The gates were of iron, swung wide to receive them. Frank waited for Rachel, leaning breathlessly with one hand gripping the bars.

'There's a tap there,' he said as she reached him.

They turned the corner. An old man stood outside the high wooden doors opening into the courtyard. He lifted one hand, watching them as Rachel fell on her knees in front of the tap, turning it on, letting the water stream cold to her elbows, drinking ferociously. She stopped, tilting her head and said to the old man, '*Tengo sed. Hace mucho calor.*'

He nodded and smiled and waited for Frank to drink. Neatly, the water barely splashing his face.

The man led them into a stony courtyard. The silence was composed of heat, of rocks and dust—the absolute absence of wind.

Feet shuffling on the cobbles.

They followed him through cool, twisting passages and up narrow, stone stairways to the very top of the castle, the ramparts. The view was immense; matted fields of sunflowers in the distance, a horizon clear of cloud. A grumble of scrub around the houses.

The old man beckoned them into a dark alcove and pointed at three symmetrical gaps in the stonework. He said something too quick for Rachel to understand. Frank looked confused, peering down at the ground that showed itself hundreds of feet below. He started to speak; stumbled, said, '*Ahí?*'

The man nodded, said something else.

'*Hombres de Francia? Aceite . . . ?*'

'*Aceite,*' agreed the old man, '*Aceite muy, muy caliente.*'

'What's he saying?' said Rachel.

'Jesus,' said Frank, peering down again, 'he's saying they used to pour boiling oil down there, on French invaders.'

'You're kidding!'

'It's like a fucking *Asterix* book up here.'

Rachel began to laugh. The distance out there was sailing with

163

light and heat. It was an impossible place—too high, too sudden in the flattened landscape.

Frank was talking to the man again, stopping to translate for Rachel. 'He says there's never usually tourists in summer. It's too hot.'

'Who lives here?'

The old man jabbed his dusty black chest with one thumb and waved down at the courtyard. His voice was grimy with age.

'Just him and some nuns. The people from the houses come here for church.'

'And the view.'

'I suppose so.'

They walked along the walled path that ringed the top of the castle, gazing at the horizon from every compass point.

'Which way's south?' said Rachel. The old man was going down the stairs.

'Over there. Beyond the sunflowers.'

Rachel chuckled.

'What?' Frank bumped her with his hip.

'Like it's after the sunflowers and not before.'

'Fuck off,' Frank laughed, 'we have to drive there, you know.'

'What, beyond the sunflowers?'

'Yes. To yon ancient town of Sevilla.'

'Cool.'

'Can't wait.'

They clattered down the stairs, jostling each other, disturbing the still air with their laughter.

He left her in Seville. She stood outside the bus station and watched the brown car disappear into the endless link of roundabouts. The signs saying *Norte*, pointing to Aracena. She could still feel the print of his fingers on her waist, lips against her cheek.

The Peugeot's engine roared as Frank changed down, beginning the haul up the mountainside. It sounded as though it was dragging along the ground.

He hadn't signed a contract with Margaret and Gil, and it would not be difficult for them to find another worker. The house was always full of English people, kids killing time between school and Oxford. They were usually related to Margaret and Gil, by blood or class. They were friendly enough, interested in having a beer down in the village occasionally, taking the drive into Seville to see an American movie, but there was a boundary between him and them. Like an electric fence, suddenly gleaming as you approached it.

He wondered if Tom had noticed it. Maybe not. With Angela to talk to in the evenings, Angela to sleep with.

He had grown accustomed to the limits, learning to enjoy his own company (the private vulgarity of his thoughts), hardly remembering to miss what he had left at home. He might never have noticed. Until Rachel arrived. Her substantial wit—dislike of the unspoken—the way she shouldered cheerfully across imagined frontiers of manners, of the unmentionable. Now he could feel his own inherited Englishness disappearing like a scarf of cloud into a blue sky.

He was serving dinner later that night. There were five guests—a couple in their thirties, peach-faced son and daughter asleep in the top bedroom, two ageing artists with black Spanish clothes and peppermint accents, and Margaret's mother, Jean, who had come over from London. She was eighty-seven, tiny beside Margaret's and Gil's pillow-padded figures. She smoked and sipped endlessly at her little gin and tonic, the same glass she had been refreshing herself from all afternoon.

Her impossibly refined voice lilted through the conversation that fled around the long table, 'Maggie, dear, everything is changing. The park is overrun with hooligans. I daren't take Scottie for a walk.'

Margaret's sausage fingers over her mother's. 'You shouldn't be walking on your own.'

Jean cackled, 'I know! But I still do!'

The telephone rang during dessert and Frank, who was in the wide tiled kitchen arranging chocolates on a plate and making coffee, answered it. It was Millicent, Margaret's sister, calling from London for their mother.

'I'll fetch her,' he said, putting the phone down.

'Jean?' said Frank. 'It's Millicent on the phone.'

'Oh!' With a leap she was up from the table, catching the cloth in her cracked fingernails and knocking her wooden chair backwards. She nearly fell, but Frank caught her, her face crashing into his chest. He set her upright and she scurried into the kitchen, sniggering. 'I must be pissed!' they heard as she disappeared under the archway.

When everyone had gone to bed and the washing-up was done, Frank took a bottle of beer from the fridge and went to join Gil on the verandah. He had started on the strawberry gin. His cigar an orange light-chunk in the darkness.

'Feeling rested?' said Gil, as Frank dragged a chair over.

'Yeah,' said Frank, sitting down, 'thanks.'

They talked idly for a while about the things Frank and Rachel had seen, about the weather, about the guests. In a week or two Millicent was coming to stay, bringing her three children. Margaret wanted the big bedroom repainted. Then Gil said, 'Rachel's a very pretty girl.'

Frank did not know what to say. They were the last words he would have used to describe her. He took a gulp of the gin Gil had handed him.

There was a pause. The amorous murmurings of the young couple upstairs. Their light flicked off, and midnight filled the valley with black oil.

'You're very lucky,' said Gil.

Frank began to feel sick. The gin was too sweet. He tried to listen to Gil, to see things from where he sat. This was exactly what made him uneasy. He could not articulate it, to Rachel, to anyone. The metamorphosis of his best friend, dirty, easygoing, always interesting to him—into a *pretty girl*. He did not want to see Rachel checking her reflection before she looked at him, worrying about the things she said, the things he said. He did not want the responsibility.

He remembered a cold afternoon in Captain's Flat, months ago, when they were driving through the fields, along the track to Sam and Florence's house. They were in the ute—Vince and Rachel sat in the front seat, the other three in the tray. They were drunk.

Florence stood up, swaying crazily, her face messy with laughter, her long curling hair flurrying around her shoulders. She shouted, 'Look! I'm Kate Bush!' and burst into the shrieking verse from 'Wuthering Heights'.

Her voice was hopeless, utterly without tune, and Frank heard himself roaring along with her, a grin of delight encasing him. She was unlovely, hilarious, making fun of herself.

It was only a second—he turned quickly back to Florence, her arms spread wide—but he caught sight of Sam watching her, serious. It was though the words were written in the air around him—*God, she's beautiful*. It made him shiver.

Gil was watching him. He took a deep breath, put the gin down and picked up his bottle of beer. 'I've been thinking about going home,' he said.

'Really?' Gil grunted and shifted his seat on the pavestones. 'What do you reckon?'

'Well, I can't stop you. I'll need some time to find someone else,' he waved a hand at the house, 'When do you want to go?'

'As soon as it's alright with you.'

'Fine.'

Easy as that.

There was another pause, and Gil refilled his glass. The smell of strawberries trickled into the night air.

'Have you been doing any writing?' said Gil.

'No,' answered Frank. 'You?'

'Nothing. No time.'

They sat there in silence, listening to the crickets beginning to chirp under the trees.

Newtown, Glebe, Henley, Coogee

It was months since Rachel and Frank had been in Spain, weeks since they had brought Sam from Captain's Flat. He had all but forgotten about early openers, happy hours, two beers for the price of one, and the number of young, bored women in the city. With a new kind of determination he launched into a drinking binge, occasionally joined by one of the group, more often than not alone at the Courthouse in Taylor Square.

He talked and talked and talked about Florence, tempering his words to suit his listener. With Frank he was tough, cursing her, speculating about her affairs with other men, comparing her unfavourably to girls who passed their table. With Rachel he wept. And with Vince he veered between the two, turning what looked to be the twist of tears into a joke.

He could not stop talking, though his voice scorched his throat like smoke. He could not believe that she had done this to him. Without Florence to fight with, reason with, hurt, his words were useless. He could do nothing. She had already done everything.

Ringing his mother in the late afternoon, trying to straighten out the slur in his voice. *Don't worry about dinner. I might not come home.*

On coming home from Spain, Frank had settled at Vince's house in Glebe, first on the living-room floor (his clothes and books stacked behind the door, where they collapsed every time some-one came in) and then, when Vince's flatmate couldn't stand it anymore, into the second bedroom upstairs. The best bedroom, with old French doors that opened onto the shaky verandah and the street. He found a desk in the lane and put it between the doors so he could look out at the people and cars meandering past.

The Stanmore house being a thing of the past, Rachel found a place in Newtown with a girl she never saw, whose presence in the tiny workers' cottage was only made apparent by the occa-sional late-night giggle and shriek as she came in with her boyfriend to pick up some clothes. In two months they met twice in front of the TV and both times Belinda was on her way to Ian's. Rachel did not ask why she didn't simply move in with him. It was too convenient, sharing rent and bills, having the house to herself. She left the front door open. Warm air from the street drifted through the low-ceilinged rooms.

When she opened her eyes, Frank was on his feet, picking his T-shirt up off the floor. She lay for a second with her face against the pillow, watching him. He pulled on his shorts and sat down on the edge of the bed to put his boots on.

'Where are you going?' Rachel said. She reached out a hand, stroked his back.

'I've got to work.'

'What at?'

'My writing.' Set his feet flat on the floor. Found an elastic in his pocket, dragging his hair together at the back. 'Where's my cigarettes?'

'In my jeans, I think.'

He kicked at them, trying to pick them up on the toe of his boot.

'Hey, Frankie.'

'What?'

'Don't go just yet. Stay here with me.'

She was wide awake now though she hadn't moved, holding her breath. 'Come on. You've got all day.' She let her hand wander up his back, travelling over the constellation of freckles on his brown skin.

His shoulders dropped slightly and he tilted his head towards her. 'I really should try and spend a whole day on it. I've got to get into the habit. I've gotta do it *now*.'

'Well then,' she took her hand away.

Long silence.

'Don't take it so personally.' he said.

'I'm not! I'm not! Give me a break, will you?'

'I'll speak to you later on or something.'

'Sure.'

Frank sighed. 'Listen, Rachel . . . '

'No, Frank, you listen. If you've got to go, you've got to go. Don't make me get into some pathetic discussion with you about it. I don't feel like it anymore. I don't want to lie here and try and convince you to stay.'

There was a pause. He glared at her, stumped.

'So go, okay?' she said.

Another pause.

'Maybe I don't want to.'

'Fucking hell.' She closed her eyes, pulling her legs up under the quilt. Felt his fingers slipping in to curl around her ankle.

'Rache . . . '

'What?'

'Just don't get upset.'

Rachel thought of screaming, tried to twist out of his grip, but couldn't. Opened her eyes and saw him looking at her. 'Well?'

'Well?' he replied.

'Come back to bed then.'

He glanced out the window, still holding her ankle. She could feel a stillness begin to freeze into her shoulders. He began to take his boots off, hooking his feet under the edge of the bed, letting them drop to the floor. Let go of her while he pulled off his shorts. Pushed her to one side and climbed back under the quilt.

They lay like that for a while, both watching the ceiling. A daddy-long-legs' jerky, drunken gait across the plaster roses. Rachel shifted closer so that her arm was against Frank's. Finally, with a deep sigh, he turned towards her, kissed the side of her cheek, slid one hand across her breast.

The treacherous shivering of desire. Rachel opened her arms wide as Frank rolled onto her, feeling the warmth, the sweet smoothness of his shoulders under her palms. Her skin like a snake's in sudden sunlight as his body pressed into hers. Relief flooded her even while her eyes, still turned to the ceiling, saw the daddy-long-legs slip and hang for a second by one crooked, fragile leg, dangling in air and space.

∞

When two people have known each other for a long time, their speech matches and meets, balancing and counterbalancing without effort, and any subject—even the most personal—can take on an almost academic quality.

Rachel and Frank had spent the morning at Coogee, Rachel as usual taking to the freezing water in the sea pool while Frank sat on the rocks and read.

Dressed but still shivering slightly, her face flushed with cold, Rachel joined him. He was reading a book that Rachel had given him, Toni Morrison's *Sula*.

'How's it going?' she said.

He closed it, and put it into the wide pocket of his leather jacket. 'I don't know. A bit—dreamy.'

'She's a fucking genius. There's nobody . . . '

'I know, I know! You told me!'

'She *makes* it look easy. Dreamy.'

'Yeah.'

Rachel tried to force her fingers through her seaweed-wet hair.

Didn't look at Frank for a moment. Then, 'Sometimes I'm not sure that you really want to be with me.'

Frank looked at her. 'Wait a second. You're kidding, aren't you.'

Rachel smiled in spite of herself. 'No, really. It's just—God, I don't know how to talk anymore! You're not happy, or something. It's like you've given up. I don't understand it.'

'You don't have to. You don't even have to think about it.'

'But it's there, right in front of me. What am I supposed to do when you seem so miserable? So pissed off?'

'I don't know. Go to the movies.'

Rachel sighed and shifted on the crumbling, salt-crusted rock. 'I didn't ever notice it, before . . . before Spain.' Not notice it. *Care* about it.

'Well, I haven't changed.' Frank considered the lie. The swell was rising. Wedding Cake Island—too far out to see movement—was a frozen turmoil of blue and thick white spray. 'Okay, maybe I have. Maybe *we* have. Sleeping together, it makes everything different.'

'But different good, I thought.'

'Yeah.'

'We're about to have one of those relationship conversations,' said Rachel. 'I can't believe it. Every way I look at it it seems wrong. I mean, we're best friends, and I didn't think there was anything we couldn't say to each other. Except now that we're sleeping together and we've got something important to talk about we have to, sort of, not know each other anymore. Because if we talk the way we usually do we don't get hold of it.'

'So what are we supposed to do?'

'I don't know! Jesus, I really don't know. I feel like I've got two lives and one of them's between the pages of a magazine, or some self-help guide.' She grimaced. 'Maybe they'd say that I should make myself less available. So you'd get jealous and come running back.'

'Should you be telling me this, then?' said Frank, sitting up to see the surf crash on the rocks below them. 'Shouldn't you kind of spring it on me?'

'Yeah, I can just imagine you responding beautifully to that sort of thing, Frank. And I can really see me pulling it off. Being intensely cool and flirting with other men. Sam. Vince.'

'That would really throw me,' Frank nodded, laughing.

'Maybe we're telling each other too much.'

'It's too late not to.'

'Okay. So why are you so fucking bad-tempered?'

Frank laughed again. 'Because I'm a fuckwit.'

The water on the horizon prickled with light.

'You really are.'

'You knew that.'

'Did I?'

Frank looked straight ahead, but out of the corner of his eye he could see Rachel's hand, pressed flat against the white sandy rock. Her silver ring with the dark green stone. Her nails carefully curved. Words unspooled in his mind. Her brown hair flicking water into his eyes.

'I remember a time,' said Rachel slowly, 'when I used to find comfort in magazines and things like that. Remember when I was into astrology?'

Frank made a face.

'Don't knock it, mate, you were as keen as anyone to have your chart read. Mr Sagittarius.' She laughed. 'Everyone wants to hear themselves talked about. That's what's so creepy about it.'

'Is there a point to this?' said Frank.

'Give me a second. What I'm trying to say is, you come to realise that you can't use it anymore. When I believed in that stuff it was like a big armchair, you could fall back into it any time things got difficult. You know—if you feel bad you just get some tarot card reader to tell you either you're about to meet your spiritual partner or that the pain you're going through is part of this incredible evolution. Like you're climbing some kind of fucking staircase to nirvana, and any minute you're about to find out you're the Angel Gabriel.'

'I think you're mixing your doctrines here.'

'But it's all the same anyway! It's all just comfort!'

'So?'

'So,' Rachel paused, aware that she wasn't really sure what she was trying to say. 'So. So I suppose I still kind of wish that someone would tell me you were my spiritual partner and everything was going to be okay.'

'You wouldn't believe them if they did,' said Frank, and unwittingly, momentarily, solved everything by putting his hand on the back of her neck.

He could feel her breathing.

She took his hand from her neck and held it, looking down at it so Frank had to move closer. Three straight lines across each knuckle, fingernails all one length. Turned it over. The creases purpling with cold.

'What's the time?'

Frank glanced back at the clock. 'Twenty past twelve.'

'I've got to go. I said I'd meet Vince, he wants to read me some stuff.'

'Slut.'

She laughed, painfully. 'Well, he'll read me something after we fuck. For appearances' sake.'

'Okay. Have a good time.'

She put his hand to her cheek, then kissed it. 'What are you going to do?'

'I don't know. Hang round. Go home and do some work.'

'I might see you later.'

'Yep.'

Letting go of his hand, she stood up. Her dress caught the wind and swirled with flowers. 'See you.'

And was gone.

Frank sat very still and stared at the island. Coogee moved silently behind his back. Hung time. The water and the sky swelled in his eyes and at the glittering, brittle edges of his mind he wondered what was happening.

Are we together for a reason, or is it just that we can go no further? Perhaps friendship is like a car crash in a deserted stretch of country—vehicles crippled, the victims set up camp. Before they know it, this new, empty place is home. They might sink a well, plant crops, build a house. Or they might simply wait, chafing at their immobility, bored, deliberately making each other suffer.

Vince was not at the cafe in Glebe, and when Rachel rang the house Frank's voice on the answering machine made her hang up without leaving a message. She went home instead, and slept for two hours, her body sinking into the heavy mattress, the smell of her mother and flowers in the pillow.

When she woke she took the black dog for a walk. There was a storm approaching, squid's ink clouds piling in the west. The sky a vast arena over the park. The wind sprang up and the trees instantly flattened their silver sides to its force. It licked the black dog seal-slick. His legs became dainty sticks. He seemed to be carried along with it, streams of air close to the ground, he was led by the nose and Rachel followed him, her chest full of surprised laughter at the wildness of the day.

They bowled through the park and cut along Albermarle Street to the railway tunnel. The dog gathered speed down the slope to the tracks. Rachel shouted at him, her voice snatched away by the wind. He waited, however, at the kerb, one paw up, glancing over his shoulder at her.

She reached him. 'Okay, you can cross.'

The dog bolted across the road and down the steps to the tunnel, his legs scattering crazily on the concrete. A train was coming—the train for Central, loaded with people and newspapers. Rachel caught up with the dog as the train howled over the tunnel and he filled the curved dark space with a great battery of barking. It shrieked back off the damp walls.

There was a cold smell in the tunnel, reminding her of the

time the four of them—five of them, Florence was still there then—had gone down to Jindabyne. It was the first time she had seen it snowing. They stayed in a wooden house with high ceilings and big leather couches.

'Like a Norsca ad,' Frank said when they arrived, tired from the drive, loaded down with bags and Vince's ever-present stereo.

Drunk every night, they played flame soccer in the dark, on the crunching white snow outside. They used a new toilet roll—tied it in a knot with string, doused it in lighter fluid or petrol, set it alight, and kicked it to each other, screaming with excitement. It swooped and arced, making the yard into a prehistoric cave of trees, lit by the flickering fireball. Their breath in great clouds of steam and pleasure. Open bottles of beer standing cold by the trees, and the occasional rattle of a wallaby as it started away through the scrub. The house waiting warm and silent for them to finish.

Rachel and Florence cooked a meal together, bumping hips in the big kitchen, taking gulps of beer and drags of Frank's cigarettes. The boys played cards on the carpet in front of the fire. They listened to the local radio station.

The rice thickening on the stove, the windows clouding over.

Vince was the only one who skied. He did it with an angry determination. He talked to no-one on the way up, hands cold on the stocks, then fought his way down with all his heavy muscles holding the skis to the crispy snow. Whack! in between the people, whoosh! against a pile of white.

The others would be at home reading or walking through the fields, or sometimes waiting for him in the Log Cabin Bar. They put Cold Chisel on the jukebox and laughed at the smooth-haired American who asked Florence if she wanted to dance. It was as many cigarettes as you could smoke, as many beers as you could drink, and driving back to the house along the twisty, icy road waiting for the lights to appear.

Vince tried to persuade Frank to come up the mountain with him but Frank laughed and said no, hunching his thin shoulders inside his coat. Looking like he had a long-barrelled pistol concealed somewhere.

It sometimes snowed down at Sam and Florence's house, but it was never so beautiful as it was at Jindabyne.

The answering machine was clicking off as Rachel and the dog reached the front door. The wind sucked the door to with a thump. She let the dog out and filled its water bowl before she played the message back.

'Rachel,' it was Frank, his slow, low voice, 'uh . . . where are you? Something's happened to Sam. His mum rang. I'm not quite sure, some sort of accident. She wants us to go over. Um . . . I was gonna drive. If you get back soon can you give us a call? Okay. See you.'

She waited a minute and then picked up the phone.

'Hello?' The sound of the TV in the background.

'It's me. What's up?'

'Oh, good. I don't really know. The pub . . . some guy jumped on him . . . '

'When? What do you mean?'

'This arvo. He must have been being an arsehole, somebody lost it and hit him. I can't tell. His mum's all over the place. Will you come with me?'

'Yeah, okay. I suppose so.' The day slammed shut. 'You driving?'

'Yeah. I'll pick you up. Ten minutes.'

'See you then.'

She hung up. The window in the kitchen pressed in and out. A photograph, propped on the television, lifted, whirled, and fell on the carpet. A car alarm went off and the dog began to bark.

Henley looked wild under the grey sky, the fat-hedged gardens awash with wind. They pulled into the driveway of Sam's mother's house, under the corrugated roof of the garage.

The front door was made of dark brown pine and never opened. They went round the side of the house, and tapped on the screen door that led into the kitchen. There was no answer.

They tapped again. The door was open—it lifted and clattered slightly.

'Should we go in?'

Frank shrugged, pushing his hands into the pockets of his leather jacket. They stepped inside, making way for each other, suddenly polite. There was a bowl on the kitchen table, a chopping board and a big knife. No sign of mayhem—no sign of Sam.

'Mrs Dalby? Sam?' said Rachel, coming forward.

There was a singing sigh from the corner. Nina sat in her chair, strapped in.

'Nina?'

Her gaze lolloped past them.

The bowl was full of hard-boiled eggs. A jar of curry powder stood beside it, and, pinned to the table by its glass edge, was a note that fluttered and crackled. Rachel picked it up and read it. *Gone to the hospital. Please look after Nina—she will have egg sandwiches for dinner. Back as soon as possible.*

She handed it to Frank.

'That's his mum's writing.' he said, and crumpled it into a ball. 'What'll we do?'

'Make dinner, I suppose.' Frank went over to Nina, holding out his hand. She grabbed it immediately. She was strong now, steely starfish fingers wrapping themselves around his wrist. 'Ah, shit! Let go!' He tried to shake her off. 'Fuck it. No, that hurts!'

Her fingers clambered up his arm. 'Sa--aam,' she crooned.

'Yes, he's coming back, Nina. Don't worry. He'll be back soon,' said Rachel. She watched as Frank prised Nina's hands apart, then glanced at the table. 'I'll make 'em, shall I? You talk to Nina.'

'Okay.' Frank went over and switched on the television and 'The Simpsons', all yellow and blue, flashed on. Nina scrabbled at the air, trying to catch Frank again, and Rachel sat down at the table.

They watched 'The Simpsons' and 'Roseanne', and Rachel used a fork to mix curry powder into the eggs. Frank found a bottle of beer in the fridge and smoked, and gave Nina things to play with—his watch, his tobacco, until she flung handfuls of it onto the lino floor. She was like a big sprawling skinny toddler.

They fed her the sandwiches, tearing them into soft, squashed pieces and pushing them into her mouth. During 'Roseanne' she had a fit—a sudden stiffening in her chair and then a high, keening scream that hurt the ears. Frank stroked the dark curling hair back from her forehead and Rachel sang to calm her down.

She tried not to feel Frank's eyes on her, tried in all her muscles not to look as though she was putting on an act—See how caring I am? See what a good mother I would make? Nina listened and began to relax, but her face was covered in vomited egg. Finally looking at each other, they both knew that she had wet her pants. It began to drip down on the footrest of her chair.

'They must keep nappies somewhere,' said Rachel.

'But we'd have to undress her.' Frank gingerly wiped some of the egg from her chin with the side of his finger.

'Jesus.'

Nina joggled up and down. Her backside squelched. Over the wind there was the sound of a car, slowing down and cutting out in the driveway.

'Thank God.'

They cleaned her face and stepped back, confused and guilty, as Mrs Dalby pushed open the screen door. She had a hand under Sam's arm—she propelled him gently into the room in front of her. He had one crutch—his left leg dragged and his face was tracked with stitches. They had shaved some of his knotted black hair which had grown, like Frank's, to his shoulders.

'Mate!' said Frank, 'What happened?'

Sam collapsed onto a chair. 'Walked into a wall,' he answered, trying to grin.

Nina squealed.

'She's wet,' said Rachel, 'I'm sorry.' She looked at Sam's mother, whose beehive had slipped to one side. 'She had a fit.'

'Ninie, are you wet?' Mrs Dalby put her bag down in the

corner and came over, small hands reaching out to Nina's long, bony ones. 'Don't worry. I'm just glad someone was here to look after her. The hospital was awful, there was a boy behind us who'd been in some kind of brawl, he had a broken nose, bleeding everywhere. You don't realise these things are going on, it's like a whole different world . . . ' Sam bent his head as his mother talked on. She was round and ruffled, at least a foot shorter than Sam. 'Can you give me a hand, Rachel? I can change her on my own, of course, but it does help to have someone to hold her . . . '

It was as though there was no-one else in the room—Sam, safely at home and Frank standing beside him were furniture. Sam said, 'Thanks Rache,' as she followed Mrs Dalby out to the bedroom, Nina's chair catching on the edge of the hall carpet.

The bedroom was blank and unlived-in. Nina was home only one weekend out of three. It had been that way for years. She lived at a hospital in Ryde.

Whenever Sam and Florence had been up in Sydney they had gone to see her. It made no difference to Nina, whose eyes saw a kind of twisted playground, alive with the comings and goings of other children who handed her toys or took them away. It was a place that could turn in on itself, carousels of colour and noise continuing even in absence.

As she struggled with Nina, who seemed to want to climb up her—she was thin, but had the slippery determination of a spider on a wall—Rachel could hear the boys talking in the kitchen. Mrs Dalby hummed gently, stripping and pinning.

'Fuckin arsehole,' Frank was saying.

'Wasn't even his drink!'

She could imagine Sam firing up—the injustice, the lack of logic—getting into a punch-up because he was so enraged that someone would be stupid enough to want to fight him. This kind of thing happened more often to Frank or Vince—Vince because he was so big (his size like an insult, an unspoken challenge to bleary-minded, fat-fisted idiots), Frank because he could not keep his mouth shut.

Rachel tried not to look at Nina's triangle of pubic hair. She was settling. Mrs Dalby pulled the sheets over her, up to her spitty chin, and kissed her forehead.

They stood back, and Mrs Dalby took a deep breath. 'Well. I think I'm going to go to bed.'

'Have you had dinner?' said Rachel, her mother's voice in her head.

'Rachel, I am just not hungry.'

Rachel heard the quivering of tears or anger in her words and found herself saying, 'I'm sorry, really . . . '

Mrs Dalby cut her off, 'It isn't your fault, dear. I don't really know what he thought he was doing, but . . . anyway. You can't be blamed, can you? I suppose you'll be staying the night?' She reached behind her and switched the light off, stepping out of the door.

Rachel tripped over some clothes, following her, as she continued, 'There are sheets in the cupboard, Sam can show you. The couch pulls out to make a bed. Try not to make too much noise.'

Every house has a silent room that is rarely used. At the Dalbys' the front room was furnished with heavy couches, obscure paintings of pre-colonial relatives and an old television. If the cat pissed in there the smell stayed for ages, clinging to the thick curtains.

Frank, Rachel and Sam sat in a row on the couch and watched the black-and-white TV. Rachel sat in the middle—she held Sam's hand. His breath was still purple with booze. Frank pulled his legs onto Rachel's lap. It was getting late. The movie was *Young Frankenstein*. They kept expecting colour in the ads but only the tones changed. Deeper blacks in the advertisements. A grainy McDonald's.

Frank fell asleep, his legs becoming heavier on Rachel's lap. The movie finished. Sam kept shifting, trying to get comfortable, his foot straight in front of him on the dark carpet.

'Where's Vince?' said Rachel softly. 'I thought he'd be here too.'

Sam said nothing.

'Wasn't he at the pub with you?'

He sniffed and pushed a stray dreadlock behind one ear.

'Sam? Hello?' She nudged him.

'Don't worry about it, okay?'

'Don't worry about what?'

Sam made a noise in his throat.

'What happened? Did he piss off when it got serious? He doesn't really like confrontations, you know,' she started to race, making excuses, 'he's hopeless. I mean, it doesn't mean . . . ' she wound down, her voice knocking at the back of her throat.

After a second, still staring at the TV, Sam said, 'Look. The fight was with him. We had a fucking fight at the pub and I lost. And I don't know where he is. Fucking celebrating. I don't know.'

Music videos. Rachel was speechless. The television flickered. She shut her eyes, swallowed, and said thinly, 'Oh.'

'Yeah.' said Sam. 'Oh.'

'Why would he do that?'

Frank turned over on his side, just missing Rachel's chin with one boot.

Sam started, 'Stuff about Florence. You know how he feels about her . . . '

'He likes her.'

'I know, and I was drunk and talking about her and he just, I don't know,' Sam shook his head, feeling the stitches wince and tighten about his eyes, 'just fucking went mad. He was saying I was a dickhead and I didn't know what I was talking about, didn't know when I had a good thing . . . '

'But . . . '

'She was the one who broke it off. Of course. I was trying to say that, but he wouldn't stop. I sort of thought it was a joke at first, but then . . . '

'Fight, fight.' said Rachel.

'Exactly. All these morons watching us, enjoying it. It was insane.'

Rachel exhaled. 'Did you tell Frank?'

'No. Not yet.'

'Jesus.' She squeezed his hand, feeling stupid. 'I wonder where Vince has got to.'

'If he thinks I'm going to apologise . . . '

'He wouldn't. Jesus, Sam, he'll be doing penance. Saying the rosary. He hates fights, you know what he's like.'

Gentle Vince, backing off with hands upraised when things looked unpleasant.

'Poor Mum, she thinks I'm a lunatic. She was scared of me. That look, you know—*is he going to turn out like his father?* She thinks I just jumped somebody in the pub. Fightin' Sam Dalby all over again.'

'Fuck that.'

'Well . . . '

'Like you have no choice but to be like him. You can decide, for God's sake.'

Frank muttered something, startling them both.

'You awake, Frank?'

'Nuh,' he sighed.

Sam and Rachel exchanged glances. 'Did you hear all that?' Sam said.

'Yeah.' He opened his eyes. 'Is the movie over?'

Vince's face was silent, his mouth closed, black eyebrows almost meeting. Eyes like smashed ice, catching the light, startling in that unmoving landscape. Coming on for twenty-six, he still walked like a teenage boy, hands half-open, brushing his thighs, knees awkwardly bent. The way he used to dance in the school gym, at the blue-light discos, was still caught fast in his body, his walk. His heavy shoulders.

Vince's mother loved Rickie Lee Jones. The lilt and swoop and catch of her voice. That was childhood for him—the last strains of 'Chuck E's in Love', caught between the swing of a calico curtain and the sea breeze, in an old house by the beach with wooden floors where the sunlight aged gracefully and the dust glittered in the late afternoon.

In the cupboard a box of powdered pink junket. His eye falls on it every time he pulls open the double doors. It has been in every house with them. The cardboard has a picture of a lady whose cheeks have faded and she holds a fluted glass of carefully finished junket. The packet smells of glacé cherries. You add milk, sweet milk, to make the junket.

Night time. He stays quiet. He runs into the kitchen from the street to snatch something to eat. His mother will be drinking a cup of tea with the next-door neighbour. Outside the cicadas are battering the night down. The kids in the street ride in tight circles on their bikes, not too slow, just fast enough to keep their balance, until Vince comes back out. Then they will ride off in a fleet around the block, to the jacaranda tree near the Forteys' where the cicadas are thick. The bark seems to move with them.

The cicada can slide its long sting into you. If you catch a male you can shake him and he will screech to split your ears. His small rib cage swells with desperate air. The females feel softer—they are not so big. You throw them up in the air and sometimes they will stay up, wings catching motion. Sometimes they will fall onto the ground with a buzzing thud, and you might not be able to find them under the streetlight.

If you throw them up during the day a magpie might crash out of a tree and beak them in. A male will holler as he is flown away. It dies into the sky.

∞

Vince fell into the house, head down, kicking the door to with one heavy foot. His hands hurt. He had been walking in the park, down by Blackwattle Bay, where the pelicans sailed like silent fighter planes over the frightening reaches of the new bridge. His head buzzed and sang with alcohol.

It was growing dark—the liquidambar in the backyard surged black against the greying sky. The wind edged under the kitchen door, wrapping cold hands around his ankles.

'Frank?' he called.

Silence, except for the rush of leaves on bricks. He did not bother to turn the light on. Unbuttoning his shirt as he went, he climbed the stairs. Sat on the edge of the bed, kicked off boots, pulled his jeans down his legs and tossed them in the corner. Got into bed, squashed pillows underneath his neck, dragged the quilt to his chin. Gradually, the kaleidoscope in his head shimmering ever slower, he fell asleep.

He woke late to the unbelievable green of leaves at his window, leaves that swallowed sunlight, their edges clean and clear. He lay still, listening to the Saturday sounds that came from the back-yards crowding their house. A hose spattering against the fence. The young professional couple next-door, voices low, scraping garden seats on the paving, plates on the table, newspapers rustling. A toddler chanting *London Bridge is falling down, falling down* . . .

A key clawing in the lock of the front door. He braced himself, expecting Frank to come thumping up the stairs, on fire with rage. He clenched his fists under the quilt.

'Vincent?'

'Up here.'

His footsteps were even, the squeak on the second last. The bedroom door swung open, the room filled with breeze. Frank was wearing a plaid shirt of Sam's, black jeans, no shoes.

There was a long pause. The woman next-door gave a trill of mirth. Frank moved over to the desk, pulled out the chair and sat down. 'G'day,' he said.

Vince turned to face him. 'Where've you been.'

'Sam's.'

'Oh.'

Frank felt in his back pocket for tobacco. 'What's . . . ah . . . what's going on?'

'I don't know.'

Arranging the tobacco into a cigarette. 'Sam's mum had to take him to the hospital.'

Vince said nothing.

'Stitches in his head. Fifteen. And his leg's fucked.'

'I didn't touch his leg.'

'No. He fell down the stairs on the way out.'

Stupid, stupid, he couldn't stop himself, Vince let out a spit of laughter. 'Sorry,' he gasped, 'it's not funny . . . '

But Frank was laughing too, his cigarette tweezed between two fingers, long hair falling forward, shoulders shaking. 'You're right! It's not funny.'

Giggles dying out. Vince pulled himself upright in bed, and nausea shuddered over him. He met Frank's eye.

'What'm I supposed to do?' said Frank.

'Arrest me.'

'Grievous bodily harm.' A grin hurt Frank's face. There was a silence.

'It's not going to be like that, is it?' said Vince. 'I mean . . . it's like . . . I didn't mean it, you know.'

'He's not going to press *charges*. But he's pretty upset.'

Vince sighed. 'Fair enough. I don't know what I'm going to say to him.'

Frank lit his cigarette. A ball of smoke unrolled towards the ceiling. 'He thought it was something to do with Florence?'

Vince let his head drop forward.

'You weren't fucking her?'

'Of course not.'

'She's not going to be around anymore, you know. We're not going to see her. There's no point in fighting about her.'

'I wasn't fighting about her!' Vince's chin jerked. 'You make it sound like some bloody tournament. Fucking knights on horseback! I got pissed off, okay, so I hit him. That's all.'

'But pissed off about what? I've never even seen you get angry!'

It was too difficult. He could not pull a single straight thread from the knotted tangle of feelings. 'I'd just had enough. On and on about what a bitch she was, but how pathetic his life's been since she left. Boring, self-obsessed . . . '

The phone was ringing. Frank got up.

'I'll make it okay. I'll talk to him. I'll pay his hospital bills.'

'With what?' said Frank, pressing out his cigarette and making for the door. Vince listened to him thundering down the stairs two at a time.

'With my fucking dole money!' he shouted, and got back down in the bed, dragging the quilt over his head.

Ten minutes later Frank reappeared. 'It's Rachel,' he said, 'she wants to know if we want to go to Wylie's.'

From under the quilt. 'Won't the water be freezing?' Not quite summer, the star jasmine still tightly budded.

'I don't know.'

Vince pulled the quilt off.

'You know what Rachel's like,' Frank offered, 'rain, hail or shine.'

'What about Sam?'

'He's asleep. They gave him something at the hospital.'

'Okay.'

'I'll go and tell her.' And Frank went back downstairs, leaving Vince to reassemble something to wear from the clothes in clotted heaps on the floor.

He tried not to notice Rachel's and Frank's hands linking as they edged ahead of him on the path down to the sea pool. Rachel had said nothing to him, only looking at him and giving him a puzzled half-smile when he climbed in the back of Frank's car. He felt he should speak, explain himself. For the first time he seemed to be setting the mood.

Rachel bent over her string bag, forcing shoes and shirt into it, pulling out her black goggles. Her breasts fit full and easy into the swimming costume that she wore. Vince looked away. Frank was lying full-length on the rock, sharp face turned up to the sun, still in jeans and shirt.

'Coming in, Vince?' Rachel stared at him, swinging the goggles in one hand.

'It looks cold.'

'It is. Coming in?'

He dragged his T-shirt over his head, shedding shorts and sunglasses. He always felt helpless in speedos. Women were much more secretive, heavy material neatly flattening across their stomachs, between their legs.

Frank did not move; his eyes shut tight.

Vince followed Rachel down the steps, along the yellowy wall that divided the pool from the sea. Water washed over their feet.

'Fuck!'

'Do you good.'

'Yeah. What doesn't kill me only makes me stronger.'

Rachel gave a short, surprised laugh. She stopped, letting Vince walk almost into her arms, their bodies bumping, the warm, firm feeling of skin on skin.

'The best way is slowly. Like this.' She squatted, then lowered her legs into the water so she was sitting on the edge of the wall. She gasped. 'Ow! Sixteen degrees!'

'How can you tell?' He copied her. The water sank its teeth into his calves. 'Jesus wept!'

She laughed again. 'Intuition mate. It was on the blackboard up the top. They test it every morning.'

'This is insane!'

'I know. But you feel so good afterwards.'

With one solid, graceful movement she slid into the water. Surfaced for a second, screaming, 'Fuck!' then struck out for the other end, her brown arms shovelling ripples away on either side of her.

Vince shut his eyes and fell in. Green closing over his head. The cold shook right through him. He pushed off from the wall, legs struggling for purchase, the water gripping his body like a muscle.

'Aah!' His face in the air. Rachel seemed to be dragging the far wall towards her. He thrashed back down again, swimming blindly after her.

Sinuous, strong, the water weaved around and into him. Rachel passed him, the thrust of her kick sending bubbles up his nose. He touched the wall and turned back, swimming more regularly, turning his head every third stroke to take a breath, mind beginning to unravel.

If women fought—but they didn't fight. He had once seen Rachel punch Frank but the blow was cushioned and caught, his arm instantly coming out to wrap around her. Women argued. They screamed and cried, and then discussed it. Women apologised.

Touch the wall and turn again.

They held each other, and understood. What would he say. *Sorry mate, I didn't mean it. Or I don't anymore.*

Florence leaning down to Rachel to say, *you look really good. Where did you get that dress?* She passed him once more, head down.

A green opaque kingdom. Under the sea. He forced downwards, feet hitting cold air for a moment. Pushing, pushing, till his chest scraped seaweed and rock and the sky miles away above him. The people mouthing shadows.

I didn't mean it.

And up again, striking along the surface.

There was no explanation to be made, or none that would not give him away, make him feel exposed and defeated and nowhere. The slow build of frustration and disappointment. The growing feeling of panic. Nobody—least of all him—wanted to know that they could not stay where they were forever. The friendships fracturing naturally over the years. And the knowledge (he thought he knew, he had never bothered to ask the others) that he was the weak link.

He flipped over onto his back and began to cut a diagonal across the empty pool, watching sunlit clouds flicker over the sky.

He couldn't imagine himself saying, even to Rachel—*I'm terrified. It's like you all have prospects and I have none. I'm nobody. All I like doing is talking to you. Nobody has ever loved me, and I can't see that anyone ever will, except for you.*

Salt water splashing into his eyes.

He saw Rachel climbing out of the pool and kept swimming, hoping the water and sunlight would swallow him up.

And Sam thought he had lost everything. To lose everything you must have something in the first place.

Sixteen laps, and Rachel hauled herself out of the pool, new-tender knees bruising against the wall. Frank had taken his shirt off, turned over onto his stomach. Vince was still swimming, black head bulldozing the water.

Rachel picked her way back to Frank, hair streaming, feet leaving spattered prints on the bone-dry concrete. Her skin felt cold with intelligence and energy; always after swimming, as though she could ruthlessly make decisions for the best. She would say, *Let's finish this.* Swallowing, however, she knew that the sun was too hot; soon her skin would be dry and before she had even spoken she would be left parched and uncertain.

And Frank was turning over again, sitting up as she approached, holding his arms out to her. He hugged her clumsily around the thighs, pulling her off balance so that she collapsed into his lap, dropping her towel.

'You look like a seal.'

He pressed his mouth against her shoulder and she felt his tongue smoothing the salt away. She could not help but begin to cry, snuffling into his chest, cool water and warm mixing. The hard clod of words that had been blocking her throat began to dissolve.

'I was fast asleep,' he murmured, containing her whole body in his.

She butted her head away so he couldn't see her face.

He pulled her tighter, her face slipped up against his shoulder and she caught a look from one of the copper-coloured ladies who sat in deckchairs along the edge of the pool. Disapproval glimmering in dingo eyes. She felt Frank's hand slide into the front of her swimming costume and shivered, from eyes to toes.

∞

Morning noises. His mother did not believe in sleeping-in, or had some idea that she was invisible, silent, as she moved around the house, cleaning, talking to Nina. Sam turned his aching neck to look at the grandfather clock that stood like a spectre against the far wall. Twelve-thirty.

As if by some instinct his mother appeared at the door. 'Sweetheart?' she said. Her hair was pinned tightly again, an upturned bowl of brown-grey.

'Hi Mum.'

'It's very late.'

'Yeah.'

'Are you hungry?'

'I don't know.' He heaved himself up, pain suddenly freezing behind his eyes. 'There's some curried egg from last night. Or I could fry you some, with bacon.'

He groaned. The thick taste of egg clogging his mouth. 'Any coffee?'

'Of course, but you should eat something. You had nothing last night, and . . . '

'I need my strength. It's okay Mum. I'll get up.' Such a horrible pain. He wished his mother would come forward, somehow take him onto her lap, oh God, soothe him, stroke away some of this misery. But she had grown so small. He could not believe she had produced him. As he got to his feet, swaying, he saw his shadow cut out the faint light reflected in his mother's eyes, light creaming its way through the heavy lace curtains.

'Do you need any help? I could run a bath.'

'Maybe later. I just want a cup of coffee.'

She shrugged, a strangely young gesture. It had been only a month since Florence left him, since Frank, Rachel and Vince had brought him back from Captain's Flat, and in that time his mother had said nothing to him. He was half-grateful—afraid she would tell him Florence had never been any good (I never trusted that girl, she had said of the distant cousin his father had disappeared with), perhaps even re-introduce him to some of his old schoolmates. Turning up in Mitsubishi Magnas to have Sunday barbecues with their parents. Pink smiles, pretty skin, voices like chainsaws. *Do you still see Vince Cook?*

She had made a place for him on the verandah. The cane chair draped with crocheted blankets, a stool for his leg, a jug of orange juice on a doily that fluttered in the breeze. The glass sparkling.

She brought the coffee, looked out at the river while she was pouring it. Glancing down to make sure she did not spot the tablecloth.

'The Morgans,' she said, nodding at the water.

It was the kind of weather that makes people stop each other in the street, lean over shop counters to tell each other, 'Great day.' The next-door neighbours and their friends swarmed over their barrel-chested speedboat. Mrs Morgan stood on the pier, holding a basket with both hands. He watched as Antony, her son—three days older than him—leaned forward, taking the basket, propping it behind him, and then held out his hands for his mother, swinging her bulk easily up onto the deck.

The boat turned slightly—a sword of light flashed along the rail.

'Where's Nina?' he said.

'Inside.' His mother stepped over to the edge of the verandah, and the sunlight greedily gathered her into its embrace.

Gardening with Florence, whistling at the black dog, laughing as it pounced on a stick and waited, tail wagging, for them to snatch at it. The blue sky smiling gloriously on them. Life seemed open-ended—the land around them widening, places to put things, furnish the country with their happiness. He wanted it to be that way always. Their old age would not be spent in some transit lounge of feeling, where people sat moodily as though waiting for the plane home after a holiday. Counting the hours, the smell of sun and frangipani wearing off their skins, disgruntled and disappointed.

The warmth filling her face, Bertha Dalby remembered sitting in the cafeteria at a country train station. Sam's father reading the newspaper. It was before Nina was born, and Sam was four, his hair just beginning to darken and thicken. He sat on a plastic chair, eating a pie with both hands. His legs dangled airily, swinging with the movement of his body as he ate. He gave her a tomato saucey grin when he saw her looking at him. The baby shifting in her stomach, pressing against her heart. She wanted to swallow him. All of him, belonging to her.

She turned around. This black-eyed man. His sweet mouth become sardonic.

'Mum?'

'Yes?' A strand of her hair slipped out of place, unfurling softly in the breeze.

'Nothing.'

And some things never change. She leaned over and kissed his forehead, below the frown of stitches, and went back into the house, where Nina sat, gurgling and cooing, in her corner of the kitchen.

∞

With his left leg pressing stiff and straight on the clutch, Sam drove out to Ashfield to see his grandfather. His mother's usual basket of groceries on the seat beside him. The afternoon sun sheering off the windscreen, clashing on the duco of the cars in front.

Col was sitting on the long, wide couch in the grand living room of his house, a glass of yellow Pernod slowly turning milky on the coffee table. He was sick—had a cold that had hung on for weeks, wasn't sure whether to take something for it on top of the stomachful of tablets he had to swallow every day. His cheeks lapped at the collar of his shirt, blistered with broken blood vessels and liver spots, his blue eyes heavy with tears.

They talked about Sam's leg, his fading black eye, the bastards who couldn't keep to themselves in the pub, always making trouble. Did Sam have a job?

'You want to look for one in one of those clothing shops. Men's clothing shops. You've got your hair cut now.'

'Maybe,' said Sam.

'I used to work in one of them, when I was young. Before I started my apprenticeship. Pearson's, in town. King Street, and Sydney Arcade, huge shops. Oh, they had some beaut clothes.' Col held his hand to his chest as a cough struggled out of him. 'Used to nick some stuff too.'

'Yeah? What sort of thing?'

'Ties. You know. Of course, when I worked at the factory I realised everybody was light-fingered. Before I took over I had a mate who nearly died, nicking stuff.' He coughed. 'He got himself some hose—you know, rubber hose—and wrapped it round his body, put his shirt on over that. But he'd had it on all day, and the chemical reaction, the heat, it tightened up. Well, we were going for the bus, and he had this sort of fit. Ha! Kicking across the road like a stricken horse! Nearly killed him!'

Sam laughed, and so did Col, patting his chest again and saying, 'Ooh. Mustn't laugh.'

They sat in silence for a while, Sam fingering the newspaper clipping of his parents that Col had found for him. *Miss Bertha Casterton and Mr Samson Dalby at the Engineer's Ball, Sydney Town Hall. Guest of Honour was His Excellency the Governor of New South Wales.* Fact drips down and forms an ever-widening puddle, a swamp of history, impossible to avoid. He imagined telling his grandchildren—his and Florence's grandchildren— about the terrible bust-up they'd had. Almost finished us!

Because who knows, even now Florence might be reading, re-reading, one of the letters Sam left around the house for her.

I stepped off the verandah this morning and nearly got run over by a tumbleweed the size of a Volkswagen.

And what difference will it make if she is? She will finish the letter and the Sam that she will see is a Sam no longer in existence. As each moment passes, each flicker of the light, everything changes.

Letters from people once loved, still loved, are useless as trophies. Even if you could wear them, paste them on your body, have everybody read them and know that you were loved, they would mean nothing.

Yesterday, outside his mother's house, a sudden shriek and tear of brakes and a terrified series of yelps. Sam had limped round the side to see what had happened. A woman standing beside her car, her boyfriend? husband? friend? bent over the Morgans' dog. It did not seem to be moving, and as Sam approached, the woman said, 'It ran out from nowhere! I didn't even see it coming.'

Still, it was alive—a taut, brindled bulldog, stretched out on the road.

'Wal,' called Sam softly. It tilted its head to look at him; eyes bright with pain, its nose wet and drooling. And beside it, on the black tarmac, an oily splash of mulberry red. Its sides heaved, its tongue hung out.

Sam sent the man to tell the Morgans and ring the vet; awkwardly, he knelt down and stroked the dog's flat forehead, smoothing where its eyebrows would have been.

It reminded him of when Florence had said she was leaving him—the dog moved its head again, watching him, watching the woman. The terrible surprise, your mouth open with it, unable to catch your breath, tears like hot metal at the back of your eyes.

Mrs Morgan came out with the man, who was now bored rather than worried, glancing at his watch. The woman's legs were shaking as Sam and Mrs Morgan gently lifted the dog to carry it into the house, but he did not put an arm round her or even say anything. The dog squirmed and whimpered, but didn't yelp.

'I think he's going to be okay,' said Sam.

'Oh, Wally,' crooned Mrs Morgan. 'Don't worry, Wally. The vet will be here soon.'

The woman followed them, her face stiff with shock.

'I'll wait for you in the car,' the man called.

Sam left Col still sitting on the couch, the aspirin that he was supposed to take like two white buttons on the coffee table.

'What are you going to do now?' he called to his grandfather as he was going out the door.

'To be honest with you, I don't know.'

'Take those tablets.'

Col waved a heavy jellyfish-mottled hand. 'Yeah, yeah.'

'See you soon.'

'Righto. Drive carefully. Liverpool Road's a bugger at this hour.'

'Okay.'

When he pulled up outside the house at Henley, Mrs Morgan was standing in her front garden, watering the plants. The hedge of star jasmine glittered with drops like a chandelier. The bulldog lay on the sun-warmed path, one white bandaged leg uncomfortably extended.

'He looks pretty good,' said Sam, feeling his knee ache in sympathy as he walked towards them.

Mrs Morgan looked up and smiled. 'Oh yes. A simple fracture. She paid for it all, you know.'

'I know.' The woman proffering her credit card, as though that could save the dog's life.

'It would have been a tragedy if we'd lost him. And not just for me,' Mrs Morgan shook her head. 'Oh no. Nina loves that dog. Her face just lights up when she sees him. I know she looks forward to coming home and seeing Wally.'

Bullshit, thought Sam. A smile made the stitches in his forehead grip.

'Dogs are wonderful for the disabled.'

'Well I'm glad he's okay.' He turned to go.

'And thank you for your help, Sam.'

'My pleasure,' he called over his shoulder, and stumped round the side of the house, where the screen door still swung and clattered in the river breeze.

Vince came round a couple of days later, when he was sitting on the verandah, watching the river and reading. His mother was out shopping. Her cat lay on Sam's lap, a purr grinding in its throat.

One foot on the first step, hands clenching and unclenching by his side. 'G'day,' he said.

Sam put his book down. The cat opened its eyes.

'Can I come up?'

'If you want.'

Vince trod up the steps. He stood at the edge of the verandah, gaze flicking nervously to the river. 'What've you been doing?'

Sam said nothing for a moment. 'Reading, mostly.'

'Yeah? What?'

Sam waved at his book. Vince reached out and picked it up. His hands, Sam noticed, were shaking.

'Jane Austen. Didn't we do this at school?'

'*Pride and Prejudice*. We did *Pride and Prejudice*. This is *Emma*.'

'Any good?'

'Excellent.'

'I should read more.'

Sam sighed.

'I haven't been doing much either. Swimming. Walking the earth.' This was a favourite phrase of Frank's—despite himself, Sam made the usual response.

'See anything good?'

Vince laughed. 'Nuh. Swedes from the youth hostel. Nordic tanning machines.' He paused. 'Do you, ah, do you want a beer? Sun's over the yardarm.'

'Not if it's gonna turn you into a psychopath.'

Vince exhaled—what could have been a laugh, could have been relief. 'No. I'll go and get some.'

Sam stopped him. 'There's some in the fridge. Rachel brought it over yesterday.'

Rachel was always faster than the rest of them when it came to doing the right thing. Maybe it was because she was a girl. It was irritating sometimes. Smoothing things over, making them see reason.

Vince went and got the beer, found a couple of glasses and set them on the table, where the sun swilled into them. He handed one to Sam, poured himself one and took a long drink.

'You can sit down.' said Sam. The beer was bitter and cold.

Vince creaked into one of the wicker chairs, shaking his black hair out of his eyes. There was a short quiet, and then Sam spoke.

'I keep wondering . . . '

'Yeah? About what?' said Vince, too quickly.

'I keep wondering about what we're all doing.'

'Jobs, you mean?'

'Well, that. Just everything. I mean, where are we all going to be in ten years?'

Vince gulped at his beer. 'We said that when we were at school. We're there now. You know. Nearly ten years later.'

'Yeah, but where's there?'

'I'm not sure yet.'

Sam grimaced. 'I don't know if we'll ever be sure. That's what scares me.' He thought for a second. 'I like it, too. I mean, I don't want to have some fucking five-year plan.'

Vince shook his head.

Sam went on, 'But I think maybe somewhere I got the idea I'd know. Like getting a telegram. This is your life, one of those Yoko Ono things. You are now here. Breathe.'

'Poor John Lennon.'

'Pussy-whipped.' said Sam.

They caught each other's eye, shuddered, and burst out laughing. The cat jumped off Sam's lap, landing with a sound halfway between a pant and a miaow. It trotted off, its crooked tail held angrily in the air.

'Anyway.' said Sam. 'Do you reckon Frank'll ever finish his book? Rachel'll get a poem published? You'll write your thesis?'

'I don't know. Sometimes when I get up in the morning Frank's working.'

'Yeah, but . . . ' Sam moved, trying to straighten his sore leg. 'I didn't expect it to be like this. When I asked Mum to take me to the dole office she looked at me like I had a disease. It was totally different in Captain's Flat. I wasn't doing anything except making stuff and waiting for Florence to come home.' His breathing was faster. Vince watched him intently. 'It was fine. All those frames I made for Rachel's mum, the vegetable garden, walking the dog. When the landlord asked me to move the cows out of the front paddock I felt like I was really doing something. It took me all fuckin' day. And then when Florence got back from work I'd made dinner. It was like it didn't matter. The DSS didn't care if I had a job or not. Here they keep asking me about my qualifications. I haven't fucking got any.'

'You could edit stuff, like at uni.'

'I could not. I haven't done shit for ages, and I was ready never to.'

There was a long silence. Then Vince said, 'I always had this feeling, you know, that when I met the right woman, it'd all fall into place. I'd have kids, and . . . and I'd look after them.'

'Exactly. And where is she? Where are they?'

Vince ducked his head. 'I thought I might have them with Soula.'

Soula. Dark eyes, a strident voice, weighted with laughter and insults. She'd pushed Vince along for years after they left school, and then suddenly given up, disappearing overseas.

'Yep.' said Sam heavily. 'I had mine and Florence's already named.'

'What were you going to call them?'

Sam swallowed some beer. 'Daisy. Lily. Flower names.'

Vince smiled. 'Mine were going to be Greek, after Soula's family. Aphrodite.'

'Zeus,' Sam grinned.

'Is that Greek?'

'I don't know.'

Vince stood up and went over to the railing, staring out at the river. A windsurfer unzipped the water. He shaded his eyes. 'Looks like Brett Hillyard out there.'

'It probably is. They all still live round here.'

'I wonder what he's doing.'

'He's an accountant I think.'

'Wow.' Vince leaned forward, feeling the warm wood against his thighs.

Wandering up the main street of Captain's Flat, they swivel and swing around each other like boats attached by ropes on a twisting tide. It's mid-afternoon. Frank and Vince are sharing a carton of chips, fingers hot and delicate, catching their pale faces in shop windows.

Rachel, Florence and Sam drift ahead. Florence has one hand in the back pocket of Sam's jeans, the other on Rachel's shoulder. The sun, of course, is shining.

They sat there until Mrs Dalby came home, plastic bags full of food cutting into her soft hands. Vince jumped up to help her. Somehow, without working at it, his muscles had become hard as wire. He took the bags from Mrs Dalby and swung into the kitchen, dumping them easily on the table. She appeared behind him, taking her cardigan off and draping it around the back of a chair.

'Are you staying for dinner, Vincent?'

'No. No thanks. I've got to go.' He stepped around her and back onto the verandah, where Sam still sat. The table held an array of empty long-necks. 'Listen, mate, I'm off now.'

'Okay.'

'There's a party, though, tomorrow night? In Leichhardt. I wanted to see if you felt like coming.'

Sam stretched and got awkwardly to his feet. 'Yeah, why not. I'm not doing anything else.'

'Are you still going to come to the mountains?'

Sam looked at him and laughed. 'No, mate. The friendship's over.'

There was a moment as they each retreated again, to their separate corners of the ring, but Vince pulled it together, coming forward with his hand held out. 'I really . . . I'm so, so sorry.'

'Nah, it's okay.' Sam shook himself, and took Vince's hand. He watched the river; Vince gazed at the darkening wooden floor. 'Give us a buzz tomorrow.'

'Sure. Sometime in the afternoon.'

'Yep. See ya.'

''Bye.'

Their hands released, Vince thudded down the steps, swaying slightly as he hit the stone path. Sam watched him, and as he disappeared, called, 'Take it easy!'

'Okay!'

And he was chewed into the hedge, gone in a second.

Mrs Dalby came out onto the verandah. Sam raised his eyebrows, surprised; she was holding a glass of wine.

'Hey Mum,' he limped towards her and she turned a smile on him that frightened him slightly. The sharp corners of her mouth softened.

She pulled out one of the chairs and sat down, her bunchy body relaxing.

'Long day?' said Sam, following suit.

'Not really.'

Sam began to feel a familiar panic. What would he say next? He did not know how to talk to his mother.

'I went to see Ninie at the hospital.'

Sam said nothing.

'There's a new doctor there. She's trying a different kind of therapy. She thinks she can get her to walk.'

'Yeah?'

Mrs Dalby drank half her glass of wine in one gulp, and Sam braced himself. He had had this conversation a hundred times before; it was what made him miss his father so much. It should have been him, the older Sam, who listened to this. He could not bear the endless repetition of hope. It was too painful to engage with, time after time. The disappointment was always the same.

Years ago they used to make a pen for Nina between the couches and the spit-and-handprint smeared television. She would stagger around like a drunk, ricocheting uselessly off the cushions, tripping forward and banging her head on the carpeted floor. When she grew bigger it became easier to just strap her into her chair. The damage she could do was too great.

Mrs Dalby set her glass down. 'It's a bloody waste of time.'

Frank lit another cigarette. The street outside gave off the occasional roar of a car, and he turned the sunlight coming through the window into a square of thick smoke. Ash lilting down onto the keys of the typewriter. Smudged it off j and it fell into the little canyon below.

'Hel–lo!' Downstairs. It was Vince, coming back from Sam's.

Gratefully, Frank pushed his chair back, calling, 'How did it go?'

'Fine.' There was the sound of the fridge opening, a bottle hissing air as Vince twisted the top off, then his heavy feet, coming up the stairs. 'Oh, sorry,' he said, stopping at the door. 'I didn't realise you were writing.'

'I wasn't.' said Frank. 'Not really. How was he?'

'Okay,' Vince nodded, 'okay. He's going to come tomorrow night.'

'Good.'

'What are you working on?'

'The book. I don't know.'

'You haven't done any for ages.'

'I know.' Frank took a deep breath then exhaled, stretching his arms. 'What'll we do for dinner?'

'What's Rachel up to?'

'No idea. Walking the dog or something. I haven't spoken to her.'

Vince took a swig from the bottle of mineral water he was holding. 'I was thinking I could make something, and we could ask her over.'

'Nah.'

'Something wrong?'

'No, not really,' Frank shrugged.

They both looked out the window.

'Curry, maybe.'

'Sure,' said Frank.

Rachel woke with a jerk to find herself staring down the barrel of the black dog's nose. She laughed shakily, put out a hand to push it away and rolled out of bed. The window showed bright grey light, the lemon tree bending and twisting in the wind. She stood there with the dog beside her and said to it, 'How are you, dog?' as though her words could anchor her to the house again.

When the dog got excited it would try and clamber into her lap, long red tongue lolling over her knees. She found later that its spit dried and hardened on her leg like a scab. It seemed to be quite happy with its change of scene. Except for the car alarms. When one went off, even in the next street, it would rush into the backyard screaming with rage until it stopped.

And electrical storms. Visiting Sam and Florence, sitting on the verandah and watching one approach out of the black sky. Lightning, a silent wound of light in the distance. No thunder. It was the thunder that sent the dog half-mad. It lay beside her on the still-warm boards, head on paws, ears raised slightly. Inside the scrape and clatter of pans and sing-sing-sing of the radio.

The phone rang. She was standing at the window with the dog at her feet.

Blue Mountains (Fire)

There were one or two small fires at first, in outlying areas of Sydney, the places that always caught in the hot season. People dousing their roofs with hoses, calling cheerily to each other across back fences. Nothing to be frightened of.

Every couple of hours someone would walk slowly past the open door of Rachel's house, shouldering a slab of beer. That happy, holiday amble.

The weather was expected to turn at any minute. Each evening Rachel leaned out her bedroom window, waiting for the southerly to kick in. The trees still hot shadows against a thickening sky.

But the weather never did turn. Everyone had Christmas at home: Vince between his parents at the dinner table, thirstily drinking wine until he could leave and meet the others; Rachel laughing and shouting to be heard in a room alive with noise and relatives; Frank picking at his food and listening to Tom and Angela planning their wedding. Sam's Christmas moved between two hospitals—the one in Ryde, where Nina sat like a bargain basement shop dummy in her chair, decorated with streamers and her brightest, most festive bib—and a smaller veteran's hospital in Ashfield. Col's unshakeable cold had developed into pneumonia. His voice gurgled like a kettle coming off the boil. He opened the book Sam had given him, read the inscription and laid it on the table beside him. The warm smell of powdered gravy permeated the ward.

New Year's Eve came and went—Sam jacked himself up with speed and spent the night dancing with a girl, an old school friend of Frank's. He went home with her. Frank, Vince and Rachel sat on the balcony at Glebe surrounded by half-empty bottles of champagne. Rachel with her legs slung over Vince's lap, sweat licking the underside of her thighs. Frank clutching a warming can of beer. In two days they would be driving up to the Blue Mountains.

They were going in Frank's car—he would bring Vince, and then they would pick Sam up from Henley. It was a Friday afternoon, the city still draped with the fading streamers of good cheer and festive spirit. People worked through the day with hangovers, disappearing to drink more at night.

Rachel, her bag packed, sat in the living room, waiting for the boys to arrive. They were late. She turned the television on. There was a chance the freeway to the mountains would be blocked— already it was impossible to drive north, the Pacific Highway a shimmering, angry snake of halted cars. Fires chewing forests up and down the coast.

The sun was sinking but the heat lay heavily in all the rooms of the house. The light fell through the barred window in ingots of dull red gold, weighted by smoke. You could smell it.

Standing on the crest of the park earlier that afternoon (the dog zagging across the hot concrete paths, head down, tail up) she had seen far distant, scorching orange, and silent clouds of black smoke at the horizon. Other people walking their dogs stopped to watch with her. Shook their heads. Talked in low, surprised voices.

The black dog stood up in the doorway as another car approached. The sound of Frank's horn. Rachel got to her feet, switched off the television, grabbed her bag and stepped out into the evening.

The dog scrambled into the car first, settling itself, bright tongue hanging, by the window. Vince had brought a six-pack. As Rachel threw her bag in he peeled a frosted bottle from the plastic holder and handed it to her. Frank leaned back over the seat to grin at her, revving the engine, and before she could properly close the door was off with a roar down the narrow, car-jammed street.

They collected Sam from his mother's house and listened to the radio all the way up. In two hours the Great Western Highway would be closed off. Rachel and Sam sat with their backs to Frank and Vince, watching the city as it was swallowed by the highway. As far as they could see—ringing Sydney, following itself up towards Richmond, burning through Kurrajong and as far as Bilpin—the fire danced and glittered, a bright orange tinsel trim, lacing itself along the black ridge of mountains out west. The sun was well below the horizon but the sky was lit stormily, every way they looked.

Second day. The house was clogged with termites and a backwash of burnt leaves, blown in by the fierce, hot wind. Rachel's mother's oil paints—it was her house, once lived in by her parents—had melted into a sticky mess. They were in the bathroom. Every time you went in you would be assailed by the acrid swirl of turpentine and paint. They kept the windows open.

Rachel and Frank sat together on the verandah, a silence between them. Rachel stared into the quiet, purple-soaked air of the mountains.

'Frank?'

'Uh-huh?' He was nearly asleep.

'*Say* something.'

'What sort of thing?' He opened his eyes.

'I don't know.'

She got up.

Frank put out a hand to her, palm upward. 'Tell me what to say.'

'Nah. I can't think of anything. I might go for a walk.'

'Okay.' His hand dropped to his side.

She crossed her arms and walked away, calling the dog. They went through the dried-out garden, her legs brushing against the tall, prickling grass, and out into the street. She stood still for a while, knowing that Frank would not follow her, looking this way and that. The tar on the road throbbed in the heat and the dog stood beside her, waving its tail idly while it waited for her to move.

Head down, she strode along the street to the laneway and turned into it. The silent, sun-flattened, dusty day. Hearing her own breathing, thump of feet on the rocky path, the dog plunging and rattling through the scrub. The air became cooler as they descended towards the cliff face. Leaves whacked her across the face; her ankles twisted in their thin sandals—she slithered and slipped down the last turn, where the bush fell away, opening out to soaring blue-green emptiness.

She stood by the sandstone wall, forcing the dog to sit. Imagined, for a second, its scrabbling yelps as it tumbled over the edge. Until her heart slowed and the eucalyptus chilled her eyes and nose, the echoes disappearing.

Two cockatoos floated down there, small as fragments of paper. She breathed in; thought she could do anything—breathed out and knew it would be frighteningly easy to topple over the sandstone wall. It only reached to her thighs.

Back at the house. Frank was still sitting where she had left him, feet up on the verandah rail, looking out at the valley. Sam and Vince on either side of him.

The dog clattered up the wooden steps and into the house. They could hear it lapping noisily at its bowl of water. Rachel pushed her hands in the pockets of her shorts and sat down on the rail, hitting knees with Vince.

'Rache,' said Frank, 'I was just thinking about the bank on Glebe Point Road. You know how at nine o'clock there's a queue outside, waiting for it to open? I've never been able to understand that. I mean, what's the story? Do you get fresh money at that hour?'

Sam chuckled. 'Like it's gone off by the afternoon.'

'Yeah,' said Frank, 'I can't help wondering if my money's always bad by the time I get up.'

Rachel smiled at Frank and shrugged. Mount Solitary was deepening to indigo in the distance. Vince touched her lightly with the ball of his foot and she caught his eye. It was growing dark, but the light would never entirely disappear. Sometimes, out here on the verandah, you could read by moonlight.

Saturday night, going-out night, and they decided to make themselves an elaborate dinner. Frank had some friends living in Leura, who he invited down for the meal on the proviso that they brought something to eat.

'Sausages,' Rachel heard him saying into the phone, 'and beer. Lots of beer.'

Later, Rachel and Vince were sitting at the table with a huge pile of vegetables, peeling and chopping.

Sam came back from the pub with a box of bottles. 'Gin and tonic?' he said, standing at the door. 'Bourbon and coke? Or some fine wine?'

'It's a bit early, Sam,' said Rachel, dropping a potato into a saucepan of water. 'We don't want to get too pissed.'

Sam came forward, dumping the box on the table. 'There's something wrong with that statement. Now what is it? *We don't want to get pissed.*'

'*Too* pissed,' Rachel corrected him.

'I put it to you that there is no such thing.'

'Any beer?' said Vince. 'Where's Frank?'

'Walking the dog.'

'What, bushwalking?' Vince put a carrot into his mouth, crunching it noisily.

'Doubt it. No, he wanted to go round and see those trees, you know Rache? The ones your mum painted.' Sam cracked open the bottle of gin and gave an exaggerated sigh of pleasure.

'The beech trees in Myoori Avenue. Weirdo. Give us one.'

Sam was getting out glasses and ice. 'I knew you wouldn't be able to hold out. No beer till later, Vince, Frank's friends are bringing it. What'll you have?'

'Whatever.' Vince finished the carrot and leant back in his chair. 'I feel like getting really smashed.'

Sam nodded, banging the icetray on the table. 'This should be fun.'

The crickets scraped and sang under the dry grass and the moon appeared, pink and furred like a peach, in the smoky darkness. Empty plates piled on the table beside them. Vince sat with the salad bowl in his lap, stuffing his mouth with lettuce.

'If that valley catches fire . . . ' said Frank's friend Robert, looking out towards the mountains.

'It won't' said Rachel.

'How do you know?'

'Well, unless it jumps the highway, burns down all of Wentworth Falls, Leura, Katoomba . . . '

'It could happen. It's burnt up past Bilpin.'

'Yeah. On the other side of the highway.' Rachel was getting drunk.

Frank laughed, cutting short his conversation with Sam and Mia, Robert's girlfriend. 'Let's just say for the sake of argument that it did catch fire. We'd be fucked, wouldn't we Rache?'

'Burnt to bits,' agreed Rachel, fishing behind her for the wine bottle. They stared out at the valley while she slopped it into her glass.

Robert was not having a good time, but Mia, charmed by Frank's and Sam's attention, was sloshed and happy. She wondered about Vince, who, finished with the salad, had perched himself on the unsteady wooden railing and was tipping his head back to look at the sky, rocking himself back and forth. She was sorry when Robert stood up and said abruptly, 'We better go.'

'No way!' said Frank. 'It's only . . . what's the time?'

'Feels late.'

'It's not!'

Sam joined Frank, saying, 'There's so much to do still! So much to drink!'

'Let's stay, sweetie,' said Mia, looking up at Robert. Her eyes gleamed in her white face.

'No. Really. I'm tired. I just want to get going.'

'But I don't.'

There was a silence, everyone watching Robert. He kicked at the verandah rail, hands in his pockets. 'I've got to go.'

'Mia can stay here if she likes.' said Frank.

Rachel sucked in her breath.

'There's plenty of beds,' agreed Sam.

'Could I?'

'Of course you could! No problem. That's okay isn't it Rob?' said Frank. 'You can come over in the morning, for breakfast.'

Robert stared at him and then said, suddenly, 'Okay. I'll come round tomorrow.'

Frank followed him out to his car. They saw him lurch slightly as he stepped off the verandah, grabbing at Robert's shoulder for balance. Robert hunched away from him.

'What are you looking for, Vincent?' said Sam.

'The Saucepan. See it?'

They all turned their eyes to the inky sky. The points of light prickled like the remains of glass, long after a smash, on a black tar road.

'The smoke must be clearing,' said Vince.

An hour later, and Rachel was making her way drunkenly back from the bathroom (she used both hands to push herself between the couches, banging her shoulder against the frame of the front door). Outside, Vince and Sam were sitting with their legs up. Vince was singing.

'*All that she wants, is another baby*
She's gone tomorrow,
But all that she wants is another baby . . . '

'I don't get it,' said Sam, cutting him off. 'Another kid? Or another—baby?'

'She's fucking guys, getting pregnant, and moving on,' said Vince.

'You reckon? I reckon she means another guy. She doesn't want to stay with just one guy, she's fucking them and then she's leaving them so she can fuck someone else.' Sam tipped his beer into his mouth. Some of it ran down his chin.

'No, mate. She's using them for sperm.'

Sam shouted with laughter. 'You're a fuckin' idiot sometimes.'

Rachel was standing beside them, frozen, watching as Frank lifted a stray lock of red hair from Mia's face and tucked it behind her ear.

'I am not a fucking idiot.'

'You are!' Sam's laughter was getting out of control, beer splashing out of the bottle as he leaned forward, shaking. 'You're a moron!'

'Fuck off, Sam.'

'No, you fuck off! You're a fucking moron!' He laughed and laughed, and Rachel watched, and even Frank and Mia looked up.

Vince stood up unsteadily and said, 'Just fucking watch it, okay?'

'What're you gonna do, hit me again?' Sam had tears in his eyes. He brought up a hand and wiped them away, and took another gulp of beer. Not looking at Vince, who was looming over him, swaying. 'You'll have to kill me this time.' he added.

With one movement, Vince flipped Sam's chair over so that he crashed onto the wooden slats, beer bottle rolling crankily away.

'Jesus, Vince!' Frank didn't move. 'It was a joke, you moron!'

Sam hauled himself up, smiling unstably, dangerously.

Vince backed away.

'Sam . . . ' Frank put his glass down. Sam stepped forward and Rachel reached out and grabbed his arm.

'Mate,' Sam began. Rachel tightened her grip. He looked around at them all—Frank tensed in his chair, Mia holding a bottle to her chest as though it could protect her, Vince wobbling against the railings. Rachel pulling at his arm. He shook her off and said, 'This is getting boring.'

Vince edged around him.

'If you're going to . . . ' he listed forward, ' . . . if you're going to beat me up every time I piss you off, it's not fucking worth it. Is it?'

No-one said anything.

'Is it?' he said again. 'You've just gotta put up with me. My life is . . . ' he was speaking with difficulty, his feet trying to balance on the boards, ' . . . my life is a piece of shit, and you're my oldest friend. My best friend. One of these days I'll be what I—what I was before, but right now I'm in a fucking mess. Okay? And this whole thing, this whole stupid thing, this *group* is all I've fucking well got. Come and live with me and my mother and you'll see. Okay?'

Vince didn't speak.

'Okay? Is that okay? Is anyone *listening?*' He overbalanced suddenly, and collapsed onto Vince, who fell backwards so the whole verandah shook. He brought his hands forward to catch him, but Sam did not fall easily. Somehow Sam untangled himself and began to hit at Vince, blindly, his mouth, nose and eyes a red mess of tears. He was screaming and trying to get up, trying to smash Vince in the face, screaming, 'Fuck you! Fuck all of you!' and Vince was curled up, both arms bent across his face, and Frank was on his feet, shouting, 'Sam! Sam, for Christ's sake!' and Rachel was trying to pull Sam off Vince and Mia—Mia crouched in her chair, her face pale with disgust.

Vince managed to unhook one leg and scissored it between Sam's so they rolled over, but caught Rachel's too so she was jolted forward, her chin thumping against Sam's shoulder, tears rushing instantly to her eyes. She struggled to extricate herself before Sam or Vince hit her but in that second Frank was standing over them. Vince put a heavy palm over Sam's screaming mouth and Frank said, 'Jesus. Come on.'

He was holding out his hand to Rachel. He lifted her back on her feet. She stood against him, her breath coming in panting sobs. Sam stopped kicking and slowly Vince got up.

Mia said, 'What is *wrong* with you guys?' and Vince laughed and helped Sam up.

He was shaking his head and looking around at the mangled verandah.

Frank clicked his tongue and said, 'Fightin' Sam Dalby.'

A breeze hushed its way along the dark line of trees. The moonlight made blue art out of the dirty plates, greasy glasses and broken chairs.

∞

The fires never did reach the valley. As each day passed the air cleared, the reports on the radio lost their spitting urgency, the wind changed from dragon's breath to the soft cool sigh of a baby's.

For a couple of nights Rachel shared the front room with Sam, whose sleeping pattern was entirely unlike Frank's. He slept spreadeagled and heavy in the middle of his single bed, his snores taking on a different timbre every time he moved. Rachel lay awake, watching the huntsman spiders scatter fiercely over the ceiling, listening to the creak of night. And during the days they sat around and talked or read, went for walks, drank at the pub.

Back and forth, back and forth, like water in a level, the bubble only rarely coming to rest. Evening, and Rachel sat beside Frank on the verandah, watching the valley drink up the darkness.

She was wearing a tight singlet top and a pair of his shorts. Her hip, where it showed between shorts and top, was rounded, cool in moonlight, a soft dune of skin. Frank put out his hand without thinking, letting it curve into his palm. Her sudden shiver jumped right through him.

'Sorry.'

Rachel looked at him. He could smell her, sweat and sandalwood. Her face was smooth, mouth silent, but eyes spilling with light.

At last she said, 'What are we going to do?'

Frank took a deep breath, speaking with an effort, 'Can't we just leave it?'

Rachel's stomach went freezing cold. 'Leave it where?' she said.

'Here. Please. It's fine. It'll be okay.'

'What, you think . . . '

'What do you think?' he said quickly.

'You tell me.'

There was the sound of a car at the gate; Sam and Vince coming back from the pub. 'Quick,' Rachel said. They both grinned.

Frank kicked at her chair. 'It's worth it, isn't it?'

'It must be.'

The bubble floats, suspended, steady. They relaxed in their chairs as Sam and Vince came blundering along the dark path.

One morning Sam found a big stick and threatened to kill any feral cats or dogs who ventured onto the land around the house. Frank was on a roll, said he couldn't kill dogs, it would upset the evolutionary balance.

'What do you mean?' said Sam, peering over the edge of the verandah. Stick in one hand, bottle of beer in the other.

'Think about it. If you kill the dogs, the sticks won't have a natural predator. They'll breed like crazy.'

'And take over the world,' said Vince who sat against the wall, reading one of his textbooks. Rachel was beside him, legs drawn up, chin resting on her knees.

'Exactly,' agreed Frank. 'You won't notice it at first. You know, you'll be in a cafe and you'll get served by a stick and you won't think anything of it. Next thing you know, you're coming home from holidays and a family of sticks has moved into your house.'

They laughed.

'Don't mess with the balance, man,' Frank was shaking his head.

Sam reached over, jabbing the stick into his stomach, and suddenly it was all on. He leapt over the verandah rail, landing with a staggering thud in the grass, and Frank jumped after him. They careened through the bottlebrush trees, shouting and laughing, and Rachel and Vince climbed onto the verandah rail to watch.

Sydney (Home)

Sam's grandfather died on a Friday, when he and Vince were at Bondi.

Vince is in the water. The sun is so low in the sky that the waves rising to break behind him block it out completely. When he turns back to face the beach it's like a sudden, silent holocaust—water lifting into a black wall against the lemony-blue sky. Quiet pierced by the excited screams of kids who duck under its crash of white. And then the horizon flattening out again, the kids getting to their feet, fragile silhouettes staggering towards the next wave. The sun slowly disappearing behind the buildings.

Sam is waiting for him on the beach, lying on his towel, face down, watching his fingers push through the cold, crunching sand. The end of summer is making him think of Captain's Flat again. The taste of red wine, people in llama jumpers crowded around a bonfire, the smell of dope. And Florence somewhere in the picture, her tall elegant figure framing some stupid conversation about poetry, about organic food, about living in the country and how it was so much better. He's had so many of these conversations and now he can't remember what *is* better about it.

He smells salt and catches sand in his eyes as Vince bends over to pick up his towel.

'Watch it, will ya?' he says, sitting up.

Vince is drying himself, heavy hair dripping with water. 'You should go in. It's beautiful.'

'Maybe later.'

'It's going to be dark soon.'

Vince thumps down next to him. The air freezing against his wet forehead.

And meanwhile, in a pub near Rachel's house, Rachel and Florence sit at the bar. The races on the TV behind them. Florence is visiting her parents, had surprised Rachel with a phone call in the middle of the afternoon. It was as though time had never moved, the same old voice saying, 'I'm bored. Let's go to the pub.'

The loss, the *situation*, between Florence and Sam could give them something to handle, to share. Like a baby. They could click their tongues over it, sigh and describe to each other its features. But Florence hardly mentions it.

She leans easily on the bar, elbows pointing down, and slides another scotch and coke down her throat. The afternoon sunlight pierces the dusty window, forcing a blade of light into the scarred wood. As she lifts her glass it cuts the colours in two, leaving them broken on her hand.

'This is what it's all about,' she says.

'What?' says Rachel. She can feel herself grinning.

'This . . . this afternoon. Like everything exists in here, right now. You don't want to be anywhere else. There isn't anywhere else.'

The jukebox is playing some faded familiar song. The pool table ticks.

'Nice without the boys, isn't it,' adds Florence.

Rachel laughs and nods. 'Weird, for me.'

'Yeah.' Florence looks sideways at her. There is a moment that could be snapped by some false declaration of friendship. Rachel holds her breath.

Florence smiles and says, 'Want another drink?'

And a second knife of sunlight joins the first, widening and opening out until the room is filled with the afternoon and outside is inside.

∞

And Frank at home writing, waiting for Rachel, his legs crossed under him as he leans over the typewriter. Not noticing how his ankles ache under his weight. Switching the light on, finally, when he can't pick out the black letters on the white paper, or the white letters on the black keys. Stretching till his bones crack, getting up from the desk and stumbling over to the bed where he falls, long limbs sprawling, into a deep sleep.

Vince gets home and, seeing the light on, comes up the stairs to talk. But Frank by now is turned to the wall, the quilt over his legs, bare feet pale and cold under the electric light. Vince switches the light off and goes into his own room to read. Lulled to sleep himself by the dark wash of leaves against his window in a new evening wind.

Sam stands by the hospital bed, looking down at his grandfather's body. Behind him Mrs Dalby and Nina, who has been brought from Ryde for this occasion. Someone had said, *the family must be together*. Sam wonders where his father is.

Col's face is the colour of old paper, one clouded blue eye half open. Nothing is happening. Until, behind him, Nina starts to squall and kick in her chair. She's screaming, bawling like a trapped cat. Sam turns around, his fists clenched to punch, and sees his mother.

She's staring out at the street, standing apart from Nina in her chair. Calm next to chaos. She doesn't move. Her thoughts sail and curl through the window as Sam steps forward and takes his sister's battering, smashing hands, going down on one knee to sing and soothe.

And later, much later, Rachel, letting herself into Frank's and Vince's house with the spare key, closing the door carefully behind her.

It's still not over. Each time I arrive I see this: I step into the house, fumble my way through the empty darkness to the kitchen, switch the light on, and there it is. Blood all over the floor. Knives—a clatter seeming to echo in the still, shocked air. Smashed glass. And you, face down, arms broken outwards, your hair knotted and clotted with red.

What would I do? What would I do? What would I do?

It never happens; every time I switch the light on the kitchen quivers and sings with silence, plates and glasses the way I left them, floor clean except for a stray leaf or two, pushed under the door by the long hand of the breeze.

And you will be sleeping. And I will climb the stairs, and they will make aching noises under my feet. And I will get into bed beside you, with the light still chiming in my head. Sleep will gather up the day like a bright ball of mercury, rolling this way and that until all of it is caught into one.